NANA

NANA

Brandon Massey

Dark Corner Publishing
Atlanta, Georgia

"Beauty is only skin deep, but ugly goes clean to the bone."
-- Dorothy Parker

As soon as Lily Worthy arrived home that Wednesday night after Bible study, she knew something was wrong.

A crisp October breeze followed her as she parked her Ford Escape beneath the carport and walked into her two-story Victorian. The big house was older than even her seventy-five years, and its frame swayed and creaked when subjected to the slightest pressure. Each footstep registered a squeak in the wooden floorboards; closed doors easily shook the walls.

Lily heard strange noises when she entered her home. The sounds came from upstairs. A frown creasing her oak-brown face, she placed her keys, purse, and leather Bible case on the small glass table beside the doorway. Her strong hands, shaped from thirty-four years working on the assembly line at the local Ford factory in Hapeville, were wracked with arthritis, but at that moment, they did not tremble.

Lily lived alone, much to the dismay of her granddaughter. Lord knows, her southwest Atlanta neighborhood had seen its share of trouble over the years. Packs of unruly youth breaking into the modest homes of the very people who had sustained the community for generations. Just last year, while she was out visiting the sick and shut-in, someone had kicked down her front door and helped himself to her television. Lily had stubbornly refused her granddaughter's pleas to move into her house in the northern suburbs. If all the good people abandoned the neighborhood and left it to rot, how could things ever get any better?

She cocked her head, listening. Age had not diminished her hearing. She heard a tapping noise, faint but deliberate, and it was definitely coming from above.

But the front door had been locked.

She shuffled down the main hallway, the polished floorboards groaning underneath her black leather boots.

Her house was clean as a model home, thanks to a

housekeeper employed by her granddaughter, and Lily's own meticulous ways. Photos of family and friends adorned the walls, and the rooms were full of old but comfortable furniture, and lots of thriving plants. It was an enormous house for a widower. She and her husband had bought the property almost fifty years ago, in anticipation of filling it with children and happiness. Life had altered the fulfillment of those dreams. Only one year into their marriage, her husband had died in a factory accident, crushed underneath an errant plate of sheet metal. She never remarried, but through fostering, had found plenty of children to share the home with her and fill the rooms with joy.

She saw nothing out of place. Her television still stood on its stand. When the burglar had broken in last year, he'd raged like a hurricane through every inch of the house.

She entered her bedroom. It was undisturbed, the queen-size bed made.

From a Payless shoebox on the top shelf of the closet, she withdrew the Smith & Wesson, snub-nosed .38. The gun, a gift from her long-deceased big brother, was already loaded.

She was stubborn about leaving her neighborhood, but she was no fool.

She went to the back door, off the mud room. It was locked, too. If there was truly an intruder in her home, how had he gotten inside?

Nevertheless, *something* was going on upstairs.

Although her intuition was strong, it wasn't strong enough for her to phone the police. What would she tell them? I hear a tapping noise upstairs, please come quick! She could imagine the lazy response from the 911 operator. *Eh, another lonely old lady frightened of innocent noises, probably just one of her hundred cats wandering around the house.* As Lily aged, she detected a bias against the elderly, a mockery even, as if people would rather forget they existed than deal seriously with them, perhaps because few wanted to accept that someday, they too, would grow old.

Lily went to the bottom of the staircase. Usually, it was dark up there, as she rarely ventured upstairs. The narrow steps, nineteen of them, were bad on her knees, and many years ago, she had reorganized the house to place all of her essential items on the first level.

But she saw a light glowing up there, coming from one of the several rooms on the second floor.

"Is anyone up there?" Lily asked. Her voice was clear and resonant as a bell, the voice of a woman who had conducted many a child through Sunday school for decades.

No one answered, but she heard a soft tap, like fingernails rapping against a wall. *Tap . . . tap . . . tap . . . tap . . . tap.*

She found the light switch at the bottom of the staircase and flicked it on. Harsh yellow light flooded the stairwell. She squinted, her bespectacled eyes taking a moment to adjust to the sudden brightness.

No one came out of hiding. The staircase was empty.

Sometimes, she wished she had accepted her granddaughter's offer to find a dog for her. Not only would a dog have been pleasant company, it would have been a welcome protector at a time such as this, would have barked and sounded an alarm to ward away intruders. But Lily was in and out of the house so often each day, involved in so many church and volunteer activities, that she'd worried a dog would get lonely staying home alone.

Wind swirled around the house, sifting through the eaves.

Tap . . . tap . . . tap . . . tap . . . tap . . .

"Hey, anybody up there?" she asked.

Only the soft raps answered.

She gathered her dress in her hand, and, keeping her grip on the revolver, headed upstairs, carefully navigating the creaky wooden steps. Once, as a much younger woman, she had fallen down those stairs while carrying a basket of laundry, and the mishap had landed her in the emergency room with a broken ankle. At her advanced age, ascending or descending such a steep staircase could result in far worse than a stay in the hospital—one more critical reason why she avoided it.

Careful, Lily . . .

She reached the second floor without incident, a light layer of perspiration coating her brow.

As she had suspected, the sound came from the bedroom opposite the head of the staircase. The door was ajar. Inside, the ceiling lamp burned, and the long window on the other side of the room was wide open, the exterior screen lifted, too. The tapping sound she'd heard came from the plastic tips of the cords that controlled the window blinds: the cool night breeze batted them against the wall.

Chuckling at herself, Lily lowered the gun. She was behaving like the jumpy old spinster she despised, spooked in her own house by innocent noises.

She realized why the window was open, too. Claudia, her housekeeper, had visited earlier that day, and she tended to throw open all of the windows while she cleaned, to air out the house. The girl had forgotten to shut this one and douse the light. She was good at her job, but a tad forgetful at times.

Lily tucked the gun away in the front pocket of her wool jacket. She stuck her head out the window. It overlooked the spacious back yard, and was a good fifteen feet above the ground. A lacebark elm tree towered back there, but the tree needed to be trimmed back a bit. Its wingspan came too close to the house, and besides causing possible damage during a storm, could have made it easy for a raccoon or some other agile creature to leap from a branch and right inside through the open window.

She lowered the screen back into place. Then, she placed both of her hands on the wooden edge of the sash, and pushed down.

The window lowered with a squeak and a tremble, but she got it down all the way. Her fingers throbbed from the effort. She rubbed her hands together, her stiff knuckles crackling like dry tinder.

And she noticed, in the glass, the reflection of someone standing behind her.

Lily spun, a gasp caught in her throat.

The room was empty. She was alone.

Her pulse raced, blood pounding in her skull. Had her mind, stimulated by hours of challenging reading each day, finally begun to falter in spite of her best efforts? The prospect of dementia frightened her far more than the idea of a stranger in her home.

She slipped out the gun again, held it in a shaky grip.

"Who's there?" she said. Her voice was no longer as clear as she'd hoped, and held a discernible note of fear.

A floorboard creaked out in the hallway; a sound it might have made underneath someone's weight.

An ordinary home invader would not have employed such stealth tactics. These lost kids, she knew, cared nothing for subtlety. They knocked down your door and stomped like the Gestapo through your home, overturning furniture and ransacking through your possessions without any fear of reprisal. That was what had also happened last summer to Cecil Taylor, the kind fellow who'd once lived across the street. He'd been sitting in his recliner watching *Family Feud* when two teenagers had broken in, pistol-whipped him, stolen jewelry and his TV and computer, drank the liquor in his cabinet, and urinated on his carpet. Cecil had been hospitalized for three weeks and moved to a nursing home afterward.

Whatever was happening here in her house was something different. It was either a wild flight of imagination—which she didn't accept—or something else.

Lord, give me the strength, Lily prayed. *Do not let my strength fail me now.*

She tightened her hold on the gun. She crept forward. Entering the hallway, she swung to the left, where she thought the noise had come from.

The corridor was illuminated with light streaming from the bedroom behind her, and from the fixture burning above the nearby staircase. But the hallway was empty.

She released a deep sigh, lowered the gun.

She needed to take her old, tired tail to bed. She could spend all night wandering through the house, chasing shadows and phantom noises. She would call her granddaughter, chat for a few minutes (she wouldn't tell the girl about any of this, of course), read a bit of Scripture, and let herself drift off to sleep. Tomorrow morning, she'd call Claudia and remind her to close the windows next time she visited, too, since her housekeeper's oversight had launched this foolish misadventure.

She doubled back and switched off the light in the bedroom. As she approached the staircase again, she felt something slip around her ankles. She looked down and saw a slender, pinkish appendage coiling like a rope around her leather boots.

A scream escaped her.

It was a fleshy thing, alive, and the word *snake* came to her panicked mind, but somehow she knew it was not really a snake. It was something else strange and terrifying.

The thing drew taut around her boots, lifting her off her feet. She lost her balance and plunged toward the staircase. The gun spun out of her grasp. Arms flailing, she tried to break her fall, but her head slammed against the hard edge of a step. Red-hot pain seared through her, trailed by an inky blackness that leaked into the edges of her vision.

Please, Lord, not yet, not now . . . I've got so much work left to do . . .

She was dimly aware that the tentacle still held her, looped around her boots. Floorboards shifted above her. She felt a presence near, and had the lurid vision of a monster out of a nightmare, something inhuman that possessed a giant tongue that it was using to suspend her at the top of the stairs.

Blood trickled into her eyes and mouth. Using her weakened arms, she attempted to push against the steps and lift herself up. She managed to raise her body about an inch. Trembling, she twisted her head around, blades of pain chopping down her spine.

She saw who was standing at the top of the stairs.

Her blood-stained lips formed the word: *"You . . ."*

And then she was released and was falling down the long staircase, tumbling into perfect darkness.

Part One

1

Troy was the first to meet the woman.

On Saturday, November 1st, the funeral service for Lily Worthy commenced at eleven o'clock in the morning, at Lily's longtime church home, Riverside United Methodist Church, in East Point, Georgia. Hundreds of people attended the ceremony. Over the years, Lily had touched the lives of many, and her untimely death left an indelible scar on the hearts of those who had loved her so much.

She fell down the stairs in her own damned house, Troy thought. He sat in the front pew of the sanctuary with his family, as the twelve-member choir launched into a soaring rendition of *Amazing Grace.* Lily had been seventy-five, but in excellent health. Her tragic accident was so unexpected that it was difficult to believe, like something out of a sad dream from which you soon hoped to awaken.

He knew his wife, Monica, was tortured by the same thoughts.

Troy had kept his right arm wrapped around Monica for most of the service. Monica trembled, sobs shaking her slim frame. He stroked her dark, curly hair, but said little. Nothing he could say would make Monica feel any better just then; holding her was enough.

For years, he had seen Monica trying to convince her grandmother to move out of the old house. Her pleas had grown desperate last summer, when someone had broken into Lily's home and stolen valuables. But Lily was nothing if not stubborn.

When her neighbor, Ruby Brown, had called them early in the morning last week and could barely speak through her sobs, Troy had expected the worst.

Went to see Lily so we could take our morning' walk . . . I had a key to her house, you see, since we been neighbors so long . . . and she was layin' at the bottom of the stairs and it looked like she musta been there all night . . .

Although crime had been a concern in Lily's neighborhood, foul play had never entered the picture. There had been no signs of forced entry, no evidence of a robbery, and thus, no police investigation had been opened. The conclusion, supported by an autopsy, was that Lily had gone upstairs for some reason and on the way down she'd lost her balance, tumbled down the steps, and snapped her neck. Accidental falls at home accounted for thousands of deaths each year, and many of the victims were elderly.

Troy buried his face in his wife's hair as the choir's singing echoed throughout the large, high-ceilinged sanctuary. Hot tears slid from his eyes. Lily had disliked him when he'd first begun to romance her cherished granddaughter during their residencies at Emory, considered him a silver-tongued lothario using his burgeoning medical career to entice women, but over time, he and the tough old lady had brokered a truce. He believed giving her two adorable great-grandkids had helped in that regard.

His mother, Pat, sat on his left. She was keeping his kids under control: seven-year-old Lexi and five-year-old Junior. Both of his children were in elementary school but still too young to really understand what was going on, and he questioned the wisdom of bringing them to the service, but Monica had insisted they pay tribute to the woman they knew as "Gran Nana." He was in no position to deny Monica anything she requested. Lily was the only family she had ever known.

Lily had taken in Monica's birth mother, a teenager at the time. After living for only two weeks under Lily's strict rule, the girl had come home and announced she was pregnant, the father unknown. She stayed around long enough to give birth to

Monica, signed her over to Lily's care, and cut out of sight. No one had seen her since.

Growing up without knowledge of her biological parents would have been an insurmountable obstacle for many children, but Monica had the iron-willed Lily in her corner. She had blossomed under Lily's loving but stern parenting style. Zoomed through school with stellar grades and graduated as valedictorian of her high school. Finished summa cum laude at Spelman. Went to Duke Medical School. Came back home to ATL and did her residency in pediatrics at Emory, where Troy was also completing his residency in radiology. They had been together ever since.

"She was all I had," Monica said softly. She dabbed at her eyes with a handkerchief, but couldn't stanch the steady trickle of tears.

Troy took his handkerchief and gently brushed it across her damp cheeks. He hated to see her in pain, wished there was something he could do to alleviate her anguish, but this was one of those rare times when even his considerable powers of persuasion came up short. There was nothing to do but to allow grief to burn through her.

"She was all I had," Monica said again, in a broken voice.

"You have us, baby," Troy said, and squeezed her, but he might as well have been speaking to Monica from the bottom of the sea.

The choir was singing at a feverish pitch:

Amazing Grace, how sweet the sound,
That saved a wretch like me.
I once was lost but now am found,
Was blind, but now I see . . .

The sanctuary's acoustics amplified the voices of the gifted choir. The three-piece band—keyboardist, drummer, and guitarist— played the old song with all the verve of touring musicians rocking at Phillips Arena in front of a crowd of thousands. He doubted there was a dry eye in the whole building.

His cell phone vibrated in his suit jacket pocket. His secondary phone. It was in poor taste to step out, but the truth was, he needed some fresh air or else he was going to implode.

He kissed Monica on the temple, told her he'd be right back. Immersed in grief, she barely registered his presence anyway. But as he rose from the pew, his mother gave him a questioning glance, and Junior looked as if he wanted to hop out of her lap and go with him. He ignored both of them.

The funeral attendees favored him with sympathetic looks as he hurried down the long aisle. It was a sea of grief-stricken faces, most of them black, but many white, Hispanic, and Asian, too. Lily's charity had known no color.

"God bless you, Dr. Stephens," the usher said, and opened the sanctuary doors for Troy.

Troy went through the carpeted lobby and stepped outside onto the front walkway. It was a blustery day, and his wool Armani suit failed to protect him against the biting air. Shivering, he walked down the flagstone steps and onto an island of dormant grass, taking shelter beside the thick trunk of an immense oak tree. The branches quivered in the breeze, shedding crisp leaves dipped in autumn colors. He would have appreciated the natural beauty of the scene if he hadn't been distracted with other thoughts.

He slipped his cell phone out of his pocket. The caller had left a voice mail. He listened to the message with growing annoyance.

No respect for boundaries, he thought. *I'll have to address this, but not now.*

He deleted the message. Pocketing his phone, he turned back to the church entrance.

That was when he noticed the woman.

She leaned against the wrought-iron railing that encircled the church's front entrance. She wore all black: one of those big church Derby hats with the wide brims, sunglasses, pants suit, pumps. Gazing out at the parking lot, she smoked a cigarette. From a distance, he couldn't discern her age, but she had the bearing of confidence, and sexiness, too.

There also seemed to be something . . . *familiar* about her.

Buttoning his jacket, he walked toward the church. The woman's face tilted in his direction, and why not? He was six-two, broad-shouldered, good-looking and well-dressed; he'd heard on more than one occasion that he resembled Denzel Washington. He fully expected to catch her eye.

As he mounted the steps, she smiled at him.

Willowy as a tree, she was tall for a woman, perhaps five-nine without her pumps. She had full lips, lined with cherry-red lipstick. From a distance, he'd thought she might be his age, but as he drew closer he realized his estimation was way off. This woman's face was lined with wrinkles. She was easily old enough to be his mother.

Jarred by the realization, he lost his footing on the last step and nearly fell down.

"Careful there, darling," she said, in a throaty voice that reminded him of a bluesy lounge singer. "If you hurt yourself, I'd have to go inside and find you a doctor."

He laughed, self-consciously, and smoothed down the front of his jacket.

"I am a doctor, actually," he said.

"That so?" She exhaled a wispy column of smoke, and he noticed it was a hand-rolled cigarette; the smoke smelled of a bracing, spicy fragrance, as if she were smoking some odd blend of herbs. "Then you must take issue with my smoking, hmm?"

"To each his own." He shrugged. "We all have our vices."

Offering a polite chuckle, she glanced away. Her hat shifted slightly. He noticed thick curls of white hair peeking out from underneath.

Why did she seem so familiar? He couldn't put his finger on it, but the thought wouldn't go away.

The wind swirled around them. It flapped the brim of her hat and carried her fragrance to his nostrils. She smelled of rosemary and summer flowers, and a deeper, musky odor that made his heart skip a beat.

Some of the sexiest women he had ever seen had ten or more years on him, and he was forty-one. This woman may have been in her sixties or even older, and damned if he didn't find her irresistibly compelling.

The front doors burst open, and a woman stumbled outside, sobbing, accompanied by a man who was struggling to console her. The couple went to the other edge of the platform and huddled together.

Troy's heart twisted. What was he doing out here, thinking of making the moves on a woman while his wife grieved inside? He had few scruples when it came to his sexual exploits, but this was beneath him.

He felt the woman in black watching him closely, her eyes hidden behind the dark lenses, lips curved in a faint smile.

"I better get back inside," he said. "Lily Worthy was my wife's grandmother. I need to be there for her."

"Of course." She flicked ashes away from her cigarette. "Family is important, isn't it? The ties that bind, dear."

Troy started to turn away, but a gut feeling kept him rooted in place. "Are you a family friend? Or relative? I've got this nagging sense that I've met you before."

"I'm a relative of your wife," she said. "We go way back, honey."

"Who are you?"

Smiling, the woman removed her sunglasses. She had large, beautiful hazel eyes.

Just like Monica, he thought, and his stomach suddenly felt as if it had plunged to the ground, because he realized what was coming next.

"I'm her mother."

2

It was, unquestionably, the worst day of Monica's life.

Prior to that Saturday, the worst day of her life had been the morning that she had learned that her grandmother, Lily, had died at home, alone, the victim of a something as random as a tragic fall down the stairs. She didn't think it was possible to feel any more hopeless, lost, or shocked.

But at the funeral, the full spectrum of emotions hit her with the force of a sledgehammer upside the head.

Lily had an open-casket funeral, per the instructions in her will. Monica had forced herself to get up and view the body, though every atom in her wanted to stay away. When she finally looked inside, she was jarred by the sight of the stout, dark-skinned woman that lay nestled within the starchy folds of the navy-blue dress. The mortician had done a superb job of concealing Lily's injuries; she hadn't looked this good even in life. But to Monica, something was missing. The ineffable quality of her grandmother was gone, and the body within the coffin was merely a beautiful but empty vessel, like a crystal vase void of the rose that had once bloomed within it.

She's in a better place, Monica thought, and believed it.

But she felt hollow, as if her heart had been cored like an apple.

At some point during the service, Troy had walked out. She didn't remember him leaving. She had turned to say something to him, and discovered that his spot beside her on the pew was empty. Her mother-in-law, Pat, took her hand, whispered words of encouragement and love.

Troy returned some time later as the pastor was delivering the eulogy. Troy's eyes were afire. He clasped her close to him and lowered his lips to her ear.

"After the service, there's someone that you *must* meet," he whispered.

She nodded. All she wanted to do after the funeral was go home, collapse in bed, and wake only after this nightmare had ended. The prospect of meeting anyone, of holding a coherent conversation, seemed an impossible burden to bear. Then there was still the burial at the cemetery, and the repast.

She didn't think she could handle any more of it. But she would do it for her grandmother. That was one lesson Lily had taught her well: how to keep moving forward when life tried to knock you down. She had been emotionally flattened all day, but she was going to see it through, the service and everything else that followed. She owed that to her grandmother. It was her duty.

Pastor Roger Hammond delivered the eulogy. A tall, gray-haired man in his sixties who had known Lily for decades, he was an eloquent speaker. He called Lily one of the "pillars" of the church community who had been gifted by God with the power to inspire, encourage, and nurture, and Monica noticed that nearly every head in the audience was nodding. It brought forth a fresh round of tears from her.

The service felt as though it was never going to end, but Monica eventually realized, as if slipping out of a trance, that people had lined up to greet her. She was Lily's only surviving immediate family; all of Lily's four siblings had passed on, and the children of those brothers and sisters were scattered to the wind. Lily had formed her closest bonds with the church, and Monica and her family.

Monica tried to get to her feet to meet the crush of people, but when her knees wobbled, the well-wishers insisted that she remain sitting. She greeted them all and accepted their embraces, kisses, and supportive words. A few of them even pressed envelopes into her hands that she dimly understood contained money, and she made a mental note to donate the funds to Lily's favored charities.

Troy remained at her side throughout the greetings, but he kept fidgeting and glancing over his shoulder to the back of the church. As the line finally dispersed, he helped her to stand.

"I want you to meet someone, sweetheart," he said.

"I'm exhausted, Troy. Who is it?"

"It's a surprise." His brown eyes glimmered.

"I need a few minutes." A spell of vertigo had hit her. She gripped the edge of the pew for balance. Looking around, she saw a stream of people filtering out of the sanctuary, but didn't see her children. "Wait, where are the kids?"

"Mom took them outside. They were restless."

She hadn't realized they had already left. Sniffling, she wiped her eyes with a handkerchief.

"I've got to visit the ladies room," she said.

"Sure, I'll meet you in the lobby."

In the restroom, Monica examined herself in the mirror. Predictably, her makeup was ruined from the tears she had shed, her eyes were bloodshot, and her hair looked as if it had been used as a crow's nest.

She switched on the faucet, allowed cold water to fill her cupped palms, and splashed them against her face.

Although Lily had raised her since her birth and treated her like a blood grandchild, she had sensed at an early age that she and Lily didn't share a genetic bond. They looked so different. Lily was short and heavy-boned, with an oak complexion and copper-brown eyes; Monica was slim, had always been taller than most of her female classmates, had a complexion the color of fresh honey, and striking hazel eyes. When Monica was nine, Lily had told her the hard facts of their relationship: she had adopted her at Monica's birth, loved her like her own biological grandchild, and was going to be there for her no matter what.

Although Lily's love for her never faltered, Monica wondered about her birth parents. Her father's identity was a mystery, but she wondered, especially, about her mother. As a mother herself to two children, she struggled to understand how a woman could give up a child she had carried in her belly for nine months, walk away, and never look back. Logically, she understood that depending upon the circumstances, putting a child up for adoption could be a good decision. But emotionally? It seemed incalculably difficult.

Where was her mother? Was she still alive? Did she ever think about Monica? Did she regret what she had done?

Those questions had haunted Monica for as long as she could remember. Lily had been her link to her mother, the only person in Monica's life who had ever known her, and in typical Lily fashion, she had declined to ever share much about her, pressing Monica to focus on the present. Monica had sensed that her biological mother and Lily hadn't been on the best of terms, but she had still felt a right to know.

Troy had even suggested hiring a detective to investigate birth records and piece together the story. Out of respect for Lily, Monica had turned down the idea. She respected her grandmother too much to go behind her back. If Lily had kept the details vague, Monica assumed it had to be for a good reason, as Lily had always had her best interests at heart.

But now, with Lily gone, Monica felt as if she had been cut off from everything that was and might have been.

She shuddered. Lowering her head, she pulled in several deep, stabilizing breaths.

Time to move forward. *Ever forward,* as Lily had always advised her.

Finally, she dried her face with a paper towel from the dispenser. She did a quick touch up of her makeup, and tried to do something to tame her hair.

As she stepped outside the restroom, an elderly gentleman waved at her from across the corridor. She didn't recognize him, but out of reflex, she returned the wave. He shuffled toward her, using a cane to support himself.

Is this the person Troy had wanted me to meet? She had never met this man before, and Troy wasn't around to confirm his identity.

"Young lady," the man said. He coughed into a handkerchief. He was about her height, but old age had given him a stoop that cut several inches from his stature. He was mostly bald, with a few wisps of brittle white hair clinging to his skull. He wore gold-rimmed bifocals.

"Sir?" Monica said.

He reached out and clasped her hand. His fingers were fragile as matchsticks and cool to the touch, but his chocolate-brown eyes radiated warmth and intelligence.

"I'm Reverend McBride." He smiled, displaying a set of dentures. "Miss Lily was a dear, dear friend of mine from way back. She went to my church before she joined Riverside."

"Oh? I didn't know about that."

"Young lady, the Lord has welcomed a new angel, yes, he has."

"Thank you, Reverend."

His bespectacled gaze searched her face. "Are you holding up okay, dear?"

"Lily was all I had."

He nodded. "I'm praying for you, child. And know this: when the good Lord closes one door, He opens another."

"I appreciate that, sir." She smiled tightly.

The old reverend hesitated, his gaze locked on her. Monica had the distinct impression that he wanted to say something else but was unsure how to begin. A heartbeat later, the moment was broken when Troy slipped up to them and gently grasped Monica by the arm.

"Everything okay, baby?" he asked.

"This is Reverend McBride, a friend of Lily's from back in the day," Monica said. "She used to go to his church."

"Pleased to meet you." Troy shook the reverend's hand. The reverend muttered a greeting and stepped back, seeming reluctant to turn away from Monica.

Troy steered Monica in the opposite direction. "Ready?"

Monica glanced over her shoulder. The pastor had turned and was shuffling down the hallway.

"I take it the reverend wasn't the mystery person you wanted me to meet?" she asked.

"Of course not. Come on."

"All right. Let's get this over with then."

Troy guided her down the corridor, through the thinning crowd, and back into the sanctuary.

"Up front there," Troy said.

Monica looked toward the front of the chamber, where Lily's gleaming casket still lay, flanked by several large and beautiful flower arrangements; the pallbearers had yet to cart it to the hearse waiting out front. A tall, slender woman dressed in black stood beside the coffin, her back to them, a solitary mourner paying her last respects.

As they approached, Troy cleared his throat. The woman turned.

When she revealed her identity, Monica passed out.

3

Troy caught Monica before she hit the floor. He eased her onto a nearby pew.

Monica's mouth lolled open, her eyelids fluttering. A low moan slipped out of her.

"Jesus, this really knocked her out," Troy muttered to himself. He felt a stab of guilt at how he'd handled the situation. Monica had been forced through an emotional wringer that day, and while the reveal of her birth mother could only be a good thing, it was too much for her to take right then. She was in a fragile state, and he needed to protect her, and probably should have done more to prepare her for this revelation.

But it was too late for that now.

Monica's mother had come to her daughter's side, too. She dabbed at Monica's brow with a green silk handkerchief.

"Mama's here, darling," she said. "Mama's finally here with you, yes she is."

Sounds good, but where the hell have you been all this time? Troy almost asked. He hadn't asked this woman much of anything after she'd revealed herself to him outside the church. He had been too surprised to know *what* to ask. He'd only agreed to bring Monica to her after the memorial service had concluded and before everyone left for the burial.

Hell, he hadn't thought to even ask her name.

"Make yourself useful and go fetch her some water, doctor," the woman said, in the tone of one used to dispensing orders. She waved him away. "Go on, now."

29

Troy blinked. Under any other circumstances, he wouldn't have tolerated that tone from anyone, much less a stranger, Monica's birth mother or not. But Monica needed him, and for her, he was willing to set aside his ego. He rose from the pew and left the sanctuary.

Downstairs, the church staff was setting up for the repast, which would commence after the burial. Troy grabbed a bottle of water from the beverage table, and returned back upstairs. He was about to head back into the sanctuary when he felt a tap on his arm.

He turned. The old pastor—Reverend McBride, was it?—had reached out with his wooden walking cane and prodded Troy.

"Where is your wife?" the reverend asked. "We didn't finish our conversation."

"She's preoccupied at the moment," Troy said. He wanted to get back to Monica and wasn't interested in wasting time talking to this guy. "Why don't you call her at home later on?"

Much to Troy's surprise, the old man slipped a late model iPhone out of his suit pocket. The man had to be damn near eighty, and Troy didn't know many octogenarians who were fluent with the latest technology.

"Give me the number, son," McBride said.

Troy recited their home phone number. McBride entered the digits into his phone with steady fingers, repeated the number back to Troy, and nodded with satisfaction.

"I'll be calling on her soon," McBride said. "We've much to discuss. As I told her, when the Lord closes one door, He opens another."

Brother, you ain't lying, Troy thought. He glanced inside the sanctuary at the seated figures of his wife, and her newfound mother. It looked as if Monica had regained consciousness. The two women were speaking, both of them clearly excited.

Troy decided to hang back for a few minutes, and give them some privacy. It wasn't every day that you met your mother for the very first time. They would have a lot to talk about, a lot of catching up to do. He wanted to let the moment last a little while longer.

4

An hour and a half later, after the burial at nearby Ben Hill Cemetery, they had returned to the church for the repast.

Everyone gathered in the spacious activity room in the basement that doubled as a dining hall. A couple of long serving tables had been set up, holding several silver chafing dishes full of food kept warm by low flames: fried chicken wings, baked tilapia, green beans, macaroni-and-cheese, meatballs, rice, collard greens, and more. Several dozen people sat at the circular tables spaced throughout the room, working through their meals and sipping cups of iced tea and soda. Laughter and smiles were everywhere. The repast was akin to a family reunion, an opportunity to break bread with friends and relatives who often saw one another only at the funeral of a loved one who had passed on.

Monica sat at a table in the corner with her family: Troy, Pat, the kids, and her mother. Her *mother*. Everyone else in the room might as well have been invisible to Monica, because she couldn't stop gawking at the woman.

Monica barely remembered Lily's burial service. When Troy had introduced Monica to her mother, she had passed out, apparently for a couple of minutes. Waking up to find her mother gently patting her hand and smiling at her had almost knocked her out again.

Everything since then had passed in a blur.

Her mother had waited behind at the church while Monica and her family had gone to the burial site; she claimed to abhor cemeteries and couldn't bear to set foot on those grounds. Far from being upset, Monica had been terrified that her mother would be gone when they returned for the repast.

But she was still there.

I'm finally talking to my mother.

Monica and her mother looked so much alike that it gave Monica chills. If Monica had been granted a vision of herself, twenty or so years in the future, that vision would have appeared exactly like the woman sitting next to her. Their genetic bond was unmistakable, downright jarring to witness.

"I never imagined this day would actually come," Monica was saying. "I mean, I did imagine it, but I never believed it would. I was afraid to hope for it, 'cause, you know, I never knew much about you. I didn't know if you were even still alive."

Monica knew she was babbling, but she couldn't help it. The words poured out of her: a lifetime of accumulated questions, and she craved answers to all of them.

"I understand, baby," her mother said. She held Monica's hand in her lap, and patted it gently. She had slender, but strong hands, Monica had noted, the hands of a woman who had worked hard for a living. "We've got so much we need to discuss. I feel fit to burst with it all, too."

Her mother's name was Grace Bolden. Lily had told Monica that her name was Grace Bolden, too, so Monica wondered if her mom—it felt weird to even think of that, her *mom*—had ever gotten married at some point. It was one of a million questions to which she yearned to get answers.

From across the table, Pat cleared her throat and leveled her gaze on Grace. "Grace, how did you find out about Lily? Had you kept in touch with her over the years?"

"All I can say is that she was on my heart, lately." Grace touched her chest as if to emphasize her point. "Isn't it remarkable how life works sometimes? I had been thinking of her, and I used directory assistance to locate her number. I called, but this was a couple of days after she had passed on, and I received no answer. I contacted the church. I recalled she had been a member and knew they could put me in touch with her."

"So they told you about the service," Troy said.

"Yes, and I *had* to come. I had to pay my respects." Grace looked to Monica and smiled. Monica felt her heart skip; she and her mother even smiled alike. "I had to see my child again. Lord knows it was long overdue."

"I'm so glad you came." Monica felt a fresh current of tears coming on. She blotted her eyes with a napkin.

"Where did you come in from again?" Pat asked.

"Houston, Texas," Grace said. "I've lived there for several years."

Monica wondered exactly how long her mother had lived in Texas. She didn't have an accent of any kind that Monica could identify, and she had the diction of an English teacher.

"I drove here all by myself, got in late last night," Grace continued. "I didn't want to miss one minute of Lily's home going. She did so much for me, back when I was a stupid little girl who didn't know any better."

"She helped lots of young girls," Monica said. She felt the absence of her grandmother so acutely that she had to pull in a deep breath, lest she fall back into a complete mess of sobbing.

What would Lily have said about Grace's return? Monica wondered. Lily had never had a whole lot to share about her biological mother, either positive or negative, but that was Lily for you. She hadn't been one to dwell on the past and had deflected most of Monica's questions with responses such as, *"that's water under the bridge, sugar, let's focus on today, the past is gone and tomorrow isn't promised to us."* Perhaps she had thought she was protecting Monica by being so evasive, but it had only deepened Monica's curiosity.

But there was no need to wonder any more. She planned to ask her mother everything.

"Are you married?" Troy asked.

Monica had noticed that Grace didn't wear a wedding band. In fact, multiple bejeweled rings of various metals adorned her long fingers—silver, gold, platinum—bearing diamonds, rubies, emeralds, and other stones. Several chains hung around her neck, too.

"Never married," Grace said. "I don't believe any man can be faithful to one woman."

Troy nearly choked on his drink. Monica thought it was an odd response, but she let it pass.

"Do you have other children?" Monica asked, and was almost frightened by the hope she heard in her voice.

Grace actually laughed. "Other children? Oh yes, dear. How can I put this without sounding improper? In my younger days, I guess you could say I was a baby factory."

"How many children do you have?" Pat asked.

"Seven," Grace said. She clasped Monica's hand. "That includes my girl here."

"Are you serious?" Monica felt her jaw unhinge. "I have six siblings?"

Grace was nodding. "Indeed, six sisters. All of them are grown now, of course, and quite spread out across the country."

"You've had all girls?" Pat asked. "That's really something."

"I'd love to see them." Monica shook her head, almost dizzy from the continuing stream of revelations. "My sisters—six of them. Wow."

"They'd love to meet you, too," Grace said. "Someday, perhaps we can arrange a family reunion."

"I'd like that very much," Monica said.

Monica started to ask another question, when her daughter, Lexi, decided she'd had enough of sitting at the table listening to boring grown folks' chatter. Lexi hopped out of her chair and darted across the room. Her brother, Junior, continued to sit on his chair next to Troy, eating a piece of chicken. He was the quieter, more malleable of her two children.

But Lexi was, to put it mildly, a handful. *Seven going on seventeen,* as Troy liked to say. She was a daddy's girl, with all the good and bad that came with it.

Troy noticed Lexi taking off. Eyebrows arched, he glanced at Monica, a question in his gaze.

"I can handle it," she said.

Monica pushed out of her chair and hurried after Lexi. Her daughter had arrived at a serving table. She was reaching for one of the many pre-cut slices of chocolate cake that had been laid on plastic dessert plates.

"Hold on there, little girl," Monica said. "You didn't ask if you could have cake."

Ignoring her, Lexi plucked a plate off the table.

"Put that back, sweetie," Monica said. "Please."

"But I love chocolate cake," Lexi said. She whirled her finger across the frosting, put it in her mouth.

"You can have some after you finish dinner," Monica said.

But Lexi took off running, cake in hand. Her braids, full of multi-colored beads, clattered in her wake.

Monica sucked in her bottom lip. She wasn't in the mood for Lexi's antics, not today, of all days.

Lexi raced to an empty table on the far side of the room. Once there, she plopped onto a chair and proceeded to shovel cake into her mouth with her fingers, as if determined to cram it all down her throat before it could be taken away.

Just like her father, Monica thought. *She's always got to have it all, on her terms.*

Monica navigated her way to the table, an artificial smile plastered on her face for the benefit of those watching the incident unfold. That fake smile promised everyone she was in control of the situation, but Monica's throat was tight with apprehension.

She didn't to make a scene, didn't want anyone to comment on her parenting skills. Being out in public with Lexi often worked her nerves like that.

Lexi had finished a third of the cake, crumbs flying everywhere, when Monica reached her. Monica snagged the plate and slid it out of her daughter's grasp.

Lexi shrieked, hitting an eardrum-piercing pitch that could have shattered glass. Half the heads in the room swiveled in their direction.

Has this child lost her ever-lovin mind? Good Lord.

Her face hot, Monica said in a tight voice: "Lexi, baby, quiet down, right now."

"I want my chocolate cake, Mommy." Tears were starting to flow.

"You know that you're supposed to ask for what you want," Monica said. She tried to keep a level tone. "You don't just take it."

"Give me my chocolate cake, Mommy!" Lexi climbed out of the chair and wrapped her arms around Monica's legs, beseeching her like a beggar in the street pleading for alms.

Blood pounded in Monica's head. She'd had enough. She was going to put the cake on the table and walk away, let Lexi have it just to calm her down. It wasn't worth all this trouble, not then, not there.

That's what your daughter is counting on, a voice in the back in her mind advised. *Your weakness. That's why she behaves like this with you, and only you. You always let her have her way.*

Monica felt a soft touch at the small of her back, and caught a current of Grace's rosemary fragrance.

"What's the matter, darling?" Grace said in a voice like easy-flowing honey. She knelt so that she and Lexi were eye to eye.

Lexi stared at Grace, tears glistening on her cheeks.

"I want chocolate cake," Lexi said, but in a softer tone.

"Oh, Nana knows that," Grace said. She ran her slender fingers through Lexi's braids. "You're such a beautiful girl, and you want your chocolate cake, hmmm? I understand. But Nana has something much better than chocolate cake."

By then, Lexi was transfixed, and so was Monica. She reminded herself that Grace had six other children—*my siblings*—and figured that meant she had oodles of grandchildren, too. She knew how to handle them.

Grace reached into her large, black leather purse and brought out a small glass jar. The jar held an assortment of brightly colored candies.

"These are gumdrops." Grace chuckled. "They are really quite good, if Nana says so. Would you like one, darling?"

Lexi nodded, sniffled.

"Ask your mommy if you may please have a gumdrop," Grace said.

"Mommy, may I please have a gumdrop?" Lexi's eyes shone. "Please, please, please?"

"You can have one," Monica said.

"Here you go." Grace opened the jar and deposited a red gumdrop into Lexi's palm.

"Thank you," Lexi said. She stared at the candy as if she'd been given the world's most treasured delicacy.

"You're welcome, darling," Grace said. "Now, please go back to sit with your brother at the table. You're setting an example for him and want him to see how well-behaved you are."

"Yes, ma'am," Lexi said.

Barely able to keep her eyes off the candy, Lexi quietly shuffled back across the room, to her family's table. Monica watched, shaking her head. Grace smiled at Monica.

"What a lovely child," Grace said. She sighed, clasped one of Monica's hands in hers. "You have such a wonderful family, dear. I wish I didn't have to drive back home to Houston today."

The thought of her mother leaving, so soon after they had finally connected, made Monica's heart twist.

"Can you stay a little while longer?" Monica asked.

5

Troy had hired a limousine service to pick them up from their home that morning and transport them to the funeral. That afternoon, they loaded up in the same Lincoln limo—Monica, his mother, and their kids—for the return drive back to their house in Dunwoody.

Grace was following them in a late model, white Chevy Malibu that Troy had tagged as a rental car without needing to ask. As the limo pulled out of the church parking lot, Troy glanced through the rear windshield to confirm Grace was tailing them. He noted that Monica was staring at her mother's car, too, as if she was afraid of letting the woman out of her sight and losing her again.

He could empathize with his wife. He was close to his own mother and couldn't imagine a life without her. His father had died over a decade ago from a heart attack, but Pops had been a jazz musician, always on the road doing gigs (so he said), an inconstant presence in their household. Troy, the eldest of three siblings, had long been the man of the family. In fact, three years ago, he had convinced his mom to move from Chicago to Atlanta after she'd retired from a long, distinguished career in the public school system. Mom had her own townhouse in Roswell, but she also had a guest room in their home, as she visited often. Troy would have had it no other way.

Although Monica was finally meeting Grace for the first time, he understood the pull of the biological bond between mother and child was like a magnetic force. When Monica had suggested that Grace spend the rest of the weekend at their house, he had readily agreed.

While he knew how important it was to Monica, he had his own admittedly selfish reasons for wanting to keep Grace around a little longer. With his wife preoccupied with her mother, it would give him an opportunity to slip away and handle his own business.

"I know I keep saying it, but I feel like I must be dreaming," Monica said. "Somebody, please pinch me and wake me up."

Lexi pinched Monica's leg, and giggled.

"Hey, not that hard," Monica said, but she laughed.

She looked good, Troy thought. Better, at least. They were bags under her eyes from lack of sleep the past week, but some of the brightness had come back to her gaze, and she was laughing again, too. Losing Lily had been hard on her and would continue to be a struggle, but with the entrance of her biological mom, she had a hope for a happier future.

"I'm so happy for you," Troy's mom said. "To finally meet your mother is surely a blessing."

"There's so much I need to talk to her about," Monica said. "I couldn't bear the thought of her leaving today. I'm so thankful she's able to extend her visit through the weekend."

"Do you intend to ask her why she never contacted you after all these years?" Mom asked.

"I was wondering the same thing," Troy said. "It's the million-dollar question, isn't it? Where the hell has she been?"

"Like I said, there's a lot that I need to talk to her about," Monica said. "I need to process through this in my own way. I'm just trying to take it all in."

"Of course, sweetheart," Mom said.

In normal traffic, the drive from East Point to Dunwoody might have taken an hour, but traffic was light on that Saturday afternoon. The limo turned into their neighborhood at a quarter to four.

They lived in Tulip Grove Estates, a gated community of forty custom-built homes. Designed in the French Provincial style, their residence was a six-bedroom, five-bath, three-garage house with a brick exterior. It sat on a wooded, one-acre lot at the edge of a forest.

They had built the place seven years ago. It had cost a lot more than Monica had wanted to spend, but she was a tightwad—Lily's influence on her—and Troy had, frankly, overruled her. The fact was that the house was close to their respective jobs (closer to his office, really), and hell, *both* of them were doctors. If they couldn't splurge on a grand home, then why the heck had they gone through all those arduous years of schooling and incurred a mountain of student loan debt?

Besides, Troy had been there, done that. He'd grown up on the South Side of Chicago, in a modest home where the idea of going on a vacation meant going "down south" to visit the same old boring relatives he saw every year. He had no intention of limiting his lifestyle, in any way, as a high-earning professional. You lived only once.

The limo pulled into the wide driveway, and Troy bounced out. Grace nosed her Chevy into the space beside them. As she got out of the car and appraised their house, she whistled lowly, removed her sunglasses.

"All right, now *this* is a house," she said. "But what else would you expect from a family of doctors?"

"Thanks," Troy said. "Do you have any luggage to take inside?"

"I'll take care of it myself, thank you." Coolness radiated from her gaze.

Troy hadn't honestly expected she would much have in the way of luggage since she had claimed her original intent was to leave that day, and she'd only arrived in town the night before. He didn't understand the sudden cold shoulder that he was getting from her, either, but perhaps she was one of those militant feminists who took offense to male chivalry.

Shrugging, he went to get his kids out of the limo. Out of the corner of his eye, he watched Grace open her car trunk and lift out a wheeled, black canvas suitcase. The bag had enough capacity for at least a week's worth of clothing, and it was fit to burst. Grace lifted it easily and placed it on the driveway.

Like mother, like daughter, he thought. Occasionally, he and Monica managed to get away for weekend trips, and she always packed an excessive amount of shoes and outfits, too.

"Thanks, brother." Troy gave the driver a generous tip and then turned to his clan. "Let's head inside, gang."

While Troy and his mom shepherded the children to the house, Monica and Grace trailed behind them. Mother and daughter spoke in soft, confidential tones; he heard Monica snicker. They were getting along famously, for which he was grateful.

Their Maltese, Duchess, was barking her head off when Troy opened the front door.

"Hey, you," Troy said to the dog. Duchess sniffed the cuffs of his slacks and whined, detecting that food had been consumed in her absence.

Lexi scooped Duchess up into her arms.

"Lexi, she needs to be let outside to potty," Troy said.

"I want Duchess to meet the new lady," Lexi said.

Lexi brought the dog to Grace as she stepped inside the house, and two things immediately happened: Grace recoiled as if presented with a hissing rattlesnake. And Duchess started barking furiously, baring her teeth, looking eager to rip into Grace if she could have managed it.

"I didn't know you had a dog." Grace moved back to the threshold, one hand clutching the doorknob. A scowl twisted her features.

"Oh, Duchess is always such a sweetheart," Monica said. She cooed to the dog, who would not be placated. "What's gotten into you, little girl?"

Duchess snapped and snarled, her attention focused solely on Grace. Grace glared at the dog.

She's definitely not a dog lover, damn, Troy thought. The woman looked as if she were eager to toss Duchess in front of a moving car.

Troy plucked Duchess out of Lexi's hands—his daughter was

struggling to hold onto her—and stroked the dog behind the ears. Petting her in that spot usually soothed her, but that time, it did nothing to calm her.

"I'll take her outside to pee and run around for a little while, burn off some of this energy," Troy said. "Monica, you can go ahead and show Grace to her room and let her get settled in, all right?"

Troy caught his mother's eye as he turned to take out the dog. A look passed between them, and Troy could read his mother's thoughts because they mirrored his own.

Duchess had always, without fail, been friendly to everyone.

Why didn't she like Grace?

6

Monica led her mother upstairs to one of the guest rooms. The surreal feeling of having her own flesh and blood parent in her presence was strong as ever; she could barely focus on where she was walking because she kept glancing over her shoulder at Grace.

Grace, for her part, seemed quietly amused at Monica's constant attention, her lips curved in a gentle smile. Her eyes absorbed every detail of the spacious house. Monica had never been truly comfortable with the size of their home—it seemed too ostentatious to her—but at that moment, she felt proud of what she and Troy had accomplished in owning such a place, and was eager for her mother's approval.

At the bedroom's threshold, Monica flicked the light switch.

"This is the other guest room, where you'll be sleeping." Monica hesitated, heart thudding. "Lily used to stay here when she would spend the night with us."

Her voice faltered as grief rippled across her heart. The spacious corner bedroom on the second floor still carried a trace of her grandmother's perfume, Chanel No. 5, and one of Monica's favorite photos hung on the wall opposite the queen-size bed: a recent, framed picture of Lexi, Junior, Monica, and Lily, dressed in their Sunday best and sitting on a wooden bench at the Atlanta Botanical Garden, surrounded by multi-hued roses. Her memory of that golden summer afternoon was more bittersweet than ever.

Grace gave Monica's shoulder a gentle squeeze. She strolled into the room, her suitcase trailing behind her.

"This is perfect, my dear." Grace traced her fingers across the flower-patterned bedspread. "I'm so thankful for your hospitality. With everything that you're dealing with right now, you didn't have to offer to let me stay overnight."

"Are you kidding? We have so much to talk about!" Monica laughed. She knew she sounded a bit manic, whipsawing from one emotional high to the next, as if adrenaline and nothing else was keeping her standing. Whenever she crashed later on, she was going to crash hard. "I couldn't let you leave so soon."

"Your family is as beautiful as your home," Grace said. "Those children of yours are absolutely adorable. And your husband? Goodness, what a piece of work he is."

"Pardon?" Monica's smile flickered. "Piece of work?"

"Oh, come now." Grace chuckled, eyes twinkling with mirth. "You know that man is a hopeless flirt. I lost count of how many women he'd mentally undressed at Lily's service. That includes me, before he learned my identity, of course."

Frowning, Monica glanced over her shoulder, down the long hallway, and confirmed that Troy and his mother were out of earshot.

"Troy is a great husband and father, but he's still a man," Monica said in a lowered voice. "You aren't going to stop a man from looking. I accepted that a long time ago. I'm not naive."

"Are you certain that he's only looking?" Grace settled onto the bed, crossed her long legs, and offered Monica a conspiratorial smile. "Woman to woman: he doesn't seem like the kind of man who would be satisfied with a 'look but don't touch' policy. He's got a *swagger* about him that I've recognized in many other men I've known over the years, and honey, they did a lot more than look."

"Now, hold on a minute." Monica crossed her arms, heat rushing to her face. "You just met Troy. I've been married to him for eight years. If he was fooling around on me, I promise you, I would know."

"Of course you would," Grace said, but her voice dripped with sarcasm. "I didn't mean to upset you. I've got no filter, darling, you'll come to learn that about me. It's gotten me into trouble before."

Monica hated to admit it, but Grace's remarks had gotten under her skin. Obviously, Troy had hawk eyes when it came to choice female anatomy. Men were visually stimulated, and like every guy she'd ever dated, if an attractive woman strolled past, he was going to look.

But cheating?

Troy wasn't a man known for restraint. He could be passionate about his interests to a degree that bordered on obsessiveness: fitness, eating organic foods, taking nutritional supplements, riding his Harley, following the Chicago Bears, investing in the stock market.

And let's not forget, sex.

Even eight years into their marriage, his sexual appetite showed no signs of abating. She enjoyed sex, too, loved and craved the intimacy they shared, but oftentimes, after a long day at work and then an evening spent with the children, she didn't have the energy to participate in bedroom activities. Troy usually seemed understanding, would give her a quick kiss, bid her goodnight, and roll over and drift to sleep.

Maybe he didn't push because he was wetting his whistle elsewhere.

She had no tangible evidence that he'd ever had an affair. None. He came home on time every night. No women called the house. He didn't take any unusual or frequent business trips. He answered his phone whenever she called him. He absolutely adored the children, and he showered her with affection. She had nothing to complain about. Grace's commentary should have rolled right off her back.

But it hung with her, like an eyelash stuck in her eye.

"Let's forget my little slip of the tongue, dear," Grace said with a dismissive wave. "I was, I believe, commenting on your adorable children?"

"Well, Junior is low-maintenance, easy-going. Lexi is a handful, as you've seen."

"She knows what she wants and isn't afraid to go after it. That's an admirable quality in a female and will serve her well in life. But you do need her to listen to you."

"She listens to Troy." *Because they're peas in a pod,* Monica almost said, but bit her tongue. She didn't want to delve into another character analysis of her husband. "We're working on it."

"I've had plenty of experience with headstrong children. I would be happy to offer a few tips if you'd like."

"Some of my siblings were headstrong?"

Grace laughed lightly. "I've worked for many, many years as a live-in nanny, tending the children of wealthy families. I've seen everything you can imagine, and much you probably could not. "

"Oh yes, I'm sure." Monica tried to hide her disappointment. In her childhood fantasies, her mother had held an exciting occupation, some high-flying career that explained why she had never come back to see about Monica. Discovering that her mother had spent her life taking care of someone else's children, while ignoring her, her own daughter, felt like the cruelest slap in the face imaginable.

"I know you have so much you want to discuss, and so do I, darling," Grace said. "First, I'd like to change clothes and freshen up."

"Of course," Monica said. "I'll do the same. I'll be back in a little while to give you the grand tour."

7

Once the child left her, Grace locked the bedroom door. For good measure, she grabbed a nearby upholstered chair and levered the broad back of it underneath the door knob.

The visit was going well, better than she could have anticipated. She had spent many years anticipating this encounter, wondering how it would proceed when she finally saw her child again, face to face. As she'd expected, Monica had blossomed into a truly beautiful woman.

The apple never falls far from the tree, she thought with a smile.

The visit would be full of conversation, laughter, and surprises. Grace could hardly wait to see how it all progressed.

Returning to the bed, she easily lifted her suitcase with one hand and deposited it on the mattress. The zipper unfurled with a whisper.

A black velvet sheet, folded lengthwise, lay atop her clothing, and she peeled it back. She had packed sufficient clothes for two full weeks. It was unlikely that she would stay at her daughter's home for such an extended period, but one must be prepared for all possible outcomes.

A wide mirror was bolted atop the oak dresser. Grace took the black sheet and a spool of masking tape from a compartment in the luggage, and, being careful to avoid glancing at her reflection, used the material to completely conceal the mirror surface's, using strips of tape to fix the sheet to the edges of the frame.

She exhaled deeply. *Much better*.

She could scarcely tolerate her reflection these days, and wherever she stayed, took pains to conceal any mirrors she would frequently come across. What older woman, once young and desirable, could stand constantly having to look at a graying husk of her former self?

With the mirror taken care of, Grace returned to her suitcase and began to unpack. In addition to the various articles of clothing and shoes, there was jewelry, bags of candies and teas and herbal tinctures, bundles of dry herbs, rolling paper for her special cigarettes, creams and oils, and much more.

Once she had unpacked and found appropriate places for the items, she stripped bare.

Even a brief glimpse of her naked form—flat, droopy breasts, vast swaths of winkles, the snow-white thatch of pubic hair—nauseated her. Sometimes her disgust was so intense that she would get dressed while standing in a dark closet, but she didn't have that luxury then.

The youthful version of her body had been a stunner, capable of enchanting any man, anywhere—and more than a few women, too. A twinge of nostalgia tugged at her.

Sighing, she slipped on a set of fresh undergarments. To finish, a solid purple kimono dress and matching slippers struck the tone that fit her mood.

Next, she pulled off her wig.

She slowly ran her fingers across her scalp. She was almost entirely bald—only a few strands of brittle hair bent underneath her touch. Her lips curled with distaste. She missed having a head full of dark, luxuriant hair.

From a velvet lined box she had placed on the dresser, she extracted another wig.

She had enough wigs to wear a different hairstyle every day for a whole month. If a woman must wear one, she ought to wear them with panache.

Working solely by touch, she fitted the fresh hairpiece on her head, pulled it down snug.

She removed the full set of false teeth she'd been wearing all day and dropped them in a jar full of a clear, sanitizing liquid. Her gums ached. Using a small applicator, she dabbed a homemade ointment along the ridges of her sore gums.

While the ointment settled in and worked its magic, she opened her makeup kit. The kit included a miniscule moon-shaped mirror, and everything else a woman needed: eyeshadow, blushes, powder, lipsticks, and more.

Using a cotton ball dipped in cleanser, she wiped the current layer of makeup off her skin. It required several cotton balls to complete the task. A quick check of her reflection in the kit's mirror—barely a second, which was all she could tolerate—confirmed she had cleansed away the prior face.

Goodness, I look my age, she thought. *What would my child think if she saw me in such condition?*

Monica would never get that opportunity, of course. No one, not even her closest lovers—of which she'd had several—had seen her without makeup in many, many years.

Such was the price a woman paid for beauty.

8

As she was heading toward the walk-in closet in the master bedroom, Monica happened to glance outside the balcony window. Troy was still in the backyard with Duchess. He leaned against the railing of the large wooden deck, his cellphone pressed to his ear. He was making angry gestures, face twisted with tension.

Monica paused. *What's going on?*

A pair of French doors served as the entrance to the wide, wrought-iron balcony. She pulled them open and poked her head outside.

"Troy? Is everything okay?"

Troy's gaze snapped upward as if his head bounced on a spring. His eyes simmered.

"Some bullshit with my little brother came up," he said, one palm covering the phone's speaker. "Go on back inside, baby. You don't need to worry about it."

"Does he need a loan again?"

"Baby, *don't worry about it*. I said I'll handle it."

She withdrew from the balcony, fastened the doors shut. Before she stepped away, she saw Troy wander farther away from the house, to the edge of the expansive backyard.

Out of the eavesdropping zone, she thought.

It was entirely feasible that Troy had gotten sucked into some drama of his brother's creation. Perhaps twice a year, his brother called with a story that ended in a request for money for some purpose or other—he was behind on child support payments, his

50

car needed major repairs, he'd gotten behind on rent, yada yada yada. As the eldest of his mother's three children, Troy was generous to a fault, the one that everyone called when they were in a bind.

So why did she think he was lying to her?

In the large walk-in closet, she kicked off her shoes, pulled off her black dress, peeled out of her support garments and panty hose. A full length mirror hung on the wall in the dressing area. Monica stood in front of the mirror wearing only her bra and panties, assessing herself with a critical eye.

She was thirty-nine years old, would hit forty in three months. In spite of giving birth to two kids, she had a more sculpted physique than she had enjoyed in her early twenties. It wasn't easy. She had to work harder to maintain her figure than she ever had as a younger woman, following a demanding routine of Pilates and Zumba, and adhering to a sensible diet. She thought she looked good, and not just "good for her age." When she went out in public, men half as old as her still flirted, a fact of which she was, perhaps, inordinately proud, and would smile to herself after such encounters thinking, *I've still got it.*

Nevertheless, her body was changing. Her skin wasn't as smooth. Her hair wasn't as thick. Laugh lines were settling in. Gravity was tugging at her breasts. Father Time was, slowly but surely, pulling her into middle age.

Had Troy noticed, too? Decided his wife was no longer the hot young thing he'd married and moved on to someone younger? Was he talking to that woman on the phone right then?

It was foolish to entertain such thoughts. Her mother's remarks were getting to her, kindling self-doubts. She hadn't realized her confidence in her marriage could be so easily punctured, but when you met your mother for the first time in your entire life and she gave you a biting criticism of your husband's fidelity, the words cut deep.

Let it go, she warned herself. *My mother's doesn't know Troy, and she doesn't know me, either. She's just talking. It means nothing.*

A hot shower would help clear her mind. It always did.

She stripped out of her bra and panties. As she was turning to go to the shower, Troy entered the closet.

"Hey," she said.

He grunted, edged around her, starting unbuttoning his shirt. Although she was completely nude, he didn't give her the slightest glance. She could remember a time when the spectacle of her naked body used to get him salivating.

"What's going on with your brother?" she asked.

"Don't want to get into it right now." He still didn't look at her, had his back turned as he undressed. "Maybe later."

"If you didn't know me, how old would you say I am?" she asked.

"What?" He turned, eyebrows arched.

"Do I have the body of a woman on the brink of forty?" She pulled in a deep breath, unconsciously sucking in her stomach. "Be honest."

"What the hell brought this on?" he asked.

"Can you just answer me honestly?"

"You look good for your age, and you know it," he said. "What's this inquisition all about?"

"So I look good for my age. Thanks, but it sounds like a back-handed compliment."

"Damn, baby. Don't you have other things to worry about right now instead of my opinion on your looks? I know I do. I'm done talking about this."

He snatched some fresh clothes off hangers and stormed out of the closet. She thought about pressing it further, but knew from experience that when Troy declared, *I'm done talking about this* that he was going to give her the silent treatment on the topic. His refusal to engage—when he decided he'd had enough—was a trait of his that had always annoyed her.

But this wasn't over yet. Not even close.

9

Monica tapped on the guest room door.

"It's me," she said. "Ready for the tour?"

"A moment, please," Grace said from inside.

Monica twisted the door knob, but the door was locked. Neither Pat nor Lily had ever locked their bedroom doors when they were visiting.

Shrugging, Monica waited in the hallway. She had changed into Croc flats, jeans, and a black long-sleeve blouse. Her homebody gear, as she liked to call it. She had no intention of leaving the house again that day.

She should have been exhausted after such an emotionally charged day, but she was inordinately excited about giving her mother a tour of her home. When she wasn't working at the clinic, taking the kids to some activity, or shopping, she was usually in her house; she had invested much of her time and energy into creating a beautiful, nourishing space for her family. Their home was a reflection of her, and showing her mother around, would, in a sense, illustrate the woman she had become.

A few minutes later, Grace emerged from the bedroom. She wore a simple purple kimono and matching, ballerina-style slippers. Monica noticed that she had refreshed her make-up, too, and that her thick gray hair looked different. Styled in a cute pageboy, it had the too-perfect look of a wig. Monica wondered about the condition of her mother's natural hair.

"Try a mint?" Grace asked. She offered Monica a quarter-sized wafer wrapped in silver foil.

"Thanks, but I'm not a fan of mints," Monica said.

"You'll like these. I promise you." Grace pressed the mint into her palm.

Monica unwrapped the candy. It was a greenish disc, with milky white striations across the surface. She slipped it onto her tongue. An intense burst of peppermint flavor made her pucker her lips.

"Hmm, that's strong," Monica said. "Good flavor, though."

"I make them myself. It's one of my hobbies."

"Ah, so you make mints and gum drops, too, like the one you gave Lexi at the church?"

"Straight from Nana's kitchen." Grace smiled.

"I enjoy baking as well. Interesting that we've got that in common." Monica clasped her hands together. "So. Let me show you around, okay?"

As they were already on the second floor of the house, Monica started their tour from there.

"Some logistics first. You already know where one of the restrooms is located, right across the hallway here." Monica motioned from the bathroom to another nearby door. "That's the other guestroom, where Pat sleeps. You and Pat can share the bathroom."

"I don't get my own lavatory?" Grace shook her head. "Tsk, tsk."

"Well, it's the closest one. I thought you wouldn't mind."

"I was making a joke. It's acceptable. Go on."

Monica proceeded to the open-air catwalk that bridged the various quarters on the second floor, her mother following close behind. From above, they had a view of the spacious family room below. Troy was watching a college football game on television, while his mother talked on her cell phone. Their kids played together on the floor with a set of Legos.

Duchess, sitting in Pat's lap, looked up at them. A low growl started deep in her throat.

What is her problem with my mother? Monica wondered again. *It's so unlike her.*

"This walkway, while visually striking, could pose a hazard for children." Grace ran her fingers along the decorative, wrought-iron railing that bordered both sides of the catwalk. "An adventurous youngster might be inspired to climb the railing and take a leap to the furniture below. Children do such things from time to time."

"Lexi is terrified of heights," Monica said, "and Junior's too little to climb up. I'm not concerned about it."

"Hmph." Grace's lips tightened. "Their Nana will worry about it then."

"Okay . . . so about this Nana stuff," Monica said. They reached the end of the catwalk and approached the next set of rooms. They were out of earshot from her family downstairs, but Monica nonetheless spoke in a hushed tone. "The kids have always addressed Troy's mother as 'Nana.' I think it's best if we use another name for you. I don't want to confuse them."

Grace stared at her. Monica found her forthright gaze slightly disconcerting. *Is she really angry about a name?*

"All of my other grandchildren have always called me Nana," Grace said.

"Understood, but like I said, they already call Troy's mother 'Nana,' " Monica said. "It wouldn't be right to take that name from her and give it to you."

"There can be only one Nana. I suppose I'll have to suffocate your husband's mother with a pillow tonight while she sleeps."

While Monica frowned at her, Grace grinned and playfully swatted her arm.

"It's no problem, dear," Grace said. "We can create another term of endearment that the children can use to address me."

"Thanks for understanding." Tension easing out of her, Monica tapped her bottom lip. "I've got it. How about they call you 'Miss Grace'?"

"Miss Grace? That sounds like something you would call a family friend or a neighbor, not a maternal grandmother, for goodness sake."

"Sorry." Monica stammered. "I'm struggling with this. Heck, I don't even know what to call you. I mean, I know I should call you 'mom' . . . but I don't think I'm ready for that yet."

"Take some time to think about it then, sweetheart." Grace's eyes were kind. "Let's see the rest of your home, yes?"

Monica showed her Junior's and Lexi's bedrooms—painted blue and pink respectively—and an activity area for the kids that she had designed. The room included a bookcase full of children's books, a small work table with matching chairs, educational toys stored in a large wooden bin, and a twenty-gallon freshwater aquarium teeming with darting tetras of multiple hues.

She gave Grace a brief look inside the master suite, too, and then showed her another room that served as Monica's study. In the study, Monica pointed out her collection of angel figurines that she had been collecting since she was a child, her glass display case full of medals and trophies from her many years of sprinting competitions, and a photo journal of her garden over the years.

Throughout the tour, Grace listened attentively, asked lots of questions, and shared remarks about her own experiences. *This* was the mother-daughter connection that Monica had been craving all her life, and what was fascinating was just how much she and her mother had in common, in both interests, and perspectives. She'd never had quite the same feeling with anyone else, even some of her closest girlfriends.

We've missed so much, Monica thought, fighting to hold back another wave of tears.

Afterward, they went downstairs by way of the grand spiral staircase, and entered the kitchen. It was an enormous space, equipped with track lighting, stainless steel appliances, glass-fronted cabinets, granite countertops, and a travertine floor. An array of copper cookware hung from hooks above the island, which also included a dual sink. It was one of the few areas of the house for which Monica had truly spared no expense.

"This rivals a kitchen at a restaurant." Grace traced her fingers across the six-burner Viking range. "Do you cook, or do you hire a chef to prepare your meals?"

"A chef?" Laughing, Monica leaned against the long center island. "Yes, we've got a chef, all right, and that's me. I do *all* of the cooking, always have. No one was going to live with Lily without being able to throw down in the kitchen."

"I remember that about her." Grace smiled wistfully.

"God, I miss her." Monica's chest suddenly got tight with emotion. She looked around for a box of Kleenex, but Grace snapped out a yellow handkerchief and offered it to her.

As Monica blotted her teary eyes, Grace slowly rubbed her hand in a circular motion across her shoulders and upper back. Lily had used to comfort her in the same way when she was a child, and the bittersweet memory made Monica cry harder.

"You should rest, my dear," Grace said. "No doubt, you're exhausted. You've had a terribly stressful day."

"I'm okay." Monica sniffled.

But as if Grace's words had triggered a switch, Monica yawned. Drowsiness tugged at her. The compulsion to lie down and sleep was so strong it was almost as if she had ingested a powerful sedative.

"I wanted to spend time with you," Monica said. "There's so much we have to talk about. We've barely scratched the surface."

"Pish, posh. I'm not going anywhere. Let's get you upstairs to bed. You've done enough today."

"But the kids will need to eat dinner."

"Their Nana will take care of it," Grace said, and Monica was too tired to protest her use of that name again. "Relax, darling. Nana will take care of everything."

10

Troy and his mom kept an eye on the kids while Monica showed her mother around the house. But when the clock ticked past six in the evening and Lexi asked about dinner, Troy realized that he hadn't seen Monica and Grace in a while. He'd heard them go back upstairs, but that had been some time ago hadn't it?

More than likely, the two women were diligently working on forging their mother-daughter bond, in private. Troy knew that Monica had a lot of tough questions she wanted Grace to answer, and there would be tears and accusations, justifications and apologies. It wasn't the kind of conversation that everyone needed to hear.

Like the discussion he'd had outside on his phone when they'd gotten home. Monica had inquired for details, but some things were meant to remain confidential.

"I'm going to see what they want to do for dinner." Troy pushed out of his leather recliner and stretched his arms over his head. "I'll be right back."

Mom had been reading a book to Lexi and Junior, both kids perched attentively on either side of her on the sofa. She was a natural teacher, one more reason Troy loved having her around. His children thrived in her presence.

"If they don't mind, I can reheat the leftovers I brought from the repast," she said. "It's no trouble at all."

"That's probably what we'll do, but I'll check."

Troy headed up to the second floor. He called out: "Monica? Grace? Have a minute, ladies?"

No one answered him. He shuffled down the catwalk. The door to the guest room where Grace would be sleeping was closed, but a knock brought no response. He opened the door.

The room was dark, and vacant.

The familiar scent of rosemary hung in the air. He ordinarily liked the scent, but it was so strong that it made his stomach roll. Quickly, he pulled the door shut and sucked in a deep breath, and the spell of nausea passed.

Had that smell come from something Grace had brought into the house? Some kind of weird incense or potpourri?

He looked around the second floor and wound up at the only room he hadn't checked, the master bedroom. The double doors were shut. When he turned the door lever, he found it locked.

He knocked. "Monica? Is everything okay?"

He got no reply. He knocked again, harder. A few seconds later, Grace cracked open the door a couple of inches. Her brows crinkled into a frown.

"What's going on?" Troy asked.

"My daughter is resting," she whispered. "She's had a long day, as you surely can appreciate."

"Can I come in?" He pushed the door, but Grace didn't budge.

"Let her sleep, dear," Grace said. "Go away."

He thought he must have heard her wrong. Go away? Was this woman serious?

"Listen, this is my room, too," he said. "Let me in. Right now."

Lips pressed together, Grace regarded him with a narrowed gaze full of disdain. Finally, she moved aside.

Troy entered, marveling that this woman actually had the nerve to lock him out of his own bedroom, in his own damn house. In the dim glow of a lamp, he noticed that Grace's skin was flushed. A glistening sheen of perspiration coated her face, too, and the top two buttons of her kimono-style dress were undone, giving him a glimpse of cleavage that he would have rather not seen.

He looked toward the bed, and saw Monica sprawled across the sheets, on her back. She rarely slept in that position. She wore a pink nightgown, but from the careless positioning of her limbs and her tousled hair, she looked as if she had passed out after a wild night of binge drinking.

"She's really out of it," Troy said. "How long has she been asleep?"

"Not nearly long enough, as you can see, obviously." Grace stared at him, hands bunched into fists on her waist. "Is there something I can do for you?"

"The kids are hungry. I wanted to know Monica's plans for dinner. My mom can reheat leftovers, though."

"Leftovers are unacceptable," Grace said, with a curt shake of her head. "I'll prepare dinner for the family. Was that all?"

"I think I'm going to take a shower." He nodded toward the doorway. "Do you mind giving me some privacy?"

"I doubt you have anything I haven't seen before." Slowly, she assessed him from sole to crown, gaze lingering on his crotch. She offered a hint of a smile.

"Excuse me?" he asked.

But she was strolling out of the room. On her way, she brushed past him—and lightly pinched his butt.

Hold up. Did she just pinch my ass?

"Please don't disturb my child," Grace said. "She needs her rest."

Grace closed the door behind her. Troy stood rooted to the carpet, mouth agape, wondering if that entire exchange had really happened or if he had only imagined it.

11

Pat was in the kitchen preparing to re-heat leftovers from the repast when Grace came in.

Pat felt her stomach coil into a tight knot. Try as she might to give this woman a fair chance, there was something about her that Pat had distrusted since her first encounter. She couldn't put her finger on a specific detail. It was everything about her, and the troubling feelings wouldn't go away no matter how hard Pat tried to bury them.

Where exactly had this woman been for all of Monica's life? Why make an appearance now—at a funeral? What did she want that had incentivized her to finally appear?

Whatever her motives, Pat distrusted them. Troy and Monica were a prosperous couple, with a beautiful home and children. A cunning individual could take advantage of a woman like Monica, someone enduring a terrible bout of grief. Although their genetic bond was undeniable—from the looks of her, Grace was Monica's biological mother as surely as Pat was Troy's mother—the circumstances of this emotional reunion were questionable.

The family dog, Duchess, was on edge, too. The normally sweet-tempered canine had been resting on the floor at the edge of the kitchen, but when Grace came in, her ears lifted and she started growling.

Pat didn't know why the dog disliked Grace, but Pat considered herself an astute judge of character. She had worked as a high school principal in the Chicago Public Schools district for decades. Throughout her career, time and again, her intuition had proven spot-on about teachers, administrators, and students. She had led her school to distinction as one of the best in the state, and it was partly because she had learned to balance the facts with her well-honed instincts.

Nevertheless, she was going to keep her mouth shut about Grace. Monica had dealt with enough lately, with losing Lily and all. The poor girl was desperate to create a relationship with her biological mother, and Pat's own misgivings gave her no reason to interfere.

But in the meantime, she was going to keep a close watch on Grace Bolden.

Pat had removed a stack of four, foil-wrapped plastic plates from the refrigerator and was looking for a dish to use for reheating the food as Grace strolled to the pantry. Grace was humming a tune, which Pat recognized as *Amazing Grace*. It annoyed Pat, perhaps irrationally. They had just heard the song at Lily's funeral.

"I'll be preparing tonight's dinner for the family." Grace retrieved an apron from the clothing hook on the inside of the pantry door. "My daughter is enjoying a well-deserved rest. You can go look after the children. Run along, now."

Run along, now? Please. "I'm going to reheat the leftovers in case anyone wants them."

"No one will want them." Grace knotted the apron around her waist. "Not after they've gotten a taste of Nana's famous meatloaf."

"You're going to make meatloaf?" Pat asked.

"Meatloaf, mashed potatoes, a chopped salad . . . perhaps homemade biscuits." Grace had opened the refrigerator and was rummaging through the contents. "They keep a well-stocked icebox."

"I went grocery shopping yesterday," Pat said. "Since so much has been going on with the funeral and all, I've been trying to help out as much as I can. That's what I do."

Muttering to herself, Grace was placing ingredients on the

counter: a large package of ground beef, onions, a tub of butter, various bottles of sauces. She slid a chef's knife out of the chopping block and used it to slice away the plastic wrapping around the meat.

Pat leaned against the counter and took a sip of her iced tea. It was obvious that Grace knew her way around a kitchen. She was sorting through items with the casual expertise of an experienced cook.

"Do you still work, back home in Houston?" Pat asked. "Or have you retired?"

Grace didn't reply. Humming, she washed vegetables, opened a cabinet to retrieve spices.

"Grace?" Pat asked.

Suddenly, Grace whirled toward her clutching the chef's knife. Her nostrils flared. Pat took a quick step backward, the edge of the counter stabbing into her lower back and giving her a small jolt of pain.

But there was danger in Grace's gaze. Pat had seen that same menacing glint in the eyes of a student who had attempted to knife a teacher, right in the midst of her office.

Duchess leapt from the floor and scrambled to Pat's side. She snarled and barked at Grace, seven pounds of fur and fury.

Grace's gaze flitted from the dog, to Pat, and back to the dog. Her lips curled in disgust.

"I am busy preparing dinner for the family," Grace said. "Please remove that foul, four-legged creature from my kitchen. Any animal that licks its own twat has no business in a space intended for food preparation and consumption."

"Relax, it's fine," Pat said carefully. She slid away another step, nudging Duchess backward with her foot. "Is my presence distracting, too?"

"You can stay if you wish. Perhaps you would learn something about cooking by observing me."

"Pardon me?" Pat blinked. "I'm a capable cook."

"Hah! I beg to differ. You were going to serve leftovers—not very delectable ones, at that—to growing young children.

Doubtless, you're one of those grandmothers who deem it appropriate to 'treat' her grandchildren at fast-food restaurants, too."

Pat was speechless.

"Why do the children call *you* Nana, anyway?" Grace asked.

"Well." Pat struggled to find her voice. "They always have. Why wouldn't they? They've known me since the day they were born." *Unlike you, who just showed up today,* Pat thought, but didn't say.

Grace's face briefly contorted with an emotion that Pat interpreted as either frustration, or anger. She looked, to Pat, like a child teetering on the verge of a complete meltdown, and Pat braced herself for another outburst.

Then, just as quickly, it was over. Mumbling, Grace turned back to the ingredients she had assembled on the counter.

There is something dangerously wrong with this woman, Pat thought. *I don't know exactly what, but something isn't right.*

Pat wanted to put some of the leftovers back in the refrigerator—it was a waste to re-heat all of the food if Grace was going to prepare a large meal—but she wasn't too keen on getting close to Grace while she was wielding a large knife. Picking up Duchess, she retreated to the family room.

She didn't want to intrude on Monica's reunion with her birth mother, but she had to warn Troy about this woman.

12

Dinner was, in Troy's opinion, outstanding. He hadn't eaten meatloaf in years, but Grace might have prepared the best damned meatloaf he'd ever eaten in his life. The mashed potatoes were sublime, seasoned with a flavorful blend of butter, garlic, rosemary, parsley, and salt. The chopped salad, comprised of romaine lettuce, carrots, tomatoes, and cucumbers, was drizzled with a tangy, balsamic-like dressing that made Troy salivate. The homemade biscuits were fluffy as clouds.

The kids ate their entire portions of their meals, too, a rare occurrence. Junior could be counted on to devour whatever you put in front of him, but Lexi was notoriously picky and could rarely be persuaded to eat anything outside of mac-and-cheese, pizza, yogurt, and chicken tenders.

Duchess hadn't been left out, either. Grace prepared something for the Maltese—it looked like cooked ground beef— and dished it into the dog's ceramic feeding bowl (which Troy noticed had been moved to the farthest corner of the kitchen). Duchess consumed the meat eagerly, tail wagging, and trotted back to Grace begging for more, her prior animosity toward the woman forgotten.

For his part, after comfort food of that caliber, Troy was willing to forgive Grace's earlier, inappropriate behavior toward him. Perhaps the woman was a tad bit eccentric. Maybe she didn't understand personal boundaries. He could probably accept her oddities, so long as she kept wielding her sorcery in the kitchen.

It was too bad that Monica missed out; even the delicious aromas wafting through the house had failed to rouse her. Grace insisted on letting her rest, and Troy agreed with her. Monica had endured an emotional roller-coaster that day, extreme highs and equally dramatic lows, and it was understandable that she'd be up there in their bedroom, dead to the world.

"I'll say it again," Troy said, dabbing at his lips with a napkin. "That was fantastic, Grace. You're going to have to visit us more often."

"As they say, the way to a man's heart is through his stomach." Grace smiled. "Are you sure you won't have any, Pat, before I clear away the dishes?"

"I'm full." Troy's mother offered a thin smile.

Troy noticed that Mom had eaten leftovers from the repast and hadn't touched anything that Grace had prepared. He detected an undercurrent of tension between the two women, and sensed, via the almost telepathic bond that mothers and their children shared, that his mom wanted to tell him something about Grace, but he had no idea what it might be.

"Then dinner is over." Grace pushed away from the table. She grinned at the kids. "After Nana provides dessert for the children."

"Yeah!" Lexi said, and shot her arms skyward in a victory dance. Junior saw what his older sister did and emulated her, little arms thrust into the air, which drew a chuckle from Troy.

"Dessert at this hour?" Mom frowned. "It's past eight o'clock. I don't think giving them sugar so close to bedtime is a wise idea."

"Nonsense." Grace gave a dismissive wave. She opened the freezer section of the refrigerator and removed a plastic container. "What is dinner without a dessert? Besides, I'm giving them a homemade strawberry sorbet, which happens to be sugar-free."

"Oh," Mom said in a small voice.

From the container, Grace doled out scoops of bright red sorbet into small bowls, one scoop for each child. Troy asked for one, too, but Grace shook her head.

"They're intended for the children," she said. "It's their special treat from Nana's private recipe collection."

"Sure." Troy shrugged. "But you just said what is dinner without dessert? I was hoping for something."

"How about I bake a cake for you before I leave tomorrow?" Grace said. She tilted her head. "What's your favorite, dear?"

"I've always loved German chocolate cake." He glanced at his mother. "My mom makes the best."

"Thanks, sweetheart." Mom smiled at him.

"Your opinion on that may change once you've tasted mine," Grace said, but she had leveled her unblinking gaze at his mother.

What's going on between these two? Troy wondered. Were they competing for a Grandmother of the Year award? He'd also caught Grace's repeated use of the title "nana" in reference to herself, and had seen his mother bristle at each mention. He understood his mom's discomfort. The kids had always known her as "nana," and she wasn't willing to give up that name to someone who had just arrived on the scene, maternal grandmother or not.

To help defuse the tension, Troy asked the kids to leave the table and come with him. He picked up their bowls of dessert and took the children upstairs into their activity area, planning to let them play while they ate the sorbet, and gradually nudge them toward their bedtimes.

His mother arrived soon thereafter, as he'd known she would. She settled beside Troy on the microfiber sofa, fingers clasping a glass of iced tea. Her lips curved in a wan smile.

"Grace is cleaning up the kitchen," Mom said. "Normally, I would have offered to help, but you know . . ."

"You don't like her," Troy said.

"I don't *trust* her," Mom said in a lowered voice. "That's what I've wanted to tell you."

Troy glanced at Lexi and Junior. The kids were playing with their respective toys, and didn't seem to be tuned in to their conversation, but children could be like human audio recorders and might repeat whatever they'd heard, at the most inopportune moments. He needed to be mindful to avoid giving them fodder for something later on.

"Let's be careful about little ears." He shifted on the cushions so he could face his mother. "Explain, please."

"It's difficult to articulate." Mom's eyes narrowed as she contemplated her words. "But there's this almost casual rudeness about her. Take the remark about the chocolate cake, for instance. That was simply rude, Troy."

"Definitely uncalled for, agreed. It's not a contest."

"My gut tells me that what I've observed so far is only the tip of the iceberg. You know I'm a shrewd judge of character."

He couldn't argue her point. In his entire adult life, he had brought home only three women to meet his mother. Monica was the only one his mother had actually liked; Mom had declared the others would make his life miserable. A couple of years after he married Monica, out of sheer curiosity, he had looked up those two exes online and found that one had been divorced twice already, and the other lady was serving time in prison for running an identity theft scam with her boyfriend.

He trusted his mother's judgment, implicitly.

"Point duly noted," he said. "But wow, she sure can cook."

"Don't let good cooking deceive you," Mom said. "She could have acquired those culinary skills while working in the prison kitchen."

Troy laughed, but Mom didn't.

"We don't have to deal with the situation much longer, okay?" he said. "She's only staying through tomorrow."

"Wouldn't have known that based on the size of her suitcase." Mom clinked the ice cubes in her glass, lips puckered sourly.

"Yeah, I noticed that, too."

"But as you said, it's only for one night," Mom said. "We can deal with it and send her on her way tomorrow."

"Exactly," he said. "We're doing this for Monica, remember? Let's just try to stay out of it. We don't need the drama."

"Fair enough." Mom squared her shoulders. "I'll try."

13

After Troy put the kids down to bed, he went to his bedroom and checked on Monica. He thought he would offer her something to eat, but it was like attempting to rouse Lazarus from the grave. She was in such a profound state of slumber that powers greater than his would have been necessary to wake her. If he hadn't known better, he would have declared her comatose.

He decided to let her keep on sleeping. He'd experienced a long day, too, but he was far from tired, and had plenty of energy left to burn.

The only question was: how would he choose to exert himself?

A few text messages later, he had his answer. Quickly, he changed into his workout gear: a pair of gray fleece training pants, a matching hoodie, and running sneakers. He kissed Monica on the forehead and left the bedroom. She didn't even stir.

Grace was coming up the spiral staircase as he was heading down.

"Where are you going, mister?" She blocked his path, glanced at her silver wristwatch. "It's past nine o'clock."

For a few years in his youth, Troy had attended a Catholic school. Grace's suddenly stern demeanor reminded him of one of the most feared nuns on staff, Sister Sweet—the irony of her name was a running joke in the school—who zealously monitored student behavior and was quick to punish the students for even minor infractions.

But that was a long time ago. He was a grown-ass man, in his own house, and he could come and go as he pleased. He didn't need to offer an explanation to a guest of all people.

"Step aside." He tried to brush past Grace, but she stuck out her arm to block his passage.

She stared at him, a challenge in her hazel-eyed gaze.

"You won me over with dinner, but now you're out of line—again," he said. "Do I have to remind you that you're a guest in *my* house?"

"Perhaps you see it that way." She smiled thinly. "But do you expect me to stand idly by while you violate my daughter's trust?"

Something in him wilted.

"What the hell are you talking about?" he asked.

"Oh, come now." Grace chuckled. "I'm wise to the ways of men, dear. Your duplicity has my naïve daughter fooled, but I knew your true nature the moment I laid eyes on you. You're practically a walking erection, eager to plunge into any warm hole you can find."

"Listen, you don't know a damn thing. I love my family. I'm committed to them 24/7. Monica knows that about me."

"You're dressed as if you're going to the gym." She assessed his body in that slow, sinuous way of hers, as if she were a giant black widow and he were a tasty fly that she might choose to consume. "That's the cover story, yes? A late-evening workout to blow off some steam?"

"If you must know—yes. And it's not a 'cover story.' It's the truth. I'm going to the gym."

"You have a fitness room here, in the basement of this residence. Why not use it?"

"I like to get out of the house, sometimes, not that it's any business of yours."

He stepped forward on the staircase. Their bodies were less than a foot apart. Her rosemary fragrance filled his nostrils, and the warmth of her body radiated from her in powerful waves. The combination almost made him dizzy.

"I won't ask again," he said in a low voice. "Step aside, Grace."

"Or you'll do what?" She glared at him, unblinking. "I'd love to see you *try* to manhandle me. I'd send you broken and sniveling to your mammy. You aren't the first man that I've had to quite literally whip into shape, and you won't be the last."

Christ, I know what she's doing, he thought. *This lady is a real piece of work.*

"Are you serious, old girl?" Troy had to laugh. "I honestly can't believe I'm having this conversation. Stop playing, Grace, and step aside."

"What's the magic word?" she asked.

"Please?" he said, unable to suppress a chuckle.

"Better." She nodded, and raised her arm to allow him to pass. "Although I don't trust you and know your sleazy game, I'll permit you to leave. But we've got plenty of unfinished business ahead of us, little man, mark my words. You lack discipline and must be taught better."

"Whatever you say, old girl."

As he passed by her, she swatted him on the rump with her open palm, hard enough to nearly send him spilling down the remainder of the stairs. His skin burned from the strike. She'd hit him *hard.*

"Hey, you keep your hands to yourself, dammit," he said.

"Toughen up, little man." She winked. "Next time, I may use a belt."

14

Sometime later that night, Pat exploded out of sleep with a cry on her lips, convinced that someone was trying to suffocate her. Gasping, she batted her hands at the attacker. She hit only empty air.

Only a bad dream. I'm safe.

As the realization washed over her, she collapsed against the bed. She pulled in deep, purifying breaths.

Her heart was racing as if she'd been running a sprint.

These days, she rarely had nightmares. At her golden age, she had seen so much, done so much, that few things frightened her any more. She had achieved a level of hard-won, quiet calm that typically followed her from her waking hours into the deepest depths of her sleep.

But not that time.

The dream had been so vivid that she could clearly recall the sensation of something pressing against her face, cutting off her airflow, and her lungs feeling as if they were about to rupture like cheap balloons.

The memory of it was so real she could literally still feel the impression that the obstructing object had left on her face. Like a . . . pillow.

The bedroom was dark, the only light coming from the greenish numerals of the clock on the nightstand. She reached for the lamp on the nightstand, pushed the switch. The light blazed on.

Pat let out a yelp of surprise.

She wasn't alone: Grace sat in the upholstered chair beside the bed. She wore purple pajamas and that horrid gray pageboy wig. She watched Pat quietly, her eyes glimmering, deep as wells.

Grace's hands rested on a thick bed pillow that lay across her lap.

Pat's gaze lingered on that pillow. Fear spread like foul smoke through every corner of her mind.

"What're you doing in here?" Pat asked. Her voice was thick.

"I thought you were having a nightmare. You were crying out as if under assault. I came to check on you."

Pat fumbled on her glasses. The room shifted into tighter focus. She read the bedside clock: it was a few minutes past two in the morning.

"Are you better, dear?" Grace asked. "Want me to fetch you a glass of cold water? Perhaps some warm milk?"

Although Grace used words that made it sound as if she were concerned for Pat's welfare, her eyes were as flat as a doll's. She seemed merely to be going through the motions of displaying empathy.

"I'm fine." Pat threw aside the covers. "You can go back to bed. I'm going to the bathroom."

"Sleep well, dear." Grace rose from the chair, dropping the pillow onto the seat cushion. "See you in the morning."

"Wait a minute." Pat glanced around the room. "Have you seen Duchess? She was in here when I went to sleep."

"I'm not the keeper of that animal. You were."

"She must have gone back to Monica then," Pat said.

"Perhaps." Grace strode out of the room, hips swaying. After she had gone, Pat released a pent-up breath.

That strange woman had gotten under her skin. How long had she been sitting there in the dark, watching Pat sleep? Who did such a thing?

Had she pressed that pillow against my face?

It was a serious accusation, and unfortunately, she had no proof that Grace had intended her any harm. But she was grateful that the woman was going home later that day. She hoped never to see her again.

When Pat finished her business in the bathroom, she returned to the adjoining hallway. Grace's bedroom door was closed, darkness at the bottom edge.

Perhaps the eccentric old fool had gone back to bed.

Then Pat heard a creaking noise coming from the catwalk. She stepped forward to take a closer look.

Dim light filtered up to the second floor from a small lamp located somewhere downstairs. But she saw the source of the sound.

Grace was on the catwalk. But she was not on the floor. She appeared, for a moment, to be walking on air.

I can't be seeing this.

Pat removed her glasses, rubbed her eyes, put her lenses back on.

Grace was on the catwalk's wrought-iron railing. Arms outstretched, she crept forward like a skilled gymnast on a balance beam, deftly placing one slippered foot in front of the other. It was at least a twenty-foot plunge to the floor below, but the old woman seemed to have no fear whatsoever.

Pat had to wonder if she was dreaming again.

As the thought crossed Pat's mind, Grace looked over her shoulder and found Pat staring at her. She put one index finger to her lips in the universal *shush* gesture.

The house was comfortably warm, but a chill washed like ice-water over Pat.

She hurried back into her bedroom.

That time, she locked the door.

15

When Monica awoke, she was astonished to discover that it was ten minutes past six o'clock in the morning.

If memory served, she'd lain down yesterday about twelve hours ago. She didn't recall waking once, and didn't remember a single dream. It was the deepest sleep she'd experienced in years.

She sat up in bed, blankets falling away from her. The room was still dark, the blinds shuttered against the sunrise.

Like a lounging cat, she stretched her arms above her head.

My mother is here.

The realization was like waking and remembering that it was your birthday. She regretted that she had missed those additional precious hours with Grace last night, but she had been so incredibly tired.

That day, she planned to literally make up for lost time.

Beside her, Troy continued to slumber, his body a shadowy shape in the darkened room. He was a heavy sleeper and didn't stir when she rose out of bed.

She crossed the room to the master bath. She noticed that Duchess's small cushioned bed was empty, but assumed the dog had slept in Pat's room, as she often did when Troy's mother stayed overnight.

Monica went through a quick morning-prep routine. As she was standing in front of the mirror, scrubbing her teeth with an electric toothbrush, she saw something in her reflection that made her stop.

She had several, completely new strands of gray hair.

She spat out a mouthful of toothpaste. Set aside the toothbrush and dug her fingers deep into her scalp, leaned closer to the mirror to get a better look.

Her eyes were not deceiving her, and it wasn't a trick of lighting, as she'd hoped. She was truly turning gray.

The realization hit her like a jab to the belly.

God, I'm truly getting old now. There's no denying it anymore.

Irrationally, she felt herself on the verge of crying. Her nose got that twitchy feeling that always came over her before the tears started flowing. She turned on the faucet and splashed several handfuls of cold water on her face. The urge to weep passed, at least for the moment.

Well, she reasoned, her fortieth birthday *was* next February, three months away. Many of her friends, some her age and others slightly younger, had mentioned to her that they'd begun to spot gray hairs, and Troy had some gray, too (which he artfully concealed with a never-ending supply of Dark & Natural). It was common at her age, no cause for alarm.

Nevertheless, she was surprised. Perhaps she just hadn't noticed it sooner, for it was as if the hair had turned color overnight.

The graying process could have been hastened by Lily's death, too. She had been inordinately stressed over the past week. It didn't require a suspension of disbelief to imagine rapid graying as a symptom of severe heartbreak, though she wasn't aware of any medical research into the matter.

I can ask my mother, she thought, and her heart swelled with excitement. The age at which one's hair began to gray was typically a hereditary trait. Since she finally had access to her biological mother, she could ask her these sorts of questions.

Heck, she could find out a lot more from Grace. She ought to do a complete medical history with her mom, learn about the family's prevalence of high blood pressure, diabetes, heart disease, cancer, and anything else she could. She was in touch with half of her family tree and should take full advantage of it.

She finished in the bathroom and went to check on the children. After confirming that both Lexi and Junior were sound asleep, she headed downstairs. She intended to brew a pot of herbal tea and fix something for breakfast; she was famished, hadn't eaten much of anything since yesterday afternoon. Although she was eager to spend more time with Grace, she didn't want to disturb her mother's rest.

As she descended the staircase, she noticed an electric glow coming from the kitchen and adjoining breakfast nook. She was wondering if someone had forgotten to switch off the lights last night, when she saw her mother sitting at the round table in the breakfast nook.

Wow, she's already awake. Monica couldn't suppress a giggle of childlike giddiness. *She must be an early riser, like me.*

It was going to be a good day.

16

Dressed in silky tangerine-colored loungewear and matching ballet-style slippers, long legs crossed, her mother had a ceramic mug standing at her elbow and a thick, leather-bound book in her hands. An ornately designed, cast iron teapot stood on the table; it wasn't one of those faux-vintage knockoffs but looked genuinely old, like something one might find in an antiques shop. The teapot didn't belong to Monica. She assumed her mother had brought it in her luggage.

My mother packed her own teapot for what she'd originally planned as an overnight trip? Monica thought. *She must be extremely particular about some things.*

She was smoking a cigarette, too, Monica noticed. It looked like a hand-rolled one, the glowing tip angled against a decorative crystal ashtray that Grace must have packed in her luggage; Monica and Troy were non-smokers and didn't keep a single ashtray in the house. The cigarette emitted a spicy fragrance, almost like incense.

Monica didn't approve of anyone smoking inside their home, but she was going to let it slide.

Grace looked up from her reading and grinned. Monica automatically smiled back, but she thought: *there's something different about her today. But I can't put my finger on what it is.*

Grace extinguished her cigarette. "Good morning, child. How're you feeling? Better today?"

"Much better, thank you. I slept like a stone. How long have you been awake?"

"Oh, I've always been an early riser." Grace shut her book and secured it with a tiny gold clasp. Monica had assumed it was a Bible, but on closer inspection it appeared to be a journal of some kind.

"I'm an early riser, too," Monica said. "Something else we have in common. We're like peas in a pod."

"How true." Grace indicated the teapot. "Would you like a cup of tea? I've brewed some of my own blend."

"Certainly." Monica inhaled the tempting herbal aromas swirling through the air. She eased into a chair at the table. "It smells wonderful. What are the ingredients?"

"It's a secret recipe." Grace winked as she fetched a cup and saucer from the cabinet. Returning to the table, she filled the mug with the tea and slid it to Monica. "Try it. I don't suggest you add sugar or cream, but that's a matter of personal preference."

Monica took a small sip of the steaming brew. It had a sweet, fruity flavor that reminded her of freshly picked strawberries.

"It's delicious," Monica said.

"Thank you. It has no caffeine, but one cup of this and you'll be full of energy for the entire day. I call it my Breakfast Brew."

Watching her mother wax poetic about her tea, it struck Monica what was different about her, and she was surprised she hadn't realized it straight away: her mother's hair had changed. Yesterday, she'd had gray hair styled in a pageboy, and Monica was convinced it was a wig. But that morning, her hair was even shorter, the fringe falling to the upper edges of her earlobes, and the coloring was a blend of black and silver in almost equal amounts.

Yet another wig, possibly? Regardless, Grace looked about ten years younger.

"Your hair," Monica said in what she hoped was a casual tone. "It looks different today."

"You noticed, eh?" Grace curled a finger around her bangs and giggled like a starlet with a secret. "Usually, I wear wigs, but today, I decided to go au naturel."

"I noticed some gray hairs this morning, for the first time ever." Monica ran her fingers across her scalp, sighed. "How old were you when you started to turn gray?"

"About your age, I believe. And child, I *immediately* colored my hair and started looking for wigs." Grace laughed. "I freely admit to vanity, dear. A youthful look is essential if a woman wishes to secure male companionship."

"I'm not sure yet whether I'll be coloring my hair or wearing a wig. While it was a bit of a shock to find the gray hairs this morning, I've always sort of liked the idea of growing old naturally."

"Is that so?" Grace sneered. "In your case, I doubt it matters. Whether you appear young or not, that husband of yours is going to plow the fields with reckless abandon."

Monica frowned at the remark, but decided to let it pass. She wasn't going to get lured into another debate about Troy's behavior.

Grace continued: "He stepped out of the house yesterday evening after nine o'clock. Allegedly to go to the gym. He didn't return until half-past eleven. What do you think about that?"

Grace watched her as if she'd just won a trick in a game of Spades, her lips curved in a mocking smile.

Monica carefully selected her words. "If that's what he said he was doing, I'll accept it at face value. He's given me no reason to doubt his honesty."

"You're either willfully blind, or a hopeless romantic." Grace clucked her tongue like a mothering hen. "Regardless, I'm not fooled—and I won't allow this man to make a fool of my precious daughter, either."

"Can we please talk about something else?" Monica asked.

"Of course, dear, if you wish." Grace shrugged. "What would you like to discuss?"

"You." Monica leaned forward, huddled over her tea. "I'd like to know more about you, and my family, too. We haven't talked about much of that yet. I have so many questions."

"Yes, yes, we've yet to explore that territory." Grace clasped her fingers across one knee. "Ask away, child, but I must warn you, I promise to answer truthfully, regardless of how it may taint the memory of certain, beloved individuals."

Monica's gut had tightened. But she said, "Understood. I only want the truth."

"Proceed then."

"All right." Monica pulled in a deep breath. "Why did you let Lily adopt me, and then wait all of these years to come back?"

"Ah." A bitter smile flickered across Grace's face. "It's the obvious place to begin, isn't it? The truth? I gave you up to Lily because when you were conceived, I was a wild, teenaged girl of eighteen, ill-prepared to raise a baby. I waited all these years to return to you because Lily despised me."

"Pardon me?" Monica felt rocked, as if dealt a blow to the head. "She despised you? Why?"

"In her opinion, I was a loose, immoral young woman and would have been a horrible influence upon you. I spoke to Lily via telephone on a few occasions while you were growing up. Each time, I asked her if I might come to see you. She warned me to stay away." Grace shook her head at the memories. "Lily was kind and loving, but she also could be *unyielding* in her beliefs, as people of great faith often are, child. Stubborn as the proverbial mule."

"I can't believe she denied you the right to see me." Hot tears were trickling from Monica's eyes. Grace offered her a tissue, which she accepted gratefully. "I wanted to see you. I *needed* to see you."

"Out of respect for Lily—she had raised you, after all—I acquiesced to her wishes." Grace gazed into the depths of her teacup. "But I knew the day would come when Lily would pass on, and then I would be free to unite with you, if you were willing to have me."

"Of course, I'm willing to have you!" The tears were coming so fast that even more tissues couldn't staunch them. "I just can't . . . I just can't believe how Lily knowingly kept me from you all these years . . ."

"I'm an uninhibited woman." Grace chuckled. Her eyes seemed to glow. "I freely admit it's true. I love men, *I love sex*. Nothing is as exciting to me as the feeling of a man, engorged, captured up in my essence, utterly at my mercy." Grace closed her eyes and shivered, as if enthralled by a recent memory of an erotic episode.

Monica blinked, tears wetting her face. She didn't know what to say.

"I've birthed many children, all of them from multiple fathers," Grace said. "Lily knew my nature and believed it would have been a corrosive influence on you. From her perspective, she did the right thing by keeping me away."

"Well, it wasn't right." Monica sniffled, mopped wetness away from her cheeks. "She told me you never called. She said you gave me up and walked out, and she never heard from you again. She lied to me!"

"She told you only what she thought you needed to hear." Reaching across the table, Grace took one of Monica's hands in her own, squeezed. "Don't hold this against her, child. Lily loved you as best she could, and look at how you've turned out. You're a beautiful, kind, successful woman. She did a far, far better job parenting you than I possibly could have done, and for that, she deserves both our gratitude."

"Yes." Still tearful, Monica was nodding. "Yes, you're right. It's going to take me some time to process this, but I know you're right."

"What else do you wish to know, child?" Grace asked.

"God, there's so much more. Where are you from, originally? How did you come to be taken in by Lily in the first place? Where was your family? Who is my father?"

"I'm afraid this is where the truth becomes sordid." Grace sipped tea, paused before going on. "My mother was a heroin-addicted whore in New Orleans, estranged from her own family. I never knew my father and doubt she did, either, considering her line of work. Growing up, I was passed from one friend to the next and never knew stability of any kind."

"Oh. I'm sorry."

"There's nothing for you to be sorry about—this is my story. I ran away to live on my own when I was thirteen. By then, I had learned that sex spun the gears of the world, and I was quite adept at using it to get ahead."

"At thirteen?"

"I had the body of a well-developed young woman at that age, but you must know, with certain men, that even a prepubescent girl is quite delectable."

Monica felt sick. "I think I get the idea. Good Lord."

"Sex is the way of the world and always has been," Grace said. "Anyway, my travels, if you will, brought me to Atlanta. I encountered Lily while she was doing community work for her church. I'd hit a rough patch and was living in a women's shelter. She and I connected, and she graciously brought me into her home to live."

Monica was nodding. Her mother's story was starting to align with the narrative that Lily had shared with her.

"Not long after I arrived, I got pregnant with you," Grace said.

"My father?" Monica asked, hesitant.

"I'm sorry, child," Grace said. "But you knew how I was then. The truth is, I've no clue of your father's identity. I wish it weren't so."

"I understand." Monica lowered her head.

She would never know the identity of her father; her mother had been her last hope in that regard, because Lily had been unable to tell her, either. She had lived her entire life without knowledge of her paternity, had learned to accept the situation, but she'd always had a hope that someday, she would learn the truth.

Now, that door was closed for good.

She sucked in a rattling breath, nodded at her mother to keep going.

"Lily was upset with me when she learned of the pregnancy, to put it lightly," Grace said. "In her words, I had violated her trust.

But she allowed me to stay with her until I gave birth to you. Our agreement, from the beginning, was that she would adopt you."

"Who named me?" Monica asked, and didn't know why it was important to get an answer to the question. She simply wanted to know.

"I gave you your name, of course. I wouldn't have allowed Lily to rob me of that small honor."

"Was it . . . difficult for you to give me up?"

"Yes, but as I said, I realized I was unprepared for the responsibilities of motherhood. Mostly, I was eager to escape Lily's strict household rules by that point. I left her home soon after I birthed you."

Monica went to sip her tea, found the cup was empty. She hadn't remembered drinking any of it. Grace refreshed her cup.

"Since then, I've lived in various cities, here and abroad," Grace said. "Usually, wherever I am, I've worked as a nanny. It's agreeable work, as I've got a sweet touch with children."

"I noticed that," Monica said. "You literally had Lexi eating out of the palm of your hand yesterday."

"She's an adorable child," Grace said. "It's a blessing to be here with you all, at last. My only regret is that I couldn't come sooner."

"I know, but let's simply focus on today, and the future, all right?" Monica said.

"Agreed. Let's do that."

Grace squeezed her hand, and they smiled at each other. Monica couldn't think of any other questions to ask. Her mother had laid so much to rest, and while Monica didn't like all of the answers, more than anything else, she'd craved only to learn the truth. It felt as if a burden she had borne for years had finally eased off her heart.

Both of them turned at the sound of approaching footsteps. Pat entered the kitchen. She offered a cheerful good morning, but her attention was on Monica; she seemed to be deliberately ignoring Grace. From the brief expression of disdain that flashed across Grace's face, Monica sensed there was a mutual dislike simmering between the two women. She wondered about that, but had another matter to discuss.

"Did Duchess sleep in your room, Pat?" Monica asked her. "I haven't seen her this morning and assumed she'd slept with you."

"I haven't seen her, either," Pat said, and her gaze sharpened and shifted to Grace. "What about you? Have you seen her? You've been up and about quite a bit, haven't you?"

What is going on between these two? Monica wondered. *Did something happen while I was sleeping?*

"I haven't seen the dog since Pat let her out last night to eliminate," Grace said.

"I stayed *outside* with her," Pat said, voice taut with indignation. "She came back inside, with me."

"I don't recall that." Grace shrugged. "But if that's true, we shouldn't be concerned. No doubt the animal's around this house somewhere and will turn up eventually."

"It isn't like her to wander off." Monica was getting out of her chair. "I've got to find her. Pat, will you help me look?"

"I'm right behind you," Pat said.

17

Someone was shaking Troy.

Wake up, sweetheart, it's important.

Troy awoke to Monica bending over him, one hand clutching his shoulder. Fear glistened in her eyes.

He blinked. Light from the bedside lamp stung his eyes, but it didn't burn away his memory of the dream he'd been having. He had been running through the house, all alone except for Grace. Grace wore an outfit of black leather, and she wielded a nasty leather whip. Like a dominatrix. She chased him from one room to the next, snapping the whip at him, and with each painful lash, a piece of his clothing tore away, and she taunted him: *Show me the goods, boy. I doubt you have anything I haven't seen before . . .*

He was grateful to wake from such a bizarre dream, but the anxiety in Monica's gaze immediately sent a corkscrew of tension twisting through his gut.

He sat up, wiped his eyes. "What's wrong?"

"We can't find Duchess. We've searched the entire house."

Grace, he thought, and felt coldness run along his spine. *The old woman did something to the dog, I know it. Mom was right about her.*

He got out of bed. "Who was the last person to see the dog?"

"Your mother. She let Duchess out last night to potty, but she says she came back inside with her."

"If Mom says she did that, then that's what happened. Mom wouldn't forget to let the dog in for God's sake."

"So where is she then?" Monica asked, her voice rising to an octave of panic. She hugged herself, and tears glistened in her eyes. "I've looked everywhere in here."

"Don't worry, baby. We'll find Duchess. I promise."

He could promise no such thing, but offering such automatic assurances to his wife was a habit, especially in her delicate emotional state as of late. It was his responsibility to be her rock, and if that meant lying to her sometimes, he was willing to do it.

In the walk-in closet, he threw on sneakers, warm-up pants, and a sweatshirt. As he dressed, he stifled a yawn. It was only half-past seven, earlier than he preferred to wake on a Sunday. Usually, Sunday was the only day of the week that he got to sleep in, while Monica and the kids, and oftentimes his mother, would go to a local church.

And after last night's activities, he definitely could have used the extra recuperation time.

Those warm memories threatened to intrude upon his thoughts, and he had to force them out of mind and focus on the matter at hand: looking for Duchess.

He met Monica and his mother in the hallway outside of their bedroom. Mom looked upset, her jaws clenched with tension.

"Mom, what happened?" he asked.

"I don't know, Troy. We've searched everywhere."

"No one has looked outdoors yet," Grace said, coming up the stairs.

Mom shot Grace a venomous look. "I told you, I let Duchess inside last night."

"Can you look outside, sweetheart?" Monica asked Troy.

Troy barely heard her. He was studying Grace as she strolled toward them, trying to reconcile her appearance with the woman he had seen yesterday. Her hair looked different. He thought her complexion had changed too, become smoother and more vibrant, but maybe that was just artfully applied makeup.

But didn't Monica look a little different, too? Was that gray in her hair?

He wished he could go back to bed. He felt as if he had awakened into a parallel universe, where everything was slightly askew from what he expected to see.

"Troy?" Monica said, in a sharper tone. "Can you look outside, please?"

He cleared his throat. "What about the kids' rooms?"

"I've looked in both of them," Monica said. She swallowed. "Outside's the only place we haven't checked."

"Duchess would have barked if she were abandoned outside," Mom said, "obviously."

Troy was about to agree with his mother, but the tearful look Monica turned on him kept his mouth shut.

"Fine," he said. "I'll look outdoors. In the meantime, I suggest we look under all of the beds and other furniture, too. The dog might've gotten wedged in somewhere. You remember she loved to crawl under the couch when she was a puppy?"

"Right." Monica nodded. "Got it."

The sun was beginning its morning ascent as Troy opened the French doors to the large pine wood deck attached to the back of the house. He stepped outside, a Thermos full of black coffee in one hand, and Duchess's pink leather leash dangling from his other hand. The November air had a bite to it that made him wish he was wearing a jacket, but he wanted to get this search over with and didn't want to return inside until he was done.

The deck was cluttered with patio furniture and a gargantuan Big Green Egg cooker that he had purchased only because another physician in his practice had boasted of having one, and Troy was never one to be outdone by a peer. He found no sign of the dog on the deck, but the dog usually scampered down the steps to the backyard. Sighing, he took a sip of coffee, and headed down the staircase to the ground level, vapor issuing from his lips in short bursts.

Their backyard was about half an acre, enclosed within a seven-foot-high wooden fence. The shortly trimmed grass was brown and dormant, the blades layered with frost. Elm trees dotted the perimeter, their branches naked. A children's playset occupied the center of the yard, standing within a sandbox: the massive wooden structure included swings, two slides, a rock wall, and more.

Troy was about to check the structure, suspecting Duchess had scrambled up the staircase and was lodged in one of the many nooks and crannies of the playset, when he noticed that the gate on the far right side of the yard hung wide open.

That was odd. Typically, that door was closed and locked, opened only if someone was taking out trash to toss it into the garbage bin standing on the other side of the house.

He approached the doorway. An article of clothing lay on the ground, on the threshold of the entrance.

"Aww, no," he said, under his breath.

It was his mother's green knit scarf.

He plucked it off the ground. It was stiff with frost. From the feel of it, the scarf had lain on the ground for several hours, probably all night.

"Damn, Mom, what happened?" he said.

His mother had insisted that she had let the dog in last night, but why was the gate open? Why was her scarf lying on the ground?

Had she forgotten Duchess out here, too?

He stepped through the entrance. His neighbor's house was about forty feet ahead, but what most concerned him was the densely wooded area that backed up to his property, beyond the fence. If Duchess had gone back there and gotten lost, or been attacked by some wild animal, Monica would lose her mind.

And she would blame Mom for it, too.

Troy walked toward the woods. He kept close to the edge of his fence, frosted grass crunching underneath his shoes. He studied the ground as he trod forward. Although he had no experience in tracking anything, he had a sharp eye for visual details, and figured any signs of where the dog had gone would jump out at him.

About twenty yards into the woods, on the bank of a narrow creek, he found the only sign any of them needed: a small bundle of white fur, streaked with dark blood.

"Shit," he said softly, the air feeling as if it had been sucked out of his lungs.

Something had torn Duchess apart.

Part Two

18

Troy braced himself for the worst when he returned inside to tell Monica what had happened. He got the reaction from her that he'd feared.

"What?" Her lips quivered, a sure sign that she was about to lose her composure. "You found Duchess where?"

Standing next to Monica in the kitchen, Mom's mouth had fallen open. He was certain she'd heard what he had said and didn't need him to repeat it. She held the frost-encrusted scarf of hers that he had plucked off the ground as if it were a leper's limb.

He didn't see Grace anywhere nearby. Her absence struck him as guilty behavior, though he had no proof that she'd been involved in the dog's death.

But you know she was responsible, don't you? Do you really believe Mom left the dog outside?

He repeated his findings to Monica. She shook her head, tears trickling down her cheeks.

"How . . . why?" Her gaze whipped from him, to Mom. "You left her outside, Pat?"

"I did *not*," Mom said. "I promise you, sweetheart, I would never do such a thing. Duchess was in her bed next to me when I fell asleep."

"But you forgot your scarf . . ." Monica stared at the fabric in Mom's hands. Her face flushed, Mom tossed the scarf onto the table.

It went downhill from there. Throughout their eight years of marriage, Monica had never argued with his mother. The two of them got along as well as if they were truly mother and daughter. But this situation with Duchess had opened a rift, and it was all Troy could do to keep Monica from calling his mother a dog killer.

When it was all over, Monica stomped out of the kitchen, his mother glaring at her, chest heaving. It would fall to Troy to patch things together. He was the neutral party in this situation and would need to broker a peace treaty.

But first, he had to collect the dog's corpse.

Lexi and Junior were awake by then, too. By the time the confrontation between Mom and Monica got heated, Grace had brought the children downstairs, ostensibly to fix them breakfast, but Troy suspected that the woman actually wanted the kids to have a front row seat to the chaos. Both of the kids were weepy, upset with the idea that they would never see Duchess again.

It was a helluva way to kick off a Sunday morning.

He was relieved to go back outside where he could enjoy relative quiet. He had draped the dog's bed blanket across his arm, intending to bundle her in it and place a call to the local pet crematory company. Although Duchess had been Monica's companion more so than his, he couldn't expect his wife to attend to these matters; she had enough to deal with and handling the dog's cremation was the least he could do to ease her burdens.

Outdoors, gazing at the dog's lifeless, blood-streaked body, he bit back tears. What the hell had really happened back here? Had a coyote come across Duchess? A vicious, stray dog? Some other predator that roamed the forest? He really didn't understand what could have eviscerated the sweet little fur ball.

"Such a shame," Grace said, behind him. Troy flinched; he hadn't realized that she was there in the woods, no more than ten feet away from him. Wearing a red parka with a fur-lined hood, she clucked her tongue. "She was such an adorable little mutt."

"She was AKC-certified, far from a mutt," Troy said.

"Of course." Grace smiled thinly. "Nonetheless, it's sad."

"I didn't think there was much love lost between you, too," Troy said. "I'd assume you were glad that she's gone."

Grace only looked at him, that thin smile resting on her lips as if painted in place.

"Speaking of gone," Troy said. "What time are you hitting the road today?"

"I'm not leaving." Grace chuckled. "I've decided that I'll be staying for another week. My daughter and I have so much catching up to do. This weekend we've only scratched the surface."

"You discussed this with Monica?" he asked.

"My daughter wants me here," Grace said. "I just so happen to be available and willing to stay on to help out with the family a bit longer. Goodness knows your poor, absent-minded mother isn't up to the task." Grace clucked her tongue and glanced at the dog's corpse.

Troy wasn't often rendered speechless, but he literally didn't know what to say. He knew what he *should* have said—*you're only a guest here and you can't unilaterally decide to extend your visit*—but he knew in his bones that Monica would take Grace's side, that she wanted her mother there, and he didn't want to upset her.

"You take care of this little lovely out here." Grace waved dismissively toward the dog's corpse. "I'll return to the kitchen and prepare a proper Sunday morning breakfast for the family: homemade waffles for the children, and my famous frittata for the adults. How does that sound?"

"Great," Troy said in a flat voice.

He watched her amble toward the house. She swung her hips like a model strutting down a runway.

Another week with this woman, he thought. *I don't know if I can handle it.*

He turned back to their dead dog.

And for the briefest moment, he envied Duchess.

19

For Monica, the morning passed in a blur. Upon hearing the news that Duchess was gone, she was beside herself with shock, disbelief—and anger. She couldn't believe that Pat, previously so reliable, had committed such a fatal oversight.

She couldn't stand to look at the woman without wanting to scream at her. Gratefully, Pat left soon thereafter, continuing to tearfully deny that she had done anything wrong. Monica loved her mother-in-law but her emotions were too raw to handle, and she didn't try to talk Pat out of leaving.

"Growing old is a terrible thing," Grace said to Monica after Pat had gone. She clucked her tongue. "The poor old woman has no memory whatsoever of what she's done. Imagine what errors she might unwittingly commit with your children!"

Monica didn't want to think about it, but the idea had crept across the back of her mind. She hated to entertain such thoughts but the seeds of distrust had been planted, and she would need to talk to Troy about ensuring his mother got help.

"I'll be staying here for another week," Grace declared. "I've got the time and you need my help. Besides, we've so much catching up to do, child."

That was the best news Monica had gotten thus far that day. Later that morning, Grace persuaded Monica to gather the kids, get away from the house, and spend some time outdoors at the local park. Although it was early November, the weather late that morning was pleasant, the temperature having climbed into the low sixties as golden sunshine beamed through scattered cumulus clouds.

Grace offered to drive the ten-minute trip to the park, and Monica readily agreed. Grace herded Lexi and Junior into Monica's BWM X5, expertly buckled the children into their respective car seats. Monica slumped in the passenger seat, clammy hands clutching a knot of tissues.

As her grief about losing her dog progressed, Monica had begun to blame herself, too. Whatever had happened outside had occurred while she was enjoying a deep, peaceful slumber last night. Surely, Duchess had barked, yelped, made some kind of panicked noises, but Monica had slept through it all, oblivious to her dog's suffering. How could she have done such a thing?

Grace climbed behind the steering wheel. She placed a reassuring hand on top of Monica's.

"I know it's difficult, dear," she said. "But the kids will enjoy getting some sunshine and playing with other children their age, for a time. A temporary change of scenery and fresh air will help revitalize you as well."

"I know you're right." Monica smiled weakly. "Thank you for everything."

Grace had made all of the arrangements for Duchess, though Troy had initially planned to do so. She'd contacted a local pet cremation service, and a soft-spoken young woman had arrived within an hour to collect the ravaged corpse from the garage where Troy had placed it, the body nestled within the dog's old fleece blanket. The cremation would be performed within twenty-four hours, after which time they would send Monica the remains and she could dispose of them as she saw fit.

First Lily, now Duchess. It was unimaginable that within the span of a few days, she had experienced the deaths of two beloved members of her family. While some people might have balked at the idea of shedding tears over a dead dog, Duchess had been a constant presence in their household for several years. Her infectious energy would be greatly missed.

Brook Run Park covered over a hundred acres, and included a community garden, dog run, skate park, and an enormous playground; the wide variety of swings, ladders, tube slides, jungle gyms, and other playsets could accommodate children of various age ranges. Canvas canopies protected the equipment from the elements, the ground covered in a synthetic material designed to cushion falls. A plentitude of wooden benches allowed adults to take a load off while the little ones cavorted about.

Predictably, at eleven o'clock on a balmy Sunday, the playground was crowded with children and their parents or grandparents. Junior climbed onto one of the swings, while Grace accompanied Lexi to a nearby playset to interact with older children. Monica gave Junior a good push. Her son cried with delight as he swooped through the crisp autumn air.

Watching her boy, Monica couldn't hold back a grin. Her mother had been spot on. Coming out here, removing the focus from her own troubles for a while and letting her children have fun, feeling the warm sunshine on her skin, was like medicine for her wounded spirit.

It was remarkable, really. Her mother had been in her life for barely twenty-four hours, and already, she felt indispensable. Monica appreciated that Grace was able to stay for another week, that she had more days to enjoy her mom's company and explore their burgeoning relationship. There was so much left to talk about, so many things to do together—truly, a lifetime to catch up on.

A sharp, familiar cry snapped Monica out of her reverie.

Startled, she turned from the swing and saw Lexi running toward her, face full of tears. Grace marched behind her, lips drawn in a taut line.

"Mommy, she pushed me!" Lexi cried, and flung her arms around Monica's legs, nearly knocking Monica off balance.

"Who pushed you?" Monica asked. "What happened?"

"That big girl . . ." Lexi leveled a shaky finger toward the playset from which she had fled.

Monica looked, but she couldn't distinguish the guilty child from the gaggle of children flitting back and forth.

"A big ox of a girl—who seems to have been dumped off here

by her parents—shoved Lexi down the slide, and caused her to lose her balance," Grace said, fists bunched on her waist. "Lexi may have slightly abraded her knee on the slide when she fell, but she'll be fine." Grace patted Lexi's head. "Don't worry, dearest—Nana knows *exactly* which child is responsible. It's the hellion wearing the pink *My Little Pony* jacket."

Monica spotted the kid: a husky, red-headed girl holding court near the top of the slide. She was yelling at the other, smaller children as if she were the playground queen.

Monica noticed that a joyless smile had settled on Grace's face. Something deep in Monica shifted, and she thought, *Okay, I don't think I ever want to make my mother angry, because she looks primed to dish out some serious punishment.*

"It's all right now." Monica wiped away Lexi's tears. "Let's all go play on something else, okay, honey?"

"Okay." Lexi nodded, sniffled.

Monica told Junior to stop swinging, and he reluctantly hopped off. They ambled to another, less crowded section of the playground, but Grace hung a few paces behind them, periodically casting glances over her shoulder.

"What's wrong?" Monica asked.

"I'm keeping my attention focused on that little bitch," Grace said with a hot, slitted gaze. "She's a horrible child, a bad seed, and I've yet to see her parents or a nanny watching her. She needs to be disciplined."

Little bitch? Monica thought. *Wasn't that strong language to use to describe a kid?*

"She's a typical schoolyard bully," Monica said. "We'll avoid her. We're here for only a short while, no need to make a big deal about it."

"That's one difference between you and me, child. You avoid conflict. But embracing conflict strengthens character."

Monica paused, unsure how to respond. But Grace had whirled around. Walking with long, swift strides, like a woman on a mission, she made a beeline to the restrooms on the edge of the park.

"Grace?" Monica said, but her mother ignored her.

Perhaps her mother merely had an urgent need to go to the ladies' room. If so, why was Monica's stomach wound tight with apprehension?

Junior was attempting to climb the artificial rock wall that was attached to the playset. Monica boosted up her son. Lexi, at the top already, hopped onto the slide and barreled down the tube with a gleeful cry.

Monica spent the next several minutes minding her children and trying not to worry about her mother's worrisome comments. But she didn't relax until she saw Grace coming back in their direction.

"Is everything okay?" Monica asked.

"Of course, my dear. I had some business to attend to in the ladies room." Grace bounded onto the stairs of the playset with the light-footedness of a cat, much to the delight of Lexi and Junior. "Nana is ready to play. I'll race you children to the bottom!"

They spent another half hour or so at the park. Grace, for her part, seemed to enjoy romping about as much as the children did, and Monica wondered if Grace had her own reasons for wanting this park excursion. She watched with amazement as her mother navigated the bars of a jungle gym as adeptly as a gymnast, at one point even swinging upward onto the top of the bars and stepping across them as if traversing a balance beam.

I was never that agile, Monica thought. *Not as a child, not now, and most definitely would not be as a nearly sixty-year-old woman.*

Feeding off Grace's boundless energy, the kids ran, leapt, and shouted, and were thoroughly exhausted when Grace declared that it was time for them to leave.

As they were loading the children in the SUV, Monica heard sirens approaching. An ambulance veered into the parking lot, lights ablaze, followed closely by two police cruisers.

"Let's move along now, family," Grace said, revving the engine.

Monica buckled her seat belt. "What do you think is going on?"

"It could be anything," Grace said with a shrug. "At a large, public playground such as this, with so many unsupervised children running about freely, sometimes, children get hurt. Sometimes, they deserve it."

A question formed like an ominous thundercloud in Monica's mind, and the implications of it were so unsettling that she didn't dare to speak it aloud. She shoved the thought away and switched on the radio, found the R&B station, and leaned back in her seat to let the classic grooves of Earth, Wind & Fire sweep away her worries.

"Now," Grace said, and flashed a grin that seemed almost manic in its intensity. "Who wants to go get ice cream?"

20

Later that afternoon, Troy met his good friend, Rodney Marshall, at Hoops, an athletic center in Buckhead. Troy needed to get outside of the house for a while and breathe. At home, the brew of emotions permeating the air was so thick he'd felt as though he were inhaling cotton.

It was a nice day for riding his bike, so he took his Harley Low Rider down GA-400 to Buckhead. Cruising along the highways on the motorcycle was normally a thrilling escape in itself, but he found his thoughts continuously circling back to that small heap of blood-soaked fur he'd discovered that morning in the woods.

The memory of that image was going to haunt him for a while.

Located on Peachtree Road near Lenox Square, Hoops billed itself as an "athletic center," and while the facility featured adequate sections for weightlifting, aerobic machines, and circuit training, the place was primarily devoted to basketball. Several pro quality basketball courts dominated a high-ceilinged, cavernous space. Members reserved court time via a smart phone app or kiosk in the lobby, eliminating the need for the old-school reservation system of someone milling on the sidelines impatiently declaring, "I got next."

Inside the arena, the sounds of bouncing basketballs and shoe soles squeaking against hardwood filled the air, like background music. The gym was full of men and a handful of women, mostly everyone in their twenties and thirties, though Troy did see a couple of gray-haired dudes fighting to hold their own against the younger generations.

He spotted Rod on one of the courts in the corner. Rod was launching shots from beyond the three-point arc. As Troy approached, one of Rod's attempts clanged off the rim. Troy retrieved the ball.

"You're outside your range, my brother," Troy said.

Rod laughed, and they gave each other dap.

Like him, Rod was from the South side of Chicago, born and bred, but they had gone to different high schools—Troy to Lane Tech and Rod to Simeon. They met at Morehouse, and had been close ever since, though their career paths and lifestyles had diverged years ago. Troy had gone into medicine, married and had two children; Rod was a civil rights attorney, and a confirmed, childless bachelor.

Rod wore a Chicago Bulls throwback jersey. At six-four and about two hundred thirty pounds, he was often assumed to be a pro athlete himself, and with his bald dome, actually bore a striking resemblance to the boxer, George Foreman.

"My apologies for being late," Troy said. "It's been a rough weekend, man."

"The funeral was yesterday." Rod's dark brown eyes were full of understanding. "Wish I could have been there, but I just got back in town this morning from Chicago. You all got my flowers?"

"Yeah, appreciate that—and listen, the funeral was the easy part." Troy took a jump shot from near the free throw line, swished it. "Check this out. Monica's mother was there."

"Wait a minute." Rod frowned. "Her mother?"

"Her biological mother. Thirty-nine years in, this woman suddenly decides to show her face."

"No shit. Damn, so that was a good thing, right?"

Troy gave Rod the highlights of what had happened since Grace's arrival yesterday. Grace's immediate, possessive behavior toward Monica and his children. His mother's growing distrust and fear of the woman. And, that morning, the discovery of Duchess's ravaged corpse in the woods behind their property.

"Monica thinks my mom forgot and left Duchess outside last night," Troy said. "My mom swears she didn't."

"Who do you believe?" Rod asked.

"Listen, my mother would never do something like that. Mom and I had a moment to chat in private before I got here. She thinks Grace set it up, and I believe her. She doesn't trust that woman as far as she can throw her."

"I liked that little dog." Rod was shaking his head. "Who could hurt a cute little dog like that in cold blood?"

A couple of slender, six-foot guys, both of them looking no older than twenty-one, approached the edge of their court.

"Excuse me, old heads," one of the guys said without a trace of malice. "Can we ball with y'all? All the courts are booked up."

"Did he just refer to us as 'old heads'?" Troy looked from the visitors, to Rod.

"I believe he did." Rod spun the ball in his large hands. "You just woke up a couple of sleeping giants, son. How about we go two-on-two? Me and my old man buddy here against you young cats, to eleven."

Both of the younger men laughed.

"Yo, we play ball in college," one of the guys said. "Y'all can't be serious."

"He sounds scared to me." Troy winked at Rod. "I think we'll have to spot these fellas three points."

The young dudes laughed even harder. "Y'all crazy, man. But all right, then. To eleven. And you ain't spottin' us nothing, 'cause we don't want to hear no excuses when y'all lose."

Troy peeled out of his warm-up jacket, tightened the laces on his sneakers.

"Hope you remembered to take your Geritol this morning," one of the guys said to Troy.

The comments were all in good fun, but the underlying tone rankled Troy. He was *only* forty-one, and truth be told, was in the best shape of his entire life. Of course, unlike during his younger days, he had to work hard to maintain peak physical condition, and his body took much longer to recover from injuries and overexertion. And hell, oftentimes only sitting in one spot for an hour or so, and then getting up, made his joints stiff as boards.

Still, the insinuation that he was over the hill, and easy pickings for these young dudes, pissed him off.

"Let's do this," Troy said to Rod, and they started the game.

What their younger competitors didn't realize was that not only had Troy and Rod been playing pick-up ball as a two-man tandem for over twenty years, both of them had been members of the Morehouse basketball team—and Rod had been an All-American and drafted in the second round of the NBA. He had played pro ball for three seasons before a knee injury forced him to hang up his sneakers, after which he'd returned to school to earn his law degree.

And both of them still had game, in wild abundance.

Within the first few minutes of their contest, Troy had sized up their opponents: the kids were good, but relied far too much on natural youthful athleticism than actual skill. Troy and Rod, deeply seasoned veterans, may not have been as fast, may not have jumped as high, but what they lacked in physical prowess they more than compensated for with crisply executed technique, and well-honed teamwork. Their passes were sharp; their shot selection was on target; their defense was tenacious; and they ran their beloved pick and roll plays over and over, with machinelike efficiency.

They beat the young guys easily, eleven to four.

"You guys should have taken those three points we offered to spot you," Troy said. He was breathing hard, but it felt good, damn good. "The game might have been a little closer."

"Hold up, man," one of the guys said, sweating profusely. "I can't believe this shit just happened. Who the hell are you dudes?"

"We're just a couple of old heads, remember?" Rod said. "We're out on a day pass from the local senior citizens home."

"I left my cane in the locker room." Troy grinned.

"Man, whatever," the other guy said. "You dudes are like pro ballers or something out here hustling folks."

"Want to play another game?" Rod asked.

"Hell naw," both of the guys said in unison. They made a show of looking at their smart phones, and quickly drifted away from the court.

Troy and Rod both laughed.

"We should have warned those young bucks," Rod said.

"Serves 'em right," Troy said.

"Now." Rod slowly dribbled between his legs. "Before they interrupted us, we were talking about why you suspect this woman Grace killed your dog."

"For starters, we don't know anything about Grace," Troy said. "We know a few basic pieces of info, but the bottom line is that she's a stranger. I get a weird vibe from her, too."

"What kind of vibe?" Rod's gaze was sharp.

"Like there's a lot more to her than she's shared with us," Troy said. "Like she's keeping secrets about what she's been doing since she gave up Monica."

"Something criminal, you think?"

"I don't know, but she's shady," Troy said. "Grace hated Duchess the minute she saw her, and I think the hate was mutual. Sometimes, I think a dog can be a good judge of character."

"I'm siding with you and moms on this, too," Rod said. "Grace only arrived on the scene yesterday. You all don't know anything about her, except what she's told you, and she could be lying." He stopped dribbling, lips pursed. "Dude, are you positive she's Monica's birth mother?"

"They definitely look like they could be mother and daughter," Troy said. "Personalities are totally different, though. Grace is a freak."

"Oh?" Rod stopped in mid-shot. "How's that?"

"She's tossed a few inappropriate comments at me, when we were alone," Troy said. "I get the distinct feeling that she's into some kinky stuff. She's testing the boundaries to see if I'm game."

Rod's lips puckered as if he had bitten into a lemon. "That's so wrong on so many levels. I don't even know what to say, man."

"Tell me about it. Honestly, I'm more concerned about the woman's integrity, and most of all, how Monica is reacting to everything that's happened."

"She's taking her mother's side on things," Rod said.

"Monica just lost Lily. She's fragile, vulnerable. Now, Grace arrives to fill that void, and suddenly, nothing that any of us says matters anymore."

"Blood is thicker than water," Rod said. "You're going to lose that battle every time, brother. Never try to come between a lady and her mama."

"Obviously."

"In spite of the ruckus that Grace has raised," Rod said. "I'm assuming she leaves town soon?"

Troy laughed, a bitter sound. "Don't I wish?"

"Uh oh. How long is she staying?" Rod asked.

"Grace decided that her visit will be extended for another week. She decided this on her own and I let it go. I know Monica would fight me on it and I'm going to lose that battle."

"I keep coming back to this." Rod took a swig from his bottled water. "But you don't know anything about this woman. Maybe she isn't who she says she is, yet she's staying under *your* roof, with your kids. That's a significant risk, Troy. You need to get some tangible evidence that supports her story."

"I'm open to suggestions."

"I have a guy, all right, Nick Sullivan, who does some investigative work for my firm from time to time," Rod said. "He's licensed, professional, and most of all, thoroughly competent. If this Grace character has so much as a speck of dirt under her fingernails, he'll find it."

"Give me his info and I'll give him a call," Troy said. "I'll be honest with you, Rod. I've got a bad feeling about this woman. I hope I'm wrong, but my gut is telling me that this incident with Duchess is only the beginning."

21

Hours later, Troy stood outside the closed doors to the master bedroom. He clenched his hands into fists and sucked in air as emotions clamped like iron bands across his chest.

Once again, he'd tried to go into his room. Once again, it was locked.

What the hell are Monica and Grace doing in there that requires them to lock the door?

He hadn't seen either of the women since they had gone to put the kids down, at least two hours ago, and he knew they were holed up in the bedroom again, behaving like teenage girls on a sleepover, sharing gossip and secrets. He was exhausted and had to work tomorrow, and he was in no mood for any of Grace's weird-ass behavior.

He rapped on the door, hard. "Open this door, dammit."

There was no reply. He knocked again, more forcefully. No one answered.

Are you kidding me? Now I'm being ignored in my own house?

Every interior door in their home that was capable of locking had a master key, but he had no idea where the key was being kept, hadn't used it since moving into the house seven years ago. Who needed keys inside their own house?

"I'm not having this shit." He punched the door one final time. "We're going to have a talk about locking these doors. It's going to stop."

He waited for about a half-minute. Incredibly, no one

responded. He stomped downstairs into the kitchen and switched on the lights.

The kitchen sparkled like a room in a model home. Grace had cooked dinner again, some sort of chicken seasoned with herbs, accompanied by roasted vegetables and freshly baked bread. It was an amazing meal, and she had cleaned up afterward, too. Her culinary and housekeeping skills were formidable, but in Troy's mind, failed to compensate for her other, increasingly disturbing qualities.

Such as her propensity for killing the family dog and making it look as if his own mother was at fault.

One of the corner drawers was used to store miscellaneous items—otherwise known as the infamous "junk drawer." Troy recalled he had seen some miniature keys in there the last time he had rummaged through the contents.

He snatched out the drawer to its full length and started searching, placing items on the counter as he dug through the space: old batteries, take-out Chinese menus, refrigerator magnets, rolls of tape, assorted nuts and bolts, assembly manuals for car seats and toys . . .

He had been looking for a few, fruitless minutes when he suddenly had the distinct sense that someone was watching him. He turned.

Grace stood on the threshold of the kitchen. Her face was like a granite slab, flat and unreadable. She wore pink velour pajamas and matching slippers; she must have owned coordinated nightwear in every color scheme imaginable.

The uppermost buttons of her pajama top were unsecured, giving him a generous view of her cleavage. The flesh at the nape of his neck tightened.

What's her game going to be this time?

"Hello, doctor." Her tone was oddly cheerful, out of sync with her emotionless face.

"Okay, listen." He straightened, shoved the drawer shut. "What's with the locking of the door to my bedroom? This is my house, you know. Don't ever do that again, and I'm telling Monica the same thing."

Grace stared at him, lips pursed.

"Did you hear what I said?" he asked.

She advanced into the kitchen, strolling with a flirty sway to her hips. Her skin appeared to glisten, and her lips actually looked fuller, too, plump and pouty, as if she'd recently gotten a Botox injection.

She came close enough to invade his personal space. Her fragrance enveloped him, that earthy rosemary scent that seemed to perpetually surround her.

He took a step back. "Hey. What's the matter with you?"

She put her hand on his crotch. He recoiled, backpedaled another step. The edge of the counter pressed against his lower back.

"Back off, woman." His heart slammed. "You know this shit isn't appropriate."

"I want you to fuck me, doctor." She stepped forward and grabbed his crotch again. She squeezed firmly, and he cringed.

"What?"

"You heard me right. I want to ride this big dick of yours and feel you explode inside me. I want to suck every ounce of your sperm out of you."

"Are you nuts?"

"You are *going* to fuck me, doctor, and soon. I promise you, you'll relish every moment."

"Keep dreaming, you old hag." He raised his hand to push her away.

She seized his wrist.

Her grip was like ice, and it was strong. Far stronger than seemed plausible for a woman of her age and slim stature. He strained to pull his wrist out of her grasp, his fingers tingling as the blood circulation faltered, but he could not get free.

"Old hag, eh?" Her lips parted in a predatory grin. "I could snap you like a twig, boy."

She increased the pressure of her grip; he felt the bones and joints in his wrist creak painfully, and a groan escaped him. Trembling, he lifted his other hand to try to break her hold, and she easily snared that one by the wrist, too.

A gasp slipped out of him. He couldn't believe it. He worked out regularly, could bench press three hundred pounds, and enjoyed an advantage of several inches and probably sixty pounds on the woman, but he was powerless to get away. It was like being trapped in restraints.

Something in him, perhaps his natural male bravado, wilted.

She's stronger than I am. How is that even possible?

Her hazel eyes glinted, as if she knew the fearful thoughts that circled through his mind and found them pleasing.

"You'll learn to do as I say if you know what's good for you," she said. "Now. Get on your knees."

He started to say no, but she tightened her grips and pressed forward, and the pain was so excruciating that he felt his knees crumple. As if weighted down by an anchor hanging from his neck, he dropped to his knees, the impact of hitting the travertine floor reverberating through his bones.

"Look at me, doctor." She didn't relinquish her hold on his wrists.

Perspiration seeping into his eyes, he raised his face to her.

"Good," she said. "Tell me that you're sorry for how you behaved."

"I . . . I . . ."

She gave his wrists a threatening clench, and the agony almost made him lose consciousness.

"I'm . . . sorry . . ." The words came out in a choked whisper.

"Yes. Sorry for what?"

"Sorry for . . . how I behaved . . ."

"That's a good boy." She finally released him. "I believe you've learned your lesson. If not, next time, I assure you, your discipline will be *much* more severe."

With a gentle chuckle, she patted the top of his head, as one might favor an obedient pet.

"Run along now. Remember what I said. That dick's going to be mine." She laughed.

Shaking and sweating, he crawled away from her. If he'd possessed a tail, it would have been curled between his legs. That was how he felt—thoroughly cowed. It was an unfamiliar experience.

Grace stared at him for a beat, an unvoiced threat in her gaze, and then she exited the kitchen in a swirl of fabric and fragrance.

He got to his feet, gently massaging his throbbing wrists. Blood and sensation were slow to return to his hands.

He shuffled into the powder room off the kitchen, bumped his shoulder against the light switch. Under the bright fluorescents, he examined his wrists.

Grace's slender fingers had left crimson bruises on his flesh.

I could snap you like a twig, boy.

The sight chilled him. He was a man of science, a trained physician. He could think of no logical reason that would explain how Grace had been able to do that to him. It defied everything in his experience and education.

Cautiously, he returned upstairs. He tried the knob of his bedroom door, and that time, it opened.

The room was dark. He edged inside.

"Monica?" he asked.

He heard slow, deep breathing coming from the bed. He crossed the room and thumbed on a bedside lamp.

Monica lay snuggled underneath the covers. Grace was nowhere to be seen. Perhaps she'd retired to her room for the night.

Monica wore her nightgown and appeared to be down for the night as well. He touched her shoulder, shook it.

He wanted to tell her what had happened, as crazy as it might sound to her. He could show her the bruises on his wrists. Give visible proof of her mother's menace, and share what Grace had said.

But Monica didn't stir, and typically, she was a light sleeper. It reminded him of how deeply she had slept last night, too.

She's exhausted. Maybe I should give her a break. Lily just died and now Duchess is gone, too . . .

An idea emerged in his mind like something scummy rising to the surface of a pond, briefly broke the surface, and then sank as he forcefully pushed it away with a firm shake of his head.

He withdrew his hand from her shoulder. Truthfully, if he had been able to rouse Monica, he doubted she would have believed his story, and he could imagine her suspicious response. *My mom made a pass at you? Why would she do that? Oh, and she put those bruises on you, a grown man? At her age? Are you sure that someone else wasn't responsible—someone that you willingly allowed to do it?*

He ground his teeth.

It could all backfire against him, calamitously. He had to be smart about his approach. He had to keep his cool.

In the bathroom, he switched on the shower. With the shower providing covering noise in case Monica awoke, he took out his iPhone and pulled up the contact information for Rod's private investigator: On the Move Investigative Services.

It was Sunday night and, not surprisingly, no one answered the line, but Troy left a voice mail message anyway. He had to do *something*.

Because he was getting scared.

22

Leaning toward the wide bathroom mirror, fingers digging deep into her scalp, Monica couldn't believe what she was seeing.

More of her hair had turned gray. Apparently overnight.

The change affected several regions of her head, in random, swirl-like patterns, as though a painter had gone wild with a dripping brush. Using a small handheld mirror, she located patches of gray at the back of her head, too.

Although her life had been in turmoil lately, Monica was certain the grayness hadn't been there yesterday. Yesterday, she'd seen only a few gray strands, nothing like this. Surely, if all of this had been there, she would have noticed it.

She couldn't explain how this had happened, so quickly and dramatically, and it worried her. She didn't know what to do about it, either, except strongly consider the possibility of coloring her hair, as her mother had suggested.

She dropped the small mirror on the vanity. She splashed cold water on her face, dried her skin with a wash cloth, and began to dress in her workout gear.

Although it was half past seven o'clock in the morning, long after she typically awoke on a Monday, she was taking the entire week off from her job at the clinic. She could exercise at her leisure and ask her mother to tend to the children if they awoke. Troy had already left for work.

As she pulled on her sweat pants, she winced. Since she'd gotten out of bed, her joints had felt stiff, tender. Her body felt as if she had over-trained, but that was absurd. She hadn't exercised in over a week, since she'd gotten the news about Lily, and had done nothing that would have caused such physical discomfort.

It required a major effort of will to make her way downstairs. Each stair sent a spike of pain through her tendons.

Grace was in the breakfast nook (*when did she ever sleep?*) sipping tea and perusing her leather-bound journal. Her mother somehow looked even better than she ever had before: skin bright, eyes shining, and hair a bit longer and darker than it had appeared yesterday.

I need to take whatever she's taking, Monica thought. *She looks absolutely terrific.*

Grace smiled at her entrance. "Morning, darling."

"More gray this morning." Monica sadly pulled at a strand of hair.

"So sorry." Grace clucked her tongue. "Dark and Lovely is your best resort, my dear. The product has always worked well for me. I've some in my luggage if you'd like to use it."

"Thanks, but I'll probably pick up my own supply later today. At the rate I'm graying, I'm going to need it."

"A woman's prerogative." Grace raised her teacup. "Would you like a cup of tea?"

"Thanks, but I'm going to try to work out this morning. Can you listen out for the kids, please?"

Monica planned to use their home gym in the basement, but before that, she wanted to complete a brisk walk around their neighborhood. Navigating the ever-shifting terrain of paved roads was always more challenging than any treadmill, though with her body in its present, strangely sore condition, a cushioned walk on a machine might have been better for her.

Regardless, she headed outdoors. The sun was still making its early morning ascent into a sky partially quilted with thin clouds, and the air was crisp and cool, the temperature hovering in the low fifties. She zipped up her fleece jacket all the way to the collar, and ambled down the walkway, to the sidewalk.

The neighborhood was quiet. Many of the residents had already left for work, and the public school buses would have had their morning pick-ups a short while ago. The only other person out was a blonde woman jogging, her Golden Retriever trotting at her side.

Watching the dog, Monica sighed. Duchess had usually joined her on these early-morning walks, the tiny Maltese stubbornly keeping pace with her. She felt her dog's absence as she might have felt a missing limb. Gathering her strength, she went to take a long stride across the pavement—

And fell as her hamstrings twanged painfully. She tumbled to the ground, barely managing to break her fall with her hands, her palms scraping against concrete.

The fall caused a spell of dizziness to wash over her. Lying on the cold sidewalk, she pulled in deep breaths of the cool air, trying to regain her equilibrium. Her throbbing legs felt as limp as cooked pasta.

What's the matter with me?

She wasn't fatigued; she had just enjoyed an incredibly restful night of sleep. But her body was betraying her. Everything ached, and she felt clumsy.

Grimacing, she pushed to her feet. The effort was as difficult as if she were in an ocean fighting against strong tides. By the time she got back to a standing position, she was sweating.

The tremendous exertion needed to complete something as simple as balancing on both feet reminded her of the aftermath of her second pregnancy. She'd needed a C-section, and the recuperation from that procedure had been grueling, requiring several days of strenuous effort to recover sufficiently to execute simple physical tasks.

But the rehab from major surgery was sensible, expected. What she was experiencing at the moment was downright puzzling.

Completing a walk—completing *any* exercise—was out of the question. She dragged herself back inside the house.

"Back so soon?" Grace asked, emerging from the kitchen. "Are you okay, darling?"

"I need to sit down for a few minutes." Carefully, wincing slightly with the movement, Monica lowered herself into an upholstered chair in the living room. "My joints are aching something awful. I don't know what's going on."

"Let me fetch you a cup of tea. It ought to help soothe you."

Monica nodded her thanks, but she was going to need more than herbal tea to get her through the day. She was going to need some painkillers.

If this condition persisted much longer, she would need to see her doctor, too.

23

Troy worked for North Point Radiology Associates. It was the largest radiology practice in the Atlanta area, and the exclusive radiology provider for Northside Hospital, out of which their service operated. The hospital had three locations in the metro Atlanta area, and he was attached to the largest facility, in Sandy Springs, barely a ten-minute drive from his house.

He was one of forty-eight physicians in the practice, and a key member of their interventional radiology team. For him, there was no such thing as a slow day at the office.

He'd originally been interested in radiology because it was one of the highest paying specialty professions in the medical field. To his surprise, he enjoyed the work and had a keen talent for it. The salary—a staggering sum, more money than he'd ever planned on earning—had become almost secondary to the sense of pleasure and purpose he derived from the job.

Nevertheless, in the midst of the work day's hustle and bustle, he couldn't stop thinking about Grace, the events of that weekend replaying in his mind in a lurid, continuous loop. The private investigator had yet to return his call, and Troy had resolved to ring him again as soon he stepped out for lunch.

At one in the afternoon, he finally had time to spare. He exited the hospital and was striding across the parking garage to his black BMW sedan, the car parked in a section of the deck reserved for hospital staff. As he was about to open the car door, a woman called out.

"Troy, wait up."

Lips pursed, he turned. It was Liz, of course. She was rushing to catch up to him, zipping up her forest-green jacket against the blustery November day.

Liz was thirty years old, a nurse attached to the intensive care unit. They had met two years ago, innocently enough, in the hospital cafeteria. As a general guideline, he avoided romantic involvements with women at work, but Liz was so attractive that he had let it happen. He had recently begun to regret the decision.

Ironically, Liz looked as if she could have been Monica's slightly younger sister. They had similar complexions, facial features, and body types. Years ago, one of Troy's ex-girlfriends had declared that if one had gathered all of Troy's lovers together in a room, it could have been mistaken for a family reunion.

"We can't go to lunch together," he said. "Rule number one: keep it discreet. You know that."

"I need to talk to you."

Talk about rules. In Troy's experience, whenever a woman that you were screwing said she wanted to "talk," the rules dictated that was never a good thing.

"I came over on Saturday night," he said. "We could have talked then. Has something happened?"

Saturday evening, he had slipped away from home and visited Liz at her condo in Dunwoody, under the guise of heading out to the gym. Admittedly, during the sixty-minute workout in Liz's bedroom, they hadn't engaged in much conversation, but he preferred it that way. He wasn't seeing Liz because he wanted a confidante or a best friend.

"I can take my own car if that makes you feel any better," she said. "Where were you planning to go?"

He noticed that she had avoided his question. He shrugged. "Hadn't decided. Somewhere quiet."

"You in the mood for Greek? I know a nice spot, great gyros. You'd like it."

"Fine. Lead on."

He tailed Liz out of the hospital complex. She drove a red Mercedes Benz coupe with a vanity plate that declared: CUTERN.

She led him to a small strip mall off Riverside Drive. The restaurant, called Athens in Atlanta, was a cozy spot, busy with the lunch crowd, the air redolent with the scents of grilled onions, beef, and lamb. At Troy's request, the hostess showed them to a booth near the back of the dining room. He had scanned the patrons and hadn't seen Monica or anyone else he knew, but one could never be too cautious in public.

"This is nice." Liz slipped off her jacket. "We don't do this often enough."

"Do what often enough?"

"You know, go out to eat. It's always been takeout or Grubhub delivered to my place. If we eat at all."

He gave a noncommittal grumble. He could feel her dancing toward the topic she wanted to discuss. But other, far more important matters pressed on his mind.

Such as the bruises he still bore on his wrists from last night's encounter with Grace.

He hadn't told Monica what had happened, had barely any time to talk to her before he'd left the house for work. He knew she was dropping off the children at school and intended to hang out with her mother all day; he needed to get Grace out of their house for good, but he couldn't accomplish that without some compelling evidence. Something Monica would believe. A woman such as Grace had to have at least a few skeletons in the closet.

Their server arrived. Liz ordered iced tea and a gyro platter, and Troy asked for the same. He couldn't summon any interest in the menu.

Watching him intently, Liz leaned forward. She was such a good-looking woman, a catch for any guy, and he wondered why she had agreed to their current arrangement. She could have done much better than him if she only demanded it; his heart would never belong to her.

He genuinely loved Monica. He loved her in the deepest fathoms of his soul. But he found the pull of the *new*—new women, new bodies, new sex—difficult to resist, like trying to escape the gravitational field of a black hole's event horizon. He had long ago given up fighting his body's natural cravings.

On his sixteenth birthday, his dad had pulled him aside. His father, Moses "Mo" Stephens, was a jazz guitarist, a talented musician who had played with some of the greats—Miles Davis, John Coltrane, Herbie Hancock—and even released a couple of solo albums, one of which had gained critical acclaim but enjoyed only modest commercial success. Pops had been an inconstant presence in their household, always out of town for gigs and studio recording sessions, but Troy distinctly remembered his dad rolling a joint, taking a couple puffs, passing the weed to Troy, and then telling him, in his typical, colorful way: *here's your birthday advice, son, and you're old enough to finally hear it. Your dick is meant to fly as free as the wind.*

In Troy's mind, hearing those words from his revered father was the equivalent of the President signing a bill to encourage free love. All of those raw, lustful urges that plagued him throughout his burgeoning teenage years were fine, Pops was saying—and he should indulge them to the limit.

The dick is meant to fly as free as the wind.

He had not been faithful to a girlfriend, ever. Not sexually. But he was always faithful emotionally. He loved his wife, and he loved all of his prior girlfriends with whom he had been in committed relationships. They got his heart, one hundred percent. But his body was meant to be shared freely.

He was careful about his activities. He *always* used protection, no matter what a woman promised him. He didn't have any STDs (he got tested annually), and hadn't fathered any children outside of his own marriage. He used a backup cell, a burner phone, to conduct his affairs. What he did in the streets, stayed in the streets. He owed that to Monica and his kids.

But he had powerful carnal needs. He was even willing to

consider that he might have been a sex addict. But he wasn't willing to do anything about it, and he'd made peace with that aspect of himself years ago.

The waiter brought their beverages. Liz took a slow sip from a straw, curled her finger around a strand of her dark hair, and gazed into his eyes, a look brimming with emotion that made him squirm in his chair.

"You wanted to talk about something?" he asked.

"Not much for small talk, huh?" she asked. "You want to get right to it."

"I have a lot of work to finish today, Liz. A long, leisurely lunch wasn't on my agenda."

"I want to talk about where this is going."

He almost choked on his tea. "What?"

"We've been doing this for five months. We have fun. We enjoy each other's company. Do you agree?"

"Sure, it's been good, the way things have been works well for me."

"I thought so." She smiled, tentatively. "I like you, too, a lot. I want us to talk about moving to the next level."

I knew having lunch with her was a bad idea, he thought. If they were in a private place, he would have blown his top right about then. But in a busy restaurant, surrounded by other diners and staff, he had to avoid making a scene, keep his voice down and sound reasonable.

"What do you mean, the next level?" he asked.

"Real talk," she said. "We get together at my place and we have sex. I'll be honest, you know how to make me feel good, real good, and I know I'm doing the same for you. It's mutual satisfaction. But we're just fuck buddies, Troy. I need more than that if we're going to keep doing this."

"I like you a lot, Liz," he said. "But are you forgetting what we established when we first started doing this? My *non-negotiable* rules of engagement?"

"Right." She made a look of disgust. "I don't expect you to leave your family or anything. But I need to be more than a warm body in the bedroom. I need . . . I need an emotional connection."

Their food arrived, two steaming platters of gyros and fries. It looked and smelled delicious. Troy speared a strip of lamb with his fork.

She stared at him, hadn't touched her food. "You're going to just sit there and eat after what I said?"

"I'm starving, Liz. I didn't eat much for breakfast."

"Can you at least give me some kind of answer?" She was clutching her fork.

He chewed, wiped the corner of his mouth with a napkin, swallowed.

"Again, I don't know why you're asking me about this."

"Don't you want to have some real conversations, and somewhere other than my bedroom?" she asked. "Spend real, quality time together? I know you have that Harley, for example. I love motorcycles. Why can't we have like a day trip on your bike?"

"I reserve day trips for my wife and kids."

She flinched as if struck with an open hand.

"Look, Liz." He put down his fork. "Let's not pretend that we didn't discuss all of this at the very beginning. I told you exactly what I was looking for, and you were fine with it. Now, you've caught feelings and want to change the rules. I'm not having it. Subject closed."

He spoke the words in a deliberately harsh tone, and he expected her to respond with an emotional explosion, like most women would have. In his experience, every arrangement such as this one reached a breaking point, and it seemed as if it was time to blow up this one, and move on to the next thing.

But Liz only smiled at him, as though she knew his game and had something better in mind.

"Come on, baby, don't you at least *think* about us having something more?" she asked softly. Her hand crept across the table, found his. She rubbed her thumb across his palm in a slow, circular motion. "Remember what I did for you on Saturday? What if I admitted that I was holding back?"

"Holding back?"

Nodding, she ran her tongue across her lips. "We could have gone further. A lot further. But I *reserve* that level for a man who agrees to give me an emotional commitment."

"You're lying," he said, because he couldn't think of any other response. He was still trying to wrap his mind around the possibility of what she could have been holding back, because it had already been so incredibly good. "Don't try to play me."

"Am I?" she asked, eyebrows arched. "Is that your final answer?"

He didn't say anything.

She winked. "Thought so. Think on it, Troy, and text me later." She rose from her seat, and tossed a twenty-dollar bill on the table. "Have a nice lunch."

Silently, he watched her strut out of the restaurant.

Every player gets played eventually, he realized. As long as he'd been doing this, he was overdue to run into a woman like Liz. He couldn't give her what he was asking for—the notion of taking a day trip with her was ludicrous—but was he willing to walk away from what she was promising him in return?

His main cell phone vibrated, like a bell signaling the end of a round.

It was the private investigator, finally returning his call.

24

Monica spent the day with her mother. *Girl time,* as her mom called it. She welcomed the opportunity to enjoy several uninterrupted hours in the company of her mother, one on one. They had a lot of catching up to do, and over the course of the week, Monica intended to pack in as much quality time as possible.

In the morning, after dropping off the kids at elementary school, they had breakfast at J. Christopher's, a local restaurant chain that served quasi-organic entrees such as blueberry pancakes sprinkled with granola, omelets stuffed with chicken and avocado, and turkey sausage paired with egg whites. Monica picked at her Belgian waffle and scrambled eggs, not having much of an appetite. A dose of Aleve taken earlier reduced much of the joint soreness she'd experienced, but she was still mystified as to the cause of the discomfort. The pain, along with her dramatically graying hair, had given her reason to worry that she was suffering from some underlying ailment. She'd booked an appointment for the next day with her primary care physician.

In spite of her concern for her own health, she was determined to put on a happy face and enjoy her mother's company.

Grace was in a fine mood. At the restaurant, throughout their meal, her mother flirted shamelessly with the waiter. He was a dark-haired young man who could not have been any older than twenty-five and bore a passing resemblance to Bruno Mars.

"Age is nothing but a number, my dear," Grace said to Monica after the waiter had come by to refresh their beverages. Eyes twinkling, she kept her gaze nailed on the server as he strolled away. "Look at that tight little ass on him. Yummy. I'd love to give it a good squeeze and ride him like a bronco."

"All right now." Monica blushed. She had to remind herself that her mother was single, and in her own words, "thoroughly enjoyed sex." Her mother's free-love attitude was a dramatic contrast to Lily's puritan perspective on all sexual matters. Lily had raised her to follow those same strict guidelines; before she married Troy, Monica had been intimate with only two other men, and had actually experienced some guilt about those relationships, as Lily had always advocated saving your virginity for marriage.

She could only speculate about how many sexual partners her mother had entertained over the years. She didn't plan on ever asking. Some things were better left unsaid.

Next, they went to Lenox Square in Buckhead, a huge indoor shopping center that Monica visited from time to time. Although it was early November, the mall was already decorated for the upcoming holidays. To Monica, it seemed the annual holiday shopping season kicked off earlier each year, part of the retail industry's relentless pursuit of consumer dollars.

Monica had intended only to browse, but at Neiman Marcus, she wound up falling in love with a sizzling pair of Michael Kors boots. She'd always had a weakness for shoes, to which the few dozen pairs in her closet at home were proof positive.

But the boots cost two hundred dollars. She loved a new pair of shoes as much as the next woman, but as a matter of principle, she wasn't going to drop that kind of money on an impulse purchase. She could hear Lily's admonishing voice in her mind: *save your money, sweetheart, and one day it will save you.* Lily's lessons on frugality had sunk so deep that Monica had developed a tendency to avoid buying anything, even a cup of coffee, on impulse. She would make a mental note about the item, review her monthly budget, and perhaps wait until the boots went on sale.

With a sigh, she put them back on the display shelf.

"I thought you loved those?" Grace asked.

"I don't need them." Monica shrugged.

Grace scowled. "Nonsense. If you want them, get them. You've had a difficult time lately, child. Consider it retail therapy."

"Did you see the price tag?" Monica shook her head. "Not today. Maybe later."

"I'll buy them for you." Grace reached for her purse.

"Are you kidding? You don't have to do this for me. I can live without them. They're only shoes. I have plenty at home already, I promise you."

"I haven't bought anything for you in your entire life." Grace patted her arm. "Don't deprive me of the pleasure of doing so now."

Monica paused. "Are you sure?"

"I won't have it any other way."

At the register, Grace paid for the purchase in cash, peeling away an assortment of bills from a bulging knot of rubber-banded money. Monica wondered if her mother was one of those old-school folks who didn't use bank accounts and dealt only in hard currency. Regardless, her mother worked as a nanny, was nearing retirement age, and needed to preserve her funds. Monica felt guilty about bringing them to the shopping mall in the first place, though it had been her mother's idea.

"Why don't we get something for you, too?" Monica asked as they left the department store. "My treat?"

"You don't have to do that," Grace said.

Monica smiled. "I'm a grown woman. I haven't bought anything for my mother in my entire life. Don't deprive me."

"Touché." Grace clasped her hands. "All right then. Is there a lingerie store on the premises?"

Monica's smile froze. That was not what she had expected Grace to say. She had thought her mother would request shoes, a new bag, or a dress.

"Sure, I think so," Monica said. "But listen, there are a lot of other stores here, too. I think there's a Coach shop across the way."

"I'd love to get something sexy to wear." Grace winked. "I may be older, but I'm not dead. You're only as old as you allow yourself to feel."

Someone needs to convince my body of those words, Monica thought. She was finding it difficult to keep up with Grace as her mother marched across the concourse, heels clicking, and at one point, needed to ask Grace to wait a minute, so she could sit on a bench and catch her breath.

I've got to find out what's going on with me, Monica thought. *I'm feeling completely out of sorts.*

At the lingerie store, Grace twirled around the shop like a giddy starlet, plucking pieces of clothing from the racks and posing with them, asking questions such as, "How much lift do you think this will give my boobs?" and "Is my butt too big for me to wear this?" The sales clerk on duty, a petite red-headed girl of perhaps twenty-one, appeared amused by Grace's behavior, and for her part, Monica felt her face steaming with embarrassment.

It wasn't that her mother was almost sixty—hell, she fully intended to be sexually active at that age, too—it was that she was her *mother.* Maybe she was too much of a prude, but she just wasn't interested in what her mother might choose to wear for an intimate evening with a man, and didn't want to imagine how Grace's body would be revealed in the various pieces that she was considering. In spite of her embarrassment, Monica kept up a friendly grin, offered non-committal responses to Grace's questions, and prayed that her mother would decide on something soon so they could get out of there.

At last, Grace decided on a black bra and panties set fashioned from fishnet mesh and lace.

"This is what I'm talking about," Grace said. "Girl, I love it."

"Is there . . . someone special who would like seeing you in this?" Monica asked. "Never mind. It's none of my business."

"A lady never tells." Grace smiled demurely. "But let's say I've got my eye on someone. He may not appreciate me yet, but he will."

After Monica paid for the clothing, they left the shopping mall, and on Grace's request, visited the grocery store, a Whole Foods supermarket not far from where Monica lived. Grace declared that she planned to prepare gourmet meals for the duration of her visit and wanted to stock up on ingredients. She swept like a dervish around the market, loading up the shopping cart with seafood, meats, poultry, produce, spices, oils, and more, and Monica struggled to keep up with her. After a short while, Monica finally gave in and went to the dining area to sit and rest, while Grace continued shopping, zipping the loaded-down cart through the aisles as if contained nothing more than a bundle of feathers.

When they arrived home, the cargo area of the SUV stuffed with paper grocery bags, Grace said she would unload the vehicle, and advised Monica to get some rest. Monica dragged herself upstairs and almost collapsed on the bed. Trying to keep pace with her mother had worn her out.

She was drifting off when the telephone on the nightstand chirped.

Blinking, she turned her head. The Caller ID displayed a local area code, but no name. She was exhausted, but had lately received so many calls from friends that she decided to answer.

Sitting up, she grabbed the handset off the cradle. "Hello?"

A gravelly, throat-clearing sound. Then: "Dr. Monica? This is Reverend McBride. We met at Lily's home-going service this past Saturday."

"I remember." Much of that agonizing day was lost in a mental fog, but she recalled the hunched-over old gentleman with wispy white hair and brown eyes that blazed with intelligence. "We didn't get time to chat, there was so much going on."

A hacking cough. "That's why I phoned. Your husband passed along your number to me. How're you getting along?"

"It's been tough," Monica said. Running her fingers through her hair, she examined a new strand of gray. "But God brought my biological mother into my life this past weekend, too. That's been an unexpected blessing."

Silence on the other end of the line. When McBride finally spoke, his voice was barely above a whisper. "Grace?"

"You know her?" Monica sat up straighter in the bed.

The pastor started to respond, but a series of phlegmy coughs seized him.

Monica clutched the handset. She tried to pinpoint the emotion she'd heard in the pastor's words: it sounded like fear.

But that didn't make any sense, did it?

"Do you know my mother, sir?" Monica asked again.

Before McBride could answer, Monica heard the phone picked up in another part of the house. Grace's voice boomed over the line: "Who's calling? My daughter Monica needs her rest."

A dial tone answered. McBride had disconnected.

Frowning, Monica replaced the handset on the cradle. Less than a minute later, Grace walked into the bedroom.

"Who was that?" Grace asked in a sharp tone.

The suddenness of Grace's entrance, and the suspicion in her gaze, had caught Monica off guard.

"Reverend McBride," Monica said. "I met him at Lily's service. He said Lily used to attend his church, a long time ago. Do you know him? He said your name."

"I most certainly remember him." Grace's lips twisted as if she'd bitten into a rotten apple. "How did he get your telephone number?"

"He said Troy gave it to him."

"That old man is not to be trusted," Grace said. "Lily abandoned his church due to his predilection for scandalous behavior. Among other things, he had a fondness for young girls."

"Oh." Monica wondered if the reverend had made a pass at Grace in her youth, but she didn't dare ask. The disgust on her mother's face made the answer obvious.

"I doubt he's changed with age," Grace said. "Such vile men never do."

"I can understand why Lily would have left his church then.

She wouldn't have tolerated being a member of a congregation led by a man like that."

"Indeed, you knew her well." Grace touched Monica's shoulder. "Get some rest, dear—and I'll answer the phone if it rings again."

25

Sitting in his home office in the basement that evening, eating a turkey-and-cheddar sandwich while the rest of his family ate dinner upstairs, Troy scanned the email that had arrived on his iPhone.

> Dr. Stephens –
> *Background report on Grace Bolden is attached. I know this isn't much, but this is standard for our express package. We can discuss what is needed for a more comprehensive investigation. Call me at your convenience.*
> *Nick Sullivan*
> *On the Move Investigative Services*

Earlier that day, when Troy had finally connected with the private detective, he'd shared his concerns about Grace; he hadn't mentioned how the woman had brought him to his knees last night, though, perhaps because it embarrassed him. Still, Sullivan had validated that all of Troy's worries were reasonable and had suggested that Troy purchase his "express investigative services package," which was a fancy name for a background check: a report on Grace's employment history, prior addresses, criminal records, and any other publicly accessible data. Troy realized he could have bought a background check online, but in the likely event that he would need further detective work, he thought it prudent to establish a business relationship with

Sullivan. Rod wouldn't have recommended the guy unless he was worth every penny.

Troy disliked opening pdfs on his phone. He raised the lid of his laptop, powered it on, and accessed the file accompanying the email.

Ten minutes later, he called Sullivan. The investigator answered immediately, an orchestra of revving engines and blaring horns playing in the background, the unmistakable music of a commuter navigating metro Atlanta's infamous rush-hour traffic.

"Hey, Doc," Sullivan said. He had a soft Boston accent, so the words came out as *hey, dahk*. "I'm guessing you read my report, right?"

"This doesn't help me much at all," Troy said, glancing at his computer screen. "Grace currently lives in Houston, she's fifty-nine-years-old and works for a nanny-placement agency? A few prior addresses in Oakland, Philly, and New Orleans, but no criminal record or judgements against her? No record of a marriage or divorce? Big deal. I need more than this to change my wife's mind about her. There's got to be some dirt."

"All right." Sullivan grunted. "We've confirmed her basic story checks out okay. But honestly, Doc, you gotta give me more to work with here."

Troy ground his teeth. Bruxism was a lifelong, bad habit of his, and worsened when he was under pressure. "What else then?"

"DNA samples, so we can verify maternity."

Troy was shaking his head. "I told you when we first talked earlier today, they look alike. The resemblance is uncanny. I don't have any doubt that she's my wife's mother."

"Maybe, but we need to rule it out. Don't doctors do that, too, when they make a diagnosis? Rule out all the obvious crap first?"

"Differential diagnosis," Troy said automatically, and recalled a professor's oft-repeated line from his medical school days. *When you hear hoof beats, look for horses, not zebras.*

"I have a setup with a local lab that does DNA testing," Sullivan said. "Comes up all the time in court cases. If you can get me a sample from your wife, and Grace, we can establish beyond all doubt that they're mother and daughter."

"Neither of them is going to submit to testing willingly. Especially Grace."

"You're a smart guy. You can figure out a way to get what we need. A buccal swab on the inside of the cheek is ideal, but a hair sample could work, too."

Troy wasn't convinced he could get even that much without getting uncomfortably close to Grace, but he saw no point in bringing that up, because the investigator's reasoning made sense. Why was he assuming his wife and Grace were mother and daughter? What if they were actually aunt and niece, or sisters, or cousins? Or not related at all? Merely because they looked alike didn't mean anything. It was plausible for complete strangers to look like twins—hence, the world of celebrity impersonators. His family could be the target of an elaborate con. In his gut, he was convinced that Grace and Monica were genetically linked, but he needed to rule out all other angles.

"I'll make it happen," Troy said. "Anything else?"

"It would be helpful if you could get into her purse, or luggage. I think checking out her personal belongings could give us some leads for further investigation."

"That's a tall order." Troy drew in a tight breath. "What am I looking for?"

"Photographs. Documentation like a driver's license, passport, credit cards. Unusual pieces of jewelry or unusual possessions. And oh, drugs, of course, of the prescription or recreational kind."

"Essentially, I need to search through all of her stuff." He pushed aside his sandwich, his appetite gone.

His wrists were still bruised from the punishing grip Grace had delivered, and he had yet to come up with a reasonable explanation for the woman's extraordinary physical strength. The idea of rummaging through her belongings, and her possibly finding out what he had done, made his stomach quiver.

I could snap you like a twig, boy.

"Go through her belongings with a fine-tooth comb, Doc," Sullivan said. "Snap pictures of what you find, and email them to me. I'll get right on it."

"If I'm doing all of the snooping here, what am I paying you for?" Troy asked, only half-kidding.

"You're paying me for my nicely formatted reports that pull together all of the details into a coherent story." Sullivan laughed. "Look, about the DNA sample. I don't want to insult your medical expertise, but it needs to be preserved, no contamination. I can get you a kit."

"I know what to do there. I assume we'll meet somewhere so I can hand it over?"

"Yeah, and the lab can turn it around within twenty-four hours, for an extra charge," Sullivan said.

"You'll have it in a couple days. I want everything expedited, I don't care about the additional fees. I need answers."

"That's what I thought you'd say."

Troy ended the call. He rubbed his hands together. He had no idea how he was going to implement his next steps, but having a list of purposeful actions to execute boosted his mood. He spun around in his chair, planning to grab a beer from the basement fridge and mull over his strategy.

Monica was standing in his office doorway. Arms crossed over her chest, her eyebrows were knitted with suspicion.

"Who were you talking to?" she asked.

26

He's hiding something, Monica thought.

Puzzled by Troy's avoidance of the family at dinner, she had come downstairs to see what he was doing. She had a hunch that he was up to something, and it wasn't work, as he'd claimed. When you had been married for eight years, you noticed the signs of something amiss. Troy loved to eat, and for him to pass on a hot, delicious dinner in favor of a cold sandwich was completely out of character.

She arrived at his office door as he was concluding a call on his cell phone. All she caught were the concluding words: *I need answers* . . .

When he saw her standing there in the doorway, he blinked with surprise, and it struck her that his expression matched how their daughter looked when she was caught misbehaving. Lexi had inherited her father's traits in so many ways.

"I've been working," he said. Quickly, he closed the lid of his laptop; she hadn't been able to decipher the text on the display.

"Oh." She glanced at his workstation. "But your work computer is off."

He frowned, clearly annoyed at the continued line of questioning. "I was about to turn it on after I finished my call. Is there something pressing you needed to talk about, baby? Something on your mind? I've got some things I need to check out."

He gently tugged on his left earlobe as he spoke. It was one of his tells, and she wasn't sure he realized it.

What is he hiding from me?

"You're missing out on an amazing dinner," she said. "A cold turkey sandwich seems more appealing to you?"

"Can you save me a plate? I might grab a bite later on. Probably I'll be working late and will get hungry again. Appreciate it, hon."

He turned to his workstation, pressed the power button, flipped open a folder beside the computer. An obvious sign that she had been dismissed.

But Monica didn't budge from the doorway.

"Do you have a problem with my mother?" she asked.

He spun in the chair, nostrils flared. "What?"

Bingo.

"I know that Pat has an issue with my mother," Monica said. "That's obvious. I'm getting the feeling that you don't appreciate her being here, either."

Troy leaned back in his chair, opening up to the conversation. His emotion was all over his face. He appeared relieved that she had broached the subject.

"She was supposed to go home at the end of the weekend," he said. "I'm not a big fan of unplanned visits from anyone, you know that about me."

Monica was trembling. "I'm getting to know my biological mother for the first time in my *entire life*, Troy. I think a little flexibility is warranted here. Is that too much to ask?"

"As soon as she shows up, Duchess is dead. The very next day. Don't you find that odd, Monica?"

"*Your* mother left her outside."

"That's bullshit." Troy ground his teeth. "My mom volunteers at an animal shelter, for crying out loud, there's nobody I know who's more responsible when it comes to pets."

"She's not perfect. She made a mistake."

"We don't know anything about Grace. Not a damned thing. With Lily gone, we don't know anyone who can vouch for a single thing she's told us."

She almost told him about Reverend McBride's call earlier

that afternoon—*I know one person who knows her*—but realized that was no trump card for her to play, either. As Grace had shared, Lily had abandoned the reverend's church because he'd been chasing after young girls—including Grace, mostly likely. The scandalous old man was hardly a credible source and was best avoided.

"Guess what?" Troy said. "Your mother's been flirting with me, too. Hell, I can hardly call it flirting, it's borderline assault. She grabbed my crotch and said she wanted me to fuck her."

Monica only stared at him. He showed her his wrists. She saw faint purple marks on his flesh.

"See these bruises? She grabbed me. Last night. When I refused to play along with her seduction. She's a helluva lot stronger than she looks, unbelievably so."

"Are you sure that one of your other women didn't get a little rough with you?" Monica asked.

When she saw the flash of shock in Troy's eyes, she knew the spear had struck its target. Her heart twisted.

"What the hell are you talking about?" he asked. "I'm telling you the truth, Monica. Grace is dangerous. We need to get her out of here."

"She's welcome to stay here as long as she wants," Monica said. "*She's my mother.* I don't have anything left to say on the subject."

"Dammit, you aren't listening to me!"

"I'm listening, all right. If you're really cheating on me, Troy, like I'm starting to believe you are, you'll be the one packing your bags and getting out of this house."

Without waiting for his reply, she walked out, trembling and teary-eyed, but feeling more empowered than she had felt in weeks. How dare he accuse her mother of those terrible, ridiculous things? Who could have believed any of that?

27

Troy awoke in bed sometime later that night, convinced that someone was in the room with them.

Monica slumbered beside him. She had been asleep when he'd finally crawled into the sack around midnight, immersed in her new, dead-to-the-world stage of sleep that would have kept her unconscious even if a sonic boom had sounded outside their window. He had been grateful, actually, that she was asleep when he entered. He hadn't wanted to encounter her accusatory glare.

If you're really cheating on me, Troy, like I'm starting to believe you are, you'll be the one packing your bags and getting out of this house . . .

He had no idea where she'd pulled insight that from, how she'd made the connection, and it troubled him. He had always been so careful, so meticulous in his deception, and she had never, ever questioned him. Until then.

It was a long time before sleep took him down.

But he was awake again, had emerged from another distressing dream about Grace. Someone was in their room. The only light in the bedroom came from the glow of their bedside alarm clocks, and the faint luminescence that framed the front window, the light drifting from a nearby streetlamp. Otherwise, it was too dark for him to make out anything but shadowy shapes.

Still, he felt a presence near the king-size bed, detected the displacement of air that hinted toward another occupant in the enclosed space.

The bedroom door was open, too. They slept with it closed.

Always. Beyond the doorway, the corridor was dark as a cavern tunnel.

Blinking groggily, he twisted his head on the pillow. The bedside clock said 3:04. No one could be in their room at that hour. He must have been imagining things. He was on that blurry edge of unconsciousness, too tired to pull himself up and search the room.

Something shifted, just beyond the foot of the bed. The mattress creaked, and he heard the whispery sound of bedsheets drawn back.

And then he noticed a shape burrowing underneath the sheets, right between the juncture of his legs.

Am I dreaming?

Nimble fingers peeled away his boxers and freed his member. A soft, moist mouth closed over him, pulled him in deep.

A shiver coursed down his spine. Intense pleasure paralyzed him.

Using tongue and lips, the nighttime visitor worked him slowly, skillfully brought him to the throbbing brink of what promised to be a volcanic orgasm—and suddenly withdrew. The shape retreated down the bed.

He heard the whispery sound of movement across carpet. Gasping, trembling, Troy craned his neck, squinting to see.

The visitor was crawling on the floor.

Grace? he thought, fuzzily. The shape was too big to be anything but an adult.

And crawling was an inaccurate description. It was more like *slithering*. She wasn't utilizing her hands or feet to propel her body forward. She was wriggling across the carpet in an eerily slow, smooth, sinuous motion, like a boa constrictor on the prowl.

I really must be dreaming.

Halfway across the room, she raised her head. He heard a wet, squishy sound . . . and saw the shape of what appeared to be a grotesquely long, ropy tongue protruding from her mouth.

All right, now I know I'm dreaming.

140

She drew the tongue back into her mouth with a motion like someone sucking in a strand of pasta. She slithered to the doorway, and away into the hall.

He realized he was clenching his teeth. He relaxed his jaws, exhaled a big gasp of air.

He waited for a minute, to see whether she would return. When nothing happened, he got out of bed.

His erection was so rigid it felt like a pole.

He tiptoed to the door and looked out in the hallway. No one was out there. He rubbed his eyes.

What the hell did I just see? What happened?

He retreated into the bedroom, closed the door. And locked it.

28

Monica awoke early as usual, but didn't dress in her workout clothes. It was clear to her, upon waking, that was she much was too stiff to attempt an exercise routine of any kind. She slipped on a pair of house shoes, wrapped herself in her robe, and went downstairs, taking each step slowly and carefully.

Her joints crackled with each step. She felt like a very old woman in deteriorating physical condition.

She needed to see her doctor. She could ascribe her chronic fatigue to grief, but the joint pain and stiffness was another matter altogether.

As she reached the bottom of the staircase, she heard Grace moving dishes in the kitchen, and she smelled the aroma of something baking, mingled with the spicy fragrance of Grace's cigarettes.

Doesn't she ever sleep? Monica wondered. It was a quarter to six in the morning. Monica had been looking forward to, perhaps jealously, a little time to herself. It seemed that the only time she had any solitude these days was when she was asleep.

"Good morning, dear," Grace said, sounding as cheerful as if she'd been wide awake for hours. She smiled brightly. "Did you sleep well?"

"Morning," Monica said. "Yeah, sleep was fine. I feel bad only when I get up."

Grace took a draw on her cigarette, ground it out in her ashtray, and came to Monica. She wore a red nightgown that billowed around her slim figure, an apron knotted around her waist. Her hair was in a short, curly style, the strands thick and dark. Monica assumed she had colored her hair. Grace's complexion was vibrant, too, her skin glowing as if lightly coated in oil.

She looks years younger, Monica thought. *I need to take whatever she's taking.*

Grace gently grasped Monica's hand. "Come to the table, dear, and let's get you a cup of tea and some freshly baked buttermilk biscuits."

She led Monica to the table and helped her sit. A cup of her special blend tea and a plate heaped with biscuits appeared in short order. Monica sampled a biscuit, and it was fantastic: dusted with sugar, lightly buttered, and fluffy, exactly how she loved them.

"These are amazing," Monica said. "I envy your energy level. How can you bake at this hour?"

"It's habit, sweetheart." Grace had begun sweeping the floor with a broom, whisking the bristles across the travertine with strong, swift motions. "An old spinster like me? What else would I do with my time?"

Monica sipped the tea. "Old spinster? You look great."

"Good enough to draw the eye of a younger man?" Grace grinned at her.

"I'd say, sure."

"Let's see if your husband gives me a second look." She barked a laugh. "He has no scruples when it comes to such things, I promise you."

"Speaking of Troy." Monica set down her cup. "I might as well tell you. We had an argument last night."

Grace smirked. "It was about me, was it not? Neither your husband nor his mother seemed to appreciate my presence in this home. I can imagine what he's told you, the awful lies he's fabricated."

"It doesn't matter what he said. I want you here. You're *my* mother. If you weren't here with me, today . . . I don't know how I'd manage to cope with Lily's death, at all."

Grace leaned the broom against the doorway, and came to her. She knelt beside the chair and folded Monica into a warm embrace.

"My sweet little darling," Grace said. "I'll never leave you again. I promise."

Monica clasped her mother against her, choking back tears. The feel of her mother against her, the warmth of her, touched an instinctive longing that was embedded so deeply in her soul that she hadn't known it existed. How dare Troy think he could deprive her of developing this bond with her mom?

When Grace finally let go, Monica winced.

"Ouch. My shoulder aches now." Monica kneaded the inflamed joint. "I'm looking forward to seeing my physician today. I'm concerned about these aching joints of mine."

"Of course, medical care sounds best," Grace said. "Meanwhile, I need to run an errand today. A little personal matter that I must attend to."

Monica wondered where her mother needed to go, but decided it was none of her business.

"I'm not sure if I'm up to driving," Monica said. "Perhaps you can drop me off at the doctor's office and then take care of your errand."

29

Troy took the day off from work. He rarely had unplanned absences of any kind, believed that an important factor in being successful was always showing up for duty, but that day, work could wait. His top priority was to get those DNA samples and search through Grace's luggage.

That morning, the thought of Grace made the base of his spine tingle, a strangely pleasurable yet disturbing sensation. He recalled figments of a bizarre, erotic dream of Grace giving him a blowjob in bed while Monica slept beside him, and then slithering, snakelike, out of the room, but not before displaying a grotesquely long tongue. He had no idea how such a weird fantasy would have ever occurred to him, but it lingered in the back rooms of his memory.

He volunteered to drop off Lexi and Junior at school. Monica seemed surprised by his offer, but didn't argue. She probably interpreted his offer as him extending the olive branch, after last night's argument. But she didn't appear to be feeling well at all, complained of severe inflammation in her joints, and shared that she was hoping to see her physician that day. She likely appreciated having one less errand to complete.

She looks older, Troy thought. A couple of days ago, he had noticed several strands of gray in his wife's hair, but he had kept his mouth shut about it. Most women were as hyper-sensitive to signs of aging as they were to fluctuations in their body weight. A smart man kept such observations to himself.

By eight-thirty that morning, he had dropped off both of his children. Monica sent him a text as he was about to pull out of the school parking lot: *dr appt at nine, Grace taking me, will keep u posted.*

This is much more perfect than what I'd hoped for, Troy thought. He'd had a backup plan to clear Monica and Grace out of the house for a few hours: he was going to claim that he'd spotted a few bugs and wanted to fumigate their home with insect killer. His stratagem would have worked, but Monica's doctor appointment was better as it didn't require him to lie.

He drove to a CVS Pharmacy, grabbed a few items that would come in handy, and then went back home, getting there around ten minutes to nine. The garage was empty, Grace's rented Chevy parked at the edge of the long driveway.

He had perhaps ninety minutes until they returned, longer if they ran another errand after the doctor appointment. Plenty of time to get what he needed.

The house was eerily quiet when he stepped inside. Duchess used to bark and scamper around happily whenever he returned home. Damn, he missed that little fur ball.

Upstairs, he headed along the catwalk, to the guestrooms. His heart pounded. He was in his own home, yet he felt like an intruder.

First, he checked the guest bathroom. Searching for hair samples. Unfortunately, Grace was a neat freak: he didn't find a single strand of hair in the sink, bath, or floor. He didn't see a toothbrush or set of toiletries, either. A pink body sponge hung on a hook in the shower, but it looked unused.

He backed out, into the hallway.

The door to the room in which Grace was staying was, as he expected, locked. He was prepared for that; last night, he had located the master key that fitted all of the interior doors. He slipped it out of his pocket.

But it didn't match the keyhole.

Brows stitched into a frown, he stepped to the other nearby bedroom, tried the key on that door. It slid in smoothly.

He moved back to the door of Grace's room, a sinking feeling coming over him.

Grace had swapped out the lock with a completely different one. One of her own.

30

Fists bunched on his waist, Troy glowered at the bedroom door like a boxer confronting an opponent in the ring.

His first impulse was to kick the door down. This was his house. Grace was only a guest. She had no right to change the lock. But he had every right to gain access to a room in his own residence, no matter what methods he chose to employ.

Crazy bitch, who does she think she is?

But he had never kicked down a door in his life. He wasn't a cop and sure as hell had never performed a breaking-and-entering. They made stomping down doors look easy in the movies, but he was no fool. Trying to knock down that door was probably going to make a helluva mess, leave marks on the door frame, the door, and the knob.

The likelihood of causing visible damage to the door gave him pause. He turned away, lips buttoned.

He was supposed to be gathering evidence in secret. Tearing up the door would make his intentions clear to Grace, and Monica. He might as well have hung a sign above the door that declared: I'M SNOOPING AROUND TO FIND DIRT.

He was more worried about Grace discovering his intent than he was Monica. The old bitch was cold-blooded. If alerted to his plans, she would respond with a scheme of her own, and as she'd already shown a willingness to murder their dog and pin the heinous act on his mother, there was no telling what sort of retribution she would rain down on him and his family.

He spun back to the doorway. *Think, man.*

The only other way into the room was via the exterior window. As the bedroom was on the second floor, accessing the window would require using a ladder. He had an extension ladder in the garage that he could have climbed all the way to the roof, but he was certain that the window was latched from the inside. It presented a similar conundrum.

He shifted his gaze to the lockset. It was brass-colored and shiny. Either Grace had visited a hardware store recently, or she had brought this in her luggage, in preparation.

He believed the latter. What else did she have in there?

In one of his old apartments from his bachelor days, it had been possible to bypass the lock with a thin, laminated card inserted between the door and the jamb. He opened his wallet, located a Costco card. He slid it into the narrow gap between the edge of the door and the door jamb, pushed the door knob, bent the card back and forth, trying to shimmy it against the bolt.

No luck. He cursed under his breath.

He unclipped his iPhone from his belt and did a quick Google search on using a card to bypass a door lock. As often happened when executing an Internet search, he happened across a series of pages on a related topic: picking a lock with a homemade lock pick set.

The process required an unfolded paper clip to shift the tumblers, and another tool that could serve as the tension wrench. It looked doable for a novice like him. But it was going to take time.

He checked his watch. Five past nine. Monica's appointment was at nine o'clock. He was counting on it taking a maximum of ninety minutes for them to return to the house, but that was purely a guess on his part.

He needed to move quickly.

He had started along the catwalk, going back to the staircase, when he heard a vehicle pull into the driveway. It sounded like Monica's X5.

Shit. Have they come back already?

He scrambled down the steps, dashed to the basement door,

and was halfway downstairs when the alarm beeped, a friendly notification that one of the sensor-monitored doors had been opened. He paused on the staircase, listened.

A single set of footsteps clicked across the entry hall.

Grace, he thought. *She dropped off Monica at the doctor's office but has come back. Dammit.*

The rapid pace of her footsteps led him to think she was in a hurry, intent on some pressing purpose of her own. But she didn't call out for him. It sounded as if she were going upstairs.

Grab whatever you returned for and get the hell out, he thought.

He waited on the basement staircase, heart rattling.

About three minutes later, he heard footsteps in the main corridor again. He climbed to the top of the stairs, cracked open the basement door, and poked his head out like a turtle peeking from its shell. He got a glimpse of Grace hurrying to the front door, her purse swinging from her shoulder.

Where is she hurrying off to? His distrust of the woman ran so deep that he suspected that all of her actions were bent toward making their lives a living hell. If he'd had the foresight, he would have followed her.

Grace exited the house. Their SUV grumbled out of the driveway.

Troy exhaled. He came out of the basement.

The telephone rang.

Is the entire world conspiring to distract me? He ground his teeth, but went to the handset standing on the kitchen counter.

Caller ID provided a local number that he didn't recognize, and didn't include a name. He thought it might be someone calling from the doctor's office or on behalf of one of his children, though it just as easily could have been one of the charitable foundations that phoned relentlessly when the holiday season neared. Regardless, he picked up.

A phlegmy cough answered Troy's greeting. Then: "This is Reverend McBride. May I speak to Dr. Monica?"

"She's out." Troy pursed his lips, thinking. "This is her

husband, Troy. Didn't we meet at Lily's memorial service this past weekend? I don't forget a name."

Another cough. "Indeed we did. Young man, it's vital that I speak to your wife, in private. Can you please pass along my message?"

"Sure." Troy had grabbed a pen and a Post-It notepad. "What's this all about?"

McBride responded only by giving the phone number at which he could be reached.

"She can contact me at any hour," McBride said.

"You really aren't going to loop me in here?" Troy asked. "I told you, I'm her husband. If what you have to tell her is important, I have a right to know."

"*Watch and pray that you may not enter into temptation. The spirit indeed is willing, but the flesh is weak.*'"

"Excuse me?" Troy said.

"Beware, young brother," McBride said. "God bless."

The reverend disconnected the call. Troy stared at the handset for a few heartbeats, struggling to comprehend what he'd heard.

Beware, young brother.

He had no idea what the old man was talking about.

Slowly, Troy hung up the phone, tucked the note into his pocket. The kitchen clock read a quarter past nine. His window of opportunity was gradually sliding shut.

31

Their family physician was Dr. Lamar Young. He and Troy had gone to medical school together at Meharry in Nashville. Monica liked him, professionally and personally. His children, two girls aged eight and ten, also were patients of hers.

Shortly after the nurse took her weight and her blood pressure—both of which were in the healthy range—Dr. Young entered the examination room.

"What's up, doc?" he said and grinned. He was a short, balding, dark-skinned man with the compact build of a high school wrestler. He wore a blue dress shirt set off with a red bow tie, gray slacks, and black leather loafers. Like most modern physicians, he had ditched the clipboard and pen in favor of an iPad and stylus.

Sitting on the examination table, Monica offered a brief smile. Usually when she came in for check-ups, she and Dr. Young spent a few minutes catching up on their personal lives, but she didn't have the energy to pretend that this was a routine wellness visit.

"Not feeling too hot these days," she said. "I've recently picked up what seems like chronic fatigue. I'm also battling a case of severe arthritis, throughout all of my joints. The best way I can describe it is . . . I feel *old*."

Dr. Young blinked, his jovial demeanor vanishing. He pushed up his wire-rim glasses, his copper-brown eyes intense.

"When did all of these symptoms begin?" he asked.

"Well, we had a death in the family recently—"

"I'm sorry, my condolences—"

"—so I've been feeling exhausted in general for the past week," she said. "But the joint stiffness, the inflammation, that's a new development. When I got up this morning, my knees ached so badly I could barely go down the stairs."

"Have you had any unusual level of physical activity lately?" Dr. Young checked his iPad. "You run regularly, correct?"

"I haven't been able to do any exercise. I've done nothing that would trigger this degree of inflammation. All I really do these days is sleep, to be frank."

"How is the quality of your sleep?" he asked.

"It's perfect. So deep, it's as though if I'm drugged—and no, I'm not taking any medication for that, over-the-counter or otherwise. I've been taking naproxen for the inflammation, but nothing else. "

"Does it help?" He tapped on his tablet, glanced at her.

"It's temporarily effective at reducing maybe half of the pain."

"So that's a no." He set aside his tablet on the table. "All right, let's have a closer look at you."

He asked her to remove her athletic shoes and socks. Kneeling, he examined her feet, gently clasped them in his cool hands.

"You've got a lot of swelling here," he said.

"It hurts to walk. I was going to try soaking them this afternoon."

Rising, he asked her to extend her arms. He examined her wrists

"Swelling here, too." He picked up his tablet. "How's your diet? Specifically sodium levels?"

"Lots of fruits and vegetables, lean protein, some grains. I usually steer clear of adding lots of salt to my food. My mother has been doing most of the cooking lately, though."

"Ah, Troy's mom? Give her my regards, please."

"No, my mother. My birth mother . . . she recently came into our lives. Long story."

"Is that so?" Dr. Young's eyes gleamed with curiosity. "Well, I'd count that as a blessing."

"We do." *At least some of us,* Monica thought.

"I'm going to order some blood work," Dr. Young said. He tapped on the iPad. "In the interim, I'm also going to give you a script for a stronger anti-inflammatory, celecoxib. Brand name, Celebrex."

"I'm familiar with it. I'll give it a try."

"In regard to your chronic fatigue—I suspect that may be due to the recent death in your family. Grief can be extremely draining, emotionally, physically. I could give you an antidepressant that may help."

"Sure." She dragged her fingers through her hair, noticed that her scalp felt too dry. A strand of hair came away in her fingers, too. She tried to refocus on her doctor, but the worsening condition of her hair continued to bug her.

"I've noticed some gray hairs," she blurted out. "It probably has nothing to do with anything."

"You're almost forty, correct?" Dr. Young pointed to his almost bald head. "I'm forty-two, Monica, and look at me. It's simply what happens as we age."

"Of course. I don't know why I mentioned it."

His eyes were kind. "I'll get those scripts for you and write up the blood work order. It typically takes a few days for results to come in. If I notice anything unusual, I'll call you."

32

Pat was at her townhouse in Roswell preparing to leave for her volunteer job at the Atlanta Humane Society when someone rang the doorbell.

She worked at the shelter three days a week, and sometimes on weekends, too, if they needed her. Two of her life's passions had long been education, and animals. She'd exercised her passion for education over a long career in Chicago's public school system; she'd spent her retirement years in the service of the dogs, cats, and other creatures that landed at the shelter.

When the doorbell chimed, she was in her bedroom doing her hair. Her watch read nine thirty. She wasn't expecting a visitor. Possibly it was a delivery. Sometimes the couriers rang the doorbell when completing a drop-off.

She set down the hair brush on the oak dresser, and stepped to the large window on the other side of the room. The window overlooked the front yard and narrow driveway. A white BMW X5 was parked in front of her one-car garage.

Monica's here? Odd that she would stop by without calling in advance. I wonder if something is wrong.

The doorbell rang again. Pat hurried downstairs.

She lived alone in the two-bedroom townhouse. Well, not entirely alone. She had a five-year-old tabby, named Pepper. She'd gotten Pepper from the shelter when he was just a kitten, and he had become the consummate house cat: he spent the majority of his time hidden in his favorite places, making appearances only to cuddle, eat, or use his litter box. He showed no interest whatsoever in her visitors. She was on her own when she opened the front door.

Grace stood on the doorstep, alone.

Pat did a double-take. Grace was the last person she had been expecting to visit—heck, probably the last person she would have wanted to see again, too. She talked to her son daily, via text if not verbally on the phone, and he'd told her that morning that Grace was still there at their house and would be through the end of the week, unless he convinced Monica to cut short her stay, a development that Pat considered unlikely. Monica's desire to forge a connection with her biological mother had blinded her to the woman's true nature.

"Hello," Pat said, cautiously. She glanced over Grace's shoulder, and did not see Monica waiting in the SUV. Had Grace visited on her own?

"Good morning, Pat. I hope you are well. You look good."

Although Pat hated to admit it, Grace looked *fantastic*. She wore a stylish, wide-brimmed, black felt halt and matching coat, with a decorative silk scarf. Her skin glowed, and she seemed to have applied barely any makeup at all. She could have easily passed for a woman in her forties, if not younger.

She looks even better than the last time I saw her, Pat thought.

Grace carried a gift-wrapped box, a red bow sitting on top. The box was large enough to contain a couple of hardback books. Pat wondered about the contents.

"May I come in, please?" Grace asked.

Pat glanced away from the package. She nodded, stepped aside.

Grace strutted inside in a cloud of rosemary-scented perfume, boot heels clicking on the hardwoods. She walked with the swagger of a woman who expected every eye in the room to focus on her. Although Pat doubted this woman's integrity, she respected her confidence.

Grace strolled into the family room off the entry hall. She swept her gaze around the space, nodding.

"You have a lovely home, dear," Grace said. "Do you live alone?"

"I have a cat. He's roaming around here somewhere."

"No male companion?" Grace winked.

"Living with me? No."

"Ah, I see," Grace said.

Pat felt her stomach muscles tighten. Grace's tone suggested that she was thinking: *that's exactly what I expected of you. You're just an old maid living alone with a cat. How pathetic.*

"But I have . . . friends," Pat said, and forced a laugh.

That was mostly a lie, however. She had a handful of gentleman friends with whom she enjoyed certain platonic activities—going out to a movie, having dinner, attending a play, for example—but none with whom she was intimate and would invite to stay overnight. After her husband's death ten years ago, dating had become difficult. Most of the men she encountered in her age group wanted a woman to serve as the equivalent as a live-in nurse, or they were seeking financial support to bolster their inadequately planned retirements. Pat had no intentions of taking care of anyone, physically, financially, or otherwise. She'd already raised her children.

She didn't know why Grace believed her romantic life was any of her business, or, more concerning, why *she* wanted to impress Grace in the first place. Maybe she envied Grace; she doubted Grace experienced the same challenges with men. With Grace's youthful looks and panache, Pat was certain she could have enticed men half her age.

"Every woman needs a friend . . . or three." Grace laughed lightly.

"That's right," Pat said.

"This is for you." Grace placed the gift on the coffee table. She eased onto the sofa and crossed her legs. "I realize that we had a rocky start to our friendship. Consider this a peace offering, my dear."

"That's sweet of you," Pat said. "Thank you."

"Please, open it."

Pat stripped away the wrapping paper to expose a plain cardboard box. Opening the box revealed three small, black glass jars with lids. A handwritten label, each in elegant script, was affixed to each jar: one read *Facial Rejuvenator* in elegant script; the other read *Body Butter*; the last, *Lovely Hands*. All of them had "*by Grace*" underneath the description, as if they were products in her personal cosmetics line.

Pat twisted off the lid of the facial rejuvenator. The jar contained a creamy substance the color of cappuccino; it smelled of peppermint, lavender, and traces of other fragrances she couldn't identify, but the overall aroma was appealing.

"Facial cream?" Pat asked.

"Indeed. I blend it myself, and use it myself, on a daily basis, and have done so for many years." Grace smiled. "Tell the truth, dear. Do I look like a woman nearing sixty to you?"

"Absolutely not." Pat laughed. "I was wondering what your secrets were."

"I drink plenty of filtered water and enjoy a *very* energetic sex life, but the factors I value most highly are the creams that I'm now sharing with you."

Pat dipped her index finger into the jar, dabbed the substance on her cheek. It was cool, smooth, and tingled deliciously on her skin.

"This feels wonderful," Pat said.

Grace nodded. "A tiny amount of these creams, applied twice a day, morning and evening, will do the trick. The hand lotion you can apply whenever you like. Carry it in your purse, perhaps. All of them are quite potent."

"What's in them?" Pat unscrewed the lid on the jar of Body Butter. It was the same color as the facial cream, with a similar texture and fragrance. "I smell peppermint and a bit of lavender, but I'm not sure about the other ingredients."

"My formulations are a trade secret, my dear." Grace rose from the sofa. "I must be going. My daughter is visiting her physician and I'll need to pick her up."

Pat stopped in her tracks. "Wait, Monica's at the doctor? What happened?"

"I think she's suffering the symptoms of a broken heart." Grace shook her head. "Poor girl. I've been trying my best to boost her spirits, but these things take time."

"Having you here seems to be helping her," Pat said, and meant it.

"I could never replace dear Lily. No one could. That remarkable woman was a force of nature."

"Thank you again for the gift, Grace. I'm going to use this, I promise you."

"I do hope so." Grace's eyes twinkled. "It would make me so very happy, my dear."

33

It took Troy almost an hour of fumbling about, repeatedly dropping tools and cursing in frustration, but he finally picked the lock.

He swiped perspiration away from his forehead with the back of his hand, and read his watch. A few minutes past ten o'clock. Monica and Grace could return home at any minute.

He pushed open the bedroom door.

The first thing that struck him was the odor, the same smell he'd encountered the last time he had opened the guest room door. The air was heavy with the fragrance of rosemary. While not unpleasant, it was overpowering. He didn't know how anyone could have slept in there without developing a massive headache.

The blinds were closed, and the curtains were drawn, too, immersing the room in dense shadow. He flicked the switch for the overhead light.

The queen-size bed was neatly made: the comforter arranged perfectly, decorative pillows artfully aligned. In fact, it didn't look as if Grace had ever lain on the bed at all.

He stepped deeper into the bedroom.

On his right, a mahogany, six-drawer dresser topped with a half-moon mirror stood against the wall. The surface held only a few items: a makeup kit, a hair brush, a vial of nail polish, a leather toiletries case, and a wooden bowl of potpourri, from which that strong rosemary aroma emanated. What kind of person traveled with a potpourri kit?

All of the objects were precisely arranged, as if laid on a grid.

Grace had a strong streak of OCD, he suspected. She would notice if anything in the room had been displaced.

He carefully lifted the hair brush. Using a set of tweezers he had purchased expressly for this task, he extracted several crisp hairs from between the brush bristles. He dropped them into his plastic sample bag, sealed it shut, and tucked it into his back pocket. Then he returned the hair brush to the dresser, in the exact spot from which he had lifted it.

He exhaled. He had his DNA sample. Next, he needed leads for Nick Sullivan to research.

He began to pull open the dresser drawers. All six were empty. She was keeping her clothes and other possessions elsewhere, probably in her suitcase.

Where had she stored her luggage?

He stepped around the bed. He didn't see her suitcase. He got on his knees and looked underneath the bed. Found nothing.

That left the closet.

He moved to the closet door; a full-length mirror hung on it, reflecting his anxious face. It was a simple door with a knob. He noted with relief that Grace had not installed a new lockset.

He pulled the door open.

The closet rod was packed with clothes. She had outfits in every color of the rainbow. On the hook on their interior of the door hung a set of black lace lingerie that would have shamed his mother.

He knelt to the carpet. There on the floor, pushed to the rear wall of the closet, behind a row of shoes, stood the suitcase.

He parted the shoe collection and dragged out the luggage.

A miniature padlock dangled from the handle, but it was disengaged. He laid the bag flat on the carpet. Hands trembling, he unzipped it.

The main compartment held a bundle of dry, spicy-smelling herbs, and a box of rolling papers. Ingredients for those strange cigarettes Grace liked to smoke.

He muttered under his breath. So was this it? Was there nothing else?

He ran his fingers across the suitcase's interior panels. He felt a bulge in one of the pockets, which was secured with a brass button.

What's this?

He unsnapped the button.

Two black, slender, leather-bound books lay nestled inside, bound together by a thick rubber band. He extracted them.

The leather casing of each volume was weathered by the passage of time. His late maternal grandmother had used to keep a leather-bound address book in which she recorded the names and addresses of every relative and family friend imaginable, going back for decades. Both of them brought to mind his grandma's old address log.

He laid both volumes flat inside the suitcase, and opened them. One of them appeared to be a recipe book, full of handwritten instructions for preparing cakes, pies, teas, candies, and other foods. Grace had elegant handwriting that reminded Troy, uncomfortably, of Monica's own penmanship.

For the sake of thoroughness, Troy used his phone to snap photographs of several pages. He doubted he would bother sending Sullivan something as innocuous as recipes, but knew that when building a case, even trivial details could later prove significant.

The second volume was an address book, with tabs for each letter of the alphabet, and ring-binding. It was secured with a tiny gold clasp. He snapped open the clasp and opened the book. The thin, crisp pages were yellowed with age.

He opened it at random, and wound up at letter "E."

There was one entry on the page, written in black ink in Grace's careful script:

Viola Easley – June 14, 1947
1752 Arthur Lane
Los Angeles, CA 90287
September 5, 1987 – September 16, 1987

Troy frowned at the record. He didn't understand the purpose of the dates. He could guess that the first date, in June, might have been a date of birth, but he didn't know what the dates in September signified.

Nevertheless, it might prove useful to research. He snapped a pic of the page.

He flipped to another page, under the "J" tab. There were three entries.

Mary Jackson (Williams) – December 5, 1924
22543 Cumberland Avenue
Boston, MA 54319
April 20, 1963 – May 1, 1963

Charlene Johnson (Trice) – August 27, 1968
909 Williams St, Apt 3
Milwaukee, WI 45102
October 5, 2007 – October 18, 2007

Christina Devereaux – September 17, 1978
8879 Rice Ferry Road
New Orleans, LA 24501

Troy wondered why the third record didn't have a set of dates underneath the address. Regardless, he took a photo.

He read his watch. It was twenty-five minutes after ten. His gut was tight with tension. At any second, he expected to hear Monica's SUV pulling into the driveway.

He paged to the "W" tab.

"Damn," he said.

Monica Worthy (Stephens) – February 7, 1975
368 Pine Glen Court
Dunwoody, GA 30338
November 1, 2014 –

Fresh sweat had formed on his brow. February 7, 1975 was Monica's date of birth, and the address listed was where they lived. Grace had come into their lives on November 1, at Lily's funeral.

But there was no end date—yet. He gnawed his bottom lip. What did that mean?

He quickly turned to other pages, taking photos of each. Some of the birth dates went as far back as 1883. Others were as recent as 1998. Locations spanned the United States; one was in Griffin, Georgia, a town south of Atlanta.

Every entry he found was a female name.

None of the records with more recent birth dates had a final date line assigned to them, which he had assumed meant that Grace had not yet encountered them. But that seemed like a flawed assumption, because the entry of the woman born in 1883 had "visit" dates over a twelve-day period in July 1921.

Obviously, Grace had not been meeting anyone in 1921. That was over ninety years ago. Grace was only fifty-nine-years-old, a fact the detective had already confirmed.

He pursed his lips. He was missing something.

A vehicle approached the house.

They're back. I've got to get the hell out of here.

Quickly, he gathered the leather-bound volumes, banded them together, stuffed them inside the interior suitcase pocket. He shoved the suitcase back into the closet. He arranged the shoes in front of it as best he could, but he worried that he was fudging the arrangement.

He closed the bedroom door—remembering to first engage the lock—just as he heard Grace and Monica enter the house via the garage access door. He rushed to the catwalk. He leaned against the railing and peered down at the two women as they emerged into view.

"Hey," he said to Monica, in his best nonchalant tone. "What did your doctor say?"

She answered, but he barely heard her response. As he dug his hands into his pockets, purely out of habit, he realized he had left behind his lock-picking set in Grace's bedroom.

34

"I had blood work done," Monica said to Troy. Moving slowly, she sat on a sofa in the family room. Troy had come downstairs but he remained standing, rocking from one foot to the other, like a child who badly needed to urinate. He kept glancing upstairs, where her mother had gone to her room shortly after they arrived home.

"What's wrong?" Monica asked. "You're fidgeting."

"I'm cool." With what appeared to demand a strenuous effort, he sat in the chair across from her. "Any ideas of what he hopes to find?"

"He wasn't sure. Since my symptoms began so recently it's tough to make a diagnosis. It could be rheumatoid arthritis, or something else."

"What do you think it is?"

"I know what it's not. It's not all related to my going through a grieving process. Perhaps my fatigue is tied to my emotional state, but not my other physical symptoms, it's something more than that."

"Lamar's a good doctor," Troy said absently. "He'll get to the root cause. Give him time."

"What have you been doing today? You seem distracted."

"Just puttering around the house, organizing my office, that sort of thing," he said.

He was lying to her again. It was obvious, like a replay of their discussion last night. Considering how his gaze kept shifting to the upper floor, she was of half a mind to believe he had stashed a mistress in a closet upstairs. But she didn't have the energy to press him on it.

She didn't have the energy for much of anything, actually, a trend that worsened each day. Several of her colleagues and friends had called and texted her over the past couple of days, offering condolences about Lily's passing, and some had wanted to come over and visit, to check in on her, and Monica had barely responded to any of them. She appreciated their concern, but she just didn't have the energy to be social.

"I'm going to lie down," she said.

"Have brunch before you take your nap, dear," Grace said, coming downstairs. "You don't want to nap on an empty stomach. I'll whip together some homemade waffles topped with my famous berry compote, along with my equally famous buttermilk fried chicken."

"Chicken and waffles, that sounds delicious," Monica said. "Troy, want to have brunch with us?"

Since Grace had re-appeared, the stress lines had faded from Troy's face. But he shook his head at her invitation to dine with them.

"I have an errand to run," he said. "I'll be out for a while. I'll pick up the kids from school on my way home."

35

Nick Sullivan ran his private investigations firm out of an office suite in the Toco Hills Shopping Center, in North Druid Hills. Troy was familiar with the area. Emory University, where he had completed his residency, was fewer than fifteen minutes away. He found the retail center with little trouble.

During the drive, he spun through different scenarios of exactly where in Grace's bedroom he had left behind his lock-pick set. He believed she hadn't yet found the tools. She was too cheerful when he'd left the house. Probably he had forgotten them in the closet, in an area on the floor that would have been tougher for her to spot.

Retrieving the tools seemed an impossibly difficult objective, though; unless she left the door unlocked, he would have to pick the lock *again*. He didn't know when he would get the opportunity, or if it was worth pursuing. If Grace found the set, would she actually understand its purpose and suspect him of snooping around?

On the Move Investigations was sandwiched between a tanning salon and a dentist's office. A Mexican restaurant was nearby, spicing the cool November air with the aroma of grilled meat, onions, and peppers. It was almost noon, and Troy realized he hadn't eaten anything all day. He had been so intent on his plans that the thought of food was a distraction.

He stepped inside the office suite.

"Hello there!" a woman said. She sat behind a glass desk in a small reception area. She was blonde, probably in her mid-forties, with a deep-baked bronze complexion undoubtedly maintained with regular visits to the tanning salon next door. She wore a tight, candy-red scoop neck sweater that displayed cleavage rivaling Pamela Anderson's. Troy wasn't a boob man, but the sheer girth of her breasts was mesmerizing.

Those have to be implants, he thought. He had to force himself to look away and concentrate on her blue-eyed gaze. Her eyes were such a dazzling shade of aquamarine he surmised she was wearing colored contact lenses, too.

"I'm Mandy." She adjusted the headset she was wearing. "You must be Doctor Stephens? I'll tell Nick that you're here."

"All right."

Mandy rose from behind the desk and strutted to a door behind her. She wore blue jeans fitted so tight they might have been shrink-wrapped to her body. She had an unnaturally narrow waist, and he guessed she must have gotten a liposuction procedure in her midsection.

Mandy re-appeared and conducted him back to Sullivan's office.

If Mandy seemed to be preparing for the role of a middle-aged Barbie, then Sullivan could have been the Ken doll. He rose from behind his oak desk as Troy entered, and Troy did a double-take at his appearance. Sullivan was about six-two, Troy's height, with broad shoulders. He was clean-shaven and square-jawed, with golden-brown hair, and a dipped-in-bronze complexion. He wore a white button down shirt and gray slacks.

In their initial phone call, Sullivan had shared that he'd worked as an Atlanta cop for a decade. Troy had expected a man who looked as if he'd lived a rough-and-tumble existence, not a guy who probably got weekly manicures.

When they shook hands across the desk, Sullivan's grip was, reassuringly, firm and dry.

"Glad you could make it, Doc," Sullivan said. "Can I get you anything? Water, coffee? Something stronger, maybe?"

"I'm good, thanks." Troy noted the walnut veneer bar cabinet in the corner, a row of glass tumblers lined along the surface, as if in preparation for a drinking game. Troy took a closer look at Sullivan and spotted the cracks beneath the man's glossy exterior: a slight redness to his skin, touches of yellow in his eyes. He glimpsed a breath mint sliding around on Sullivan's tongue and caught a bracing whiff of peppermint. How many drinks had the man already consumed that day?

Troy eased into a leather chair with a split cushion and frayed arm rests. Including the bar cabinet, the room held a printer, a five-gallon aquarium with one sad gold fish and water that needed to be filtered, and a live cactus plant. Photos of Sullivan at various stages of his career hung on the walls: dressed in Marine blues, a shot of his graduation from the police academy. His framed pi license hung behind his desk, on which stood a battered Sony laptop.

Sullivan tented his slender fingers. He flashed a smile, showing off capped teeth.

"You got the goods, Doc?" he asked.

Troy placed two plastic bags on the desk, each containing hair samples from Grace, and Monica, respectively. Both bags were clearly marked with the woman's name, as Sullivan had instructed.

"I'll get these delivered to the lab, via courier." Sullivan ripped a sheet of paper from a notepad and used a paperclip to package the samples and his note. Then he punched a button on his phone. "Mandy, I need you to run to the lab, pronto."

"Courier, huh?" Troy said.

Sullivan winked. "The DNA lab's on the other side of the shopping center, actually. Great thing about working near Emory and the CDC. Every medical professional you could ever need is over here."

Mandy re-entered and swiped the bags off the desk. "Be back in fifteen."

"Thanks, hon." Sullivan watched her sashay out of the office, a wistful smile on his face. "Isn't she something? Sixteen years of marriage and three kids, but I never get tired of looking at her."

"What do you think of the photos I sent you?" Troy asked.

Sullivan straightened in his seat, all business again. "I haven't yet run down all of the names. But I noted that one of them was local, down in Griffin."

"I saw that. Chrisette, was it?"

"I'm thinking of taking a field trip to get a look-see." Sullivan drummed his fingers on the desktop. "If you want me to, that is. There is a charge for travel and on-site investigation."

"Why not?" Troy shrugged. "Maybe we'll learn something useful. At this point, I'm thoroughly perplexed."

"Did you find anything else that you didn't send over to me?"

"An old book full of recipes. I didn't think it was worth a follow up, but I did take a few photos."

"Due diligence, Doc, due diligence." Sullivan clucked his tongue. "Send those to me, please."

Troy accessed the recipe book pics on his phone and emailed them to Sullivan.

"Nana's lemon pound cake," Sullivan said, examining the new photos on his laptop. He peered at Troy. "Curious. Can she cook for shit?"

"She's a fabulous cook. That's about the only compliment I can give her."

"I'm going to shoot these over to my baby sister and get her take," Sullivan said. "She's a chef, the real deal, trained at Johnson & Wales, worked at restaurants in Paris and New York. For a minute it looked like she was gonna get her own show on The Food Network, but the deal fell through."

"That's everything I've got," Troy said. "So we have hair samples from Monica and Grace, a collection of women's names from an address book with indecipherable dates, and recipes for Nana's lemon pound cake, among other treats."

"And I'm going to check out Chrisette Thomas, in Griffin," Sullivan said. "We'll get DNA results back by tomorrow."

"Is there anything else I can do while I'm waiting?" Troy asked.

"Actually, yeah." Sullivan snapped his fingers. "Just remembered. You said something when we talked before, about how this woman and your wife will hole up in the bedroom with the door locked?"

"Every night." Troy wasn't going to share how Grace had squeezed his wrists and brought him to his knees. It was too embarrassing to admit to another man that such a thing had happened.

"What are they doing in there?" Sullivan asked.

"No clue. Talking, I guess. But it's damned strange."

"It's your house, Doc. I'd say you have a right to know, agreed?"

And then Sullivan reached into a desk drawer and brought out an item that, once he explained its function, brought a smile to Troy's face.

"Oh, you're good," Troy said.

36

For the second consecutive evening, Troy refused to have dinner with the family. At that point, Monica wasn't surprised. He disliked her mother and wanted her gone—fine. She would have appreciated at least a token attempt for him to put on appearances, for the sake of the children, but that was Troy for you. Selfish to a fault.

Grace had prepared another fabulous meal: lamb chops with mint jelly, au gratin potatoes, creamed spinach, freshly baked rolls. Chicken fingers and home fries for the kids. Monica considered herself a capable home cook, but Grace put her culinary skills to shame.

She made it all look so easy, that was the amazing part. Monica watched her mother as she glided about the kitchen, securing plates and flatware to set the table. In her forest-green kimono and slippers, she moved as gracefully as a Tai Chi master.

A casual observer comparing the two of us would assume I was the older woman, Monica thought. Her mother, bless her, had picked up Monica's prescription for the anti-inflammatory, Celebrex, and Monica had doubled her dosage. The drug eased the discomfort, but it left her with that disconnected, medicine-head feeling that she despised.

As everyone got settled at the table in the kitchen, Lexi rose from her chair.

"Can I eat in the TV room?" Lexi asked.

"We're eating dinner here," Monica said. "All of us are."

Lexi stared at her, her brown eyes so perceptive for a seven-year-old that Monica feared what she was thinking.

"But Daddy isn't eating here." Lexi pointed toward the basement door. "He's eating downstairs. Why do I have to eat here? It's not fair."

Monica put her fingers to her temple. *Thank you, Troy, for putting me in this position. You leave the room again and go away to sulk like a spoiled brat, forcing me to deal with the aftermath.*

"Daddy is busy working," Monica said.

"I want to eat in the TV room," Lexi said. "Please?"

"Me, too," Junior said, but her boy glanced at her as if afraid what she might say.

"We're eating together, children," Monica said. "End of discussion."

"I want to eat in the TV room!" Lexi slapped the dinette table as if it had personally offended her. She darted out of the room, beaded braids clicking. Monica sighed, glanced at her mother.

"Blame that husband of yours." Clucking her tongue, Grace set a cup of milk next to Junior. "He set the tone for this unruly behavior. Children learn by observation and example, my dear."

"I'm not in the mood to deal with this." Monica ran her fingers through her hair. "God, I'm so exhausted."

"It's a woman's burden to bear." Grace offered a wry smile. "We carry the weight of the family on our shoulders, while the menfolk play with their toys. They're good only for screwing."

Sighing, Monica snatched Lexi's plate off the table. She took the plate into the family room. Lexi was hiding in the corner behind her dollhouse, clearly expecting an angry reprimand.

Monica put the plate on the coffee table.

"Eat in here, I don't care," she said. "I'm not going to fight with you."

Lexi peeked from behind the dollhouse, lips parted in confusion. Glaring at her, Monica turned to walk out. As she did, she stepped on one of Lexi's stuffed animals, twisted her ankle, and didn't regain her balance in time to prevent a fall. She plunged forward and banged against the carpet, barely avoiding knocking her head against an end table.

The impact snapped through her so painfully that she let out a yelp. Hot tears seared her eyes.

"Mommy!" Lexi ran to her. "Are you okay, Mommy?"

Monica's entire left side pulsed, and her ankle felt full of crushed glass. She tried to draw herself upright, but couldn't manage it. The pain was too intense and left her weakened.

Help, I've fallen and I can't get up! she thought, comically, and had to choke back a burst of wild, fatalistic laughter.

"Mommy's . . . okay," Monica said, breathing hard. "I need a minute to get my bearings."

Grace entered the family room, wiping her hands on a kitchen towel. "I thought I'd heard a cry. Are you all right, dear?"

"I lost my balance. I'll be okay."

Kneeling beside her, Grace grasped her by the arm, and helped her stand. In spite of her slight frame, her mother seemed so strong and sturdy that Monica had the thought that Grace could have picked her up as easily as if she were a baby, and a remark Troy had made last night flashed through her mind: *She's a helluva lot stronger than she looks, unbelievably so.*

Monica moved to the nearest upholstered chair and eased onto it. Her left ankle throbbed. She massaged it carefully.

Grace watched her, brows furrowed with concern.

"I think it's only a sprain," Monica said. "I'll be fine. Please, go ahead with dinner. I don't want the food to get cold."

"Come along, sweetheart." Grace touched Lexi's shoulder. "Pick up your plate. We're going to eat in the kitchen, as family."

"Yes, Nana," Lexi said obediently.

Grace winked at Monica, and ushered Lexi back into the kitchen.

She's been here but a few days, and Lexi listens to her while she disobeys me, Monica thought. She couldn't help feeling a sharp sense of failure. What kind of mother was she? Her daughter fought her at every turn but a relative stranger could guide her to compliance? What was she doing wrong?

Hunched over in the chair, massaging her ankle, Monica felt a small, loose object in her mouth. She brought her hand to her lips, spat it out.

The object came out, mingled with a thick gob of saliva and dark blood.

It looked like a decaying tooth.

37

Dinner for Troy was another cold sandwich from a local sub shop. He didn't care. He refused to take another bite of anything Grace created, no matter how tempting the aromas. Throughout a good portion of his brutally demanding radiology residency, he had subsisted on a diet largely comprised of tuna fish sandwiches, coffee, and apples. He could manage for a few more days until Grace either voluntarily left their home, or he forced her out.

Upon entering his basement office with his sack of food, he found a white, business-size envelope lying on his desk. His name was inscribed on the front with black ink, in elegant script.

His stomach compressed into a tight ball. That was Grace's handwriting.

The envelope was sealed. He tore it open.

It contained two items: his homemade lock-pick set, and a folded slip of paper.

He unfolded the note. A single question was inscribed on it:

Did you find what you were seeking?

Coldness washed over him.

"Shit," he said. "She knows."

Weak-kneed, he dropped onto the desk chair. He placed the food on the desk, pushed it aside. He had lost his appetite.

The truth was, he had screwed up. Leaving behind evidence of his investigation was the worst possible outcome. He might as well have kicked the door off the hinges.

He called Nick Sullivan on his cell phone. He didn't know who else he could talk to about this turn of events.

"Hey, Doc," Sullivan said pleasantly. "I'm still working through what you turned over to me today. Everything all right?"

"She knows I was searching through her things. I was rushing, got careless, and left behind a lock pick in the guest room. She found it."

"That sucks. She threaten you?"

"Not exactly. I don't know what she's going to do, but she'll do *something*."

"Did you tell her what you found? That you're working with me?"

"Hell, no. Of course not."

"Then I'd say we're okay, for now. She's in the dark. I should have some answers by tomorrow, on the DNA if nothing else. And if our little hidden camera does its job—and it will—then you'll have some answers about what the heck she's doing in the bedroom every night with your wife."

Before Troy had left Sullivan's office that afternoon, the detective had given him a spy camera to place in the master bedroom, the device disguised as an ordinary clock-radio that stood quietly on the nightstand. It would record video and audio footage and store the data on a micro SD card that they could later transfer to a computer.

"If you're worried, my advice is to stay alert, and steer clear of her," Sullivan said.

Troy muttered a thank you, and ended the call. He spent the next few hours in the basement, wasting time on the Internet and distracting himself from his anxious thoughts. Around nine o'clock, he finally went upstairs.

The ground floor of the house was silent. All of the dishes were put away in the kitchen, and the television was shut off.

Upstairs, he checked on Lexi and Junior. Both of the children had been put to bed already, and slumbered quietly in their rooms. He ground his teeth. He hated that he had missed their bedtimes, when he would always read each of them a book of their choosing, first Junior, then Lexi, since his daughter was oldest and had developed the attention span to follow longer stories. Grace's arrival had wreaked havoc with their nightly rituals, had interrupted his treasured daily routines of fatherhood.

He approached the door to the master bedroom. It was closed, and, as he expected, locked.

He smiled to himself. Although he had located the master key, he didn't intend to use it since he had the spy camera in place allowing him to secretly record their activities. *I'll find out soon enough what you're doing in there.*

Back downstairs, he returned to the kitchen. He had eaten his sub shop sandwich and a bag of chips, but he was still hungry—famished, actually. He hadn't consumed enough food that day. It was late in the evening, but if he didn't get something else on his stomach he was going to have a tough time sleeping.

A layered chocolate cake stood on the island, prominently displayed underneath a glass dome. A Post-It note had been affixed to the lid, words scrawled in Grace's handwriting.

> *Troy,*
> *Here's the German chocolate cake I promised.*
> *Can we call a truce?*
> *-- Grace*

He chuckled. That woman, nuts as she was, understood full well that the way to a man's heart was through his stomach. German chocolate cake was his favorite dessert, and this one, with three layers, looked fantastic, like a concoction he might have seen in a display case at a bakery.

He couldn't resist.

He cut a generous slice and transferred it a plate. Poured himself a glass of pinot noir and took the dessert and wine into the family room, where, settling into his leather recliner, he switched on the TV to ESPN, intending to catching up on the day's NBA news.

The cake was actually even more delicious than it looked, the chocolate and coconut-pecan flavors perfectly balanced. It *was* better than his mother's, as much as he hated to admit it.

Within three minutes of taking the first bite, he passed out.

38

When Troy awoke sometime later, he was lying on his back on the king-size bed in the master bedroom. He was naked. Flickering candlelight illuminated the room. It was a four-poster bed, and he was bound to each post, at ankles, and wrists, with thick rope.

A towel had been stuffed in his mouth, sealed inside with a strip of duct tape across his lips.

Oh, Jesus, what is this . . .

He struggled against the restraints. The bedframe shook, but he could not get free. He was bound tight.

His chest heaved, air whistling in and out of his nostrils. Where was Monica? He screamed against the tape, shouting for his wife, but it was pointless, his words muffled and incoherent.

How had he wound up here? The last thing he remembered was eating a piece of chocolate cake and watching television. His memory was fractured, as if he'd been drugged.

Perhaps, he realized, the cake had contained more than just butter, sugar, flour, eggs, and chocolate.

Across the room, the bathroom door swung open. Grace strolled out into the candle light. She wore only the black lace lingerie set that he had seen earlier in the guest room closet, and a pair of black stilettos.

What's she planning to do to me?

Again, he struggled futilely against the ropes.

In spite of his terror, he noticed that her body was impossibly youthful: skin smooth and unblemished, breasts round and full.

Not a wrinkle or stretch mark or patch of cellulite to be found.

I've got to be dreaming because this is impossible. She's almost sixty, not thirty.

Grace took a long draw on her cigarette, and then set it upon the ashtray she'd placed atop the dresser.

"It's time for you to fuck me, doctor." She smiled. "You've been a naughty little man, pawing through my possessions, so this is how we've got to do it, my dear. You're going to give me what I need, your precious seed. I suspect you'll greatly enjoy the ride regardless of your incapacitation."

She climbed onto the bed. She knelt in the juncture of his thighs.

Cold sweat oozed from his pores. In other circumstances, this might have been his ultimate fantasy, but everything was wrong about this situation. Horribly, shamefully wrong.

She touched his testicles. Her fingers were ice-cold, and he flinched.

"Touchy, eh?" she asked. "Let's see how you like this, then."

She opened her mouth and stuck out her tongue. Except it was not a tongue of normal proportions. It slithered from the recesses of her throat, extended past her chin, and continued to stretch, like an uncoiling pink snake, several feet long. The tip of the tongue dipped all the way to his penis, and there, it tickled the underside of his testicles, warm and moist.

God in heaven I know this has got to be a nightmare . . . no way in hell any of this is actually happening.

But his body responded, a massive erection building. Although everything in him was screaming against this obscenity, he was powerless to break the growing tides of sensation.

She worked him slowly and expertly with her monstrous tongue. Soon, he was breathing hard, skin flushed.

After she had coaxed him to the precipice of an orgasm, she withdrew. She removed her bra and panties, let both pieces fall to the floor.

Her body, fully revealed, was spectacular. In spite of himself, his erection throbbed harder, in anticipation of the intimacy to come.

"I've built up quite the appetite since my last coupling." She winked, and prepared to mount him. "Abide with me, my dear. It's going to be a long night."

39

Troy opened his eyes to sunlight streaming through the shutters. He was in his bedroom. Monica's side of the mattress was empty.

He nearly leaped out of the bed. He was bare-chested and clad in a pair of cotton lounge pants, his normal bedtime wear. But he had a slight headache pulsing behind his eyes, as if he'd had too much to drink.

What the hell had happened?

There were no candles in the room. No ropes hanging from the bedposts. No gag in his mouth.

He ran his fingers across his wrists. They felt tender, as they might have if they'd been secured with rope.

He hurried toward the bathroom. As he moved, his legs and lower back ached, too.

Like I've been screwing all night, he thought.

In the bathroom's bright fluorescents, he examined his body. Redness encircled both of his wrists, and his ankles, too. There was a scatter of bite marks on his chest, and a quarter-sized welt marked his collarbone region; he hadn't gotten a hickey since he was a sophomore in college.

His penis looked normal, but it was sore to the touch.

Grace rode me like a goddamn cowboy.

Bits and pieces of memory came back to him, and much to his chagrin, it was not entirely unpleasant. He remembered the biting, the licking, the sucking . . . the relentless grinding as she milked seemingly every ounce of bodily fluids from him. He'd experienced multiple, spine-rattling orgasms. Viewed from a purely physical perspective, it was the most amazing sex he'd ever had.

Nevertheless, he felt dirty. It was his wife's *mother*.

He got into the shower enclosure and cranked the water to a temperature so hot he could barely tolerate it. But the searing jet spray burned the fog out of his mind, helped him think more clearly.

He could not stop thinking about that inhumanly long tongue of hers. It made it difficult to accept that any of what he recalled had truly happened. Or if it had, then the experience was filtered through the distorted lens of a potent hallucinogenic drug.

What had she put in that damn chocolate cake?

He could accept the theory that he'd been drugged. Liked the idea, actually. It explained a lot. It explained everything.

His passing out—obviously due to the drug. Grace didn't have the smooth skin and physique of a woman half her age. That had been the drug altering his perception. Neither did she possess a five-foot-long tongue that could twist and turn like a cobra. Drugs, again.

Learning which drugs could have had those effects on him would require research. He hadn't studied pharmacology since medical school.

He switched off the shower, stepped out, grabbed a towel to dry off.

As bizarre and upsetting as last night's incidents had been, it comforted him to realize that science could provide answers. He was a physician; he could figure this out, using the tools of logic and reason.

Speaking of tools, what about his spy cam? The clock-radio should have captured everything.

Towel wrapped around his waist, he rushed out of the bathroom.

Monica was in the bedroom. She stood in front of the dresser mirror, mouth open as she examined her teeth. She was already clothed in jeans and a sweater.

"Hey," she said, in a flat tone. "You slept in, huh?"

He muttered a reply, glanced at the nightstand. The spy camera was gone, replaced by the old clock-radio he used. The digits read 8:35. With only mild alarm, he realized he was running late for work.

"Where's the new clock I bought?" he asked.

She glanced at him in the mirror. "That ugly, cheap thing? I put it in the nightstand drawer. It didn't match the décor in here at all. I couldn't stand to look at it."

He strained to keep his tone level. "When did you do that?"

"Before I came to bed last night. Why?"

"It's my side of the bed, Monica. I wanted it there."

"Then I'll get you another clock-radio set," she said. "Seriously, that thing is hideous, and it doesn't fit your taste at all. You typically have better taste in . . . well, everything."

"Are we going to stand here and argue about what sort of clock I put on *my* nightstand?" he asked.

She turned to face him. He noticed that she had several additional strands of gray hair, more than he recalled seeing yesterday. He also noted crow's feet bracketing her eyes, a detail that he hadn't observed in the past.

Lily's death is taking a toll on her, he thought, and felt a stroke of guilt. Could he have done a better job of providing emotional support? He'd been obsessed with her mother to the point that he'd ignored everything else occurring in his household. Perhaps his focus was misplaced.

"What's the deal with you and this clock?" she asked.

"I only wanted it there, that's all."

"It's not worth arguing about." She shrugged. "Go ahead and keep your ugly clock."

He took the spy cam clock out of the nightstand and plugged it in. He would need to wait for Monica to leave the bedroom to check the feed, but he doubted it had recorded anything worthwhile during the short time it had been active. It had been unplugged long before the events of the prior night.

"I wish you would give my mother a chance," Monica said.

He glanced at her. "Excuse me?"

"I've accepted her, Troy, and so have the children. Everyone except you is on board with viewing her as a valuable member of this family. Last night, Lexi even called her 'nana.'"

"My mom is supposed to be 'nana.' Lexi is confused."

Monica gave him a pointed look.

"Maybe you're the one who's confused," she said. "My mother's role in this house is clear to everyone else."

He could only shake his head. She had no clue what was going on. He wondered if Grace was slipping Monica drugs, too, because she was delusional.

After throwing on a t-shirt and pants, he hurried out of the bedroom. On the other side of the house, he approached Grace's room.

The door was ajar. He was going to knock when Grace called out, "Come in, doctor."

Heart knocking, he pushed the door open. Grace stood in front of the full-length mirror. She wore only a set of black lace panties—the same pair he recognized from last night's erotic episode. She was rubbing her flat stomach with one hand, in slow circles. Her breasts were round and full, nipples like chocolate cherries.

He froze on the threshold, his mouth as dry as chalk.

How can she look like this? I thought what I'd seen last night had been a dream.

"Good morning." Grace winked, as if aware of his thoughts. "Here for another roll in the hay?"

His cheeks burned. He looked over his shoulder to confirm that Monica wasn't nearby. "What the hell did you do to me? You drugged me."

Smiling dreamily, Grace tilted her head sideways. She continued to rub her belly. It reminded Troy, crazily, of a pregnant woman caressing the curves of an unborn child.

"Did you enjoy it?" she asked. "Your little friend was quite responsive to my coaxing."

She wriggled the tip of her tongue at him.

He stammered. "I don't know what you did, but you stay away from me."

"My milk will come in soon; I'm rather unique in that fashion." She slid her hands to her breasts, cupped them, and glanced at him with a sly smile. "I'll need someone to suckle. Interested? I'll ride your dick while you suck the teat."

"What? *No.* I don't want anything to do with you."

She laughed. "Oh, I got what I wanted from you, doctor. And you had a wonderful erotic experience you'll never forget. I'd say we're square. Run along now, dear. I truly don't need you anymore."

She stepped forward and slammed the door in his face.

40

Pat had awakened at her usual time, seven-thirty, and followed her usual weekday routine, with one variation: after a shower, she applied both of the creams that Grace had given her the day prior.

Her skin tingled pleasantly as she rubbed in the treatments. It was her third application. She'd used them twice yesterday; the first time immediately after Grace had visited, and again before going to bed. It was probably too soon to expect any noteworthy effects, but her skin certainly *felt* different. Softer. Smoother. More vibrant. She had used anti-aging products in the past, but these were unlike anything she had tried before, at least in the respect of how they felt while being absorbed into her skin.

Perhaps it was time to reconsider her harsh characterization of Grace. The woman's generosity had surprised and delighted her.

By nine o'clock, Pat was driving her Toyota Camry to the humane society. She'd gotten in late yesterday and wanted to make up for lost time. Although she was only a volunteer and the minimum commitment for volunteers was just five hours per month, Pat's service far exceeded the minimum. She'd become an indispensable member of the staff.

The Atlanta Humane Society campus was located on Howell Mill Road. The parking lot was already getting full, but she found a space in the area of the parking lot reserved for volunteers.

The campus was a light gray building with lots of windows and a huge canvas awning at the front entrance. A poop-bag dispenser and can stood near the front doors, since many dogs tended to eliminate in the area around the entrance, but a volunteer always wound up stepping outside several times a day to attend to any messes.

Inside, the adoption area, where she worked, was already full of activity. She signed in. The adoption supervisor, Fran, looked relieved to see her.

"It's raining cats and dogs in here," Fran said, one of her favorite sayings. Like Pat, Fran was a retiree. She was on the permanent staff.

"Morning," Pat said. She consulted the team work responsibilities log behind the front desk. "Need me here at the front desk, or somewhere else?"

"Can you walk some dogs?" Fran asked. "We're short back there."

"On my way." Pat nodded crisply, unsurprised. An organization that relied so heavily on volunteers could occasionally suffer resource gaps. Although the team work log delineated areas of responsibility, she usually wound up pitching in wherever she was needed.

The campus was home to dozens of dogs awaiting adoption: over sixty dog runs and nearly forty puppy pens. In the course of a day, all of those canines needed play time, and they needed to be walked, one-on-one.

The canine containment area was filled with a cacophony of barking, yelping, and whining. Would-be adopters wandered the wide rows, dogs competing for their attention.

Pat snagged a leash from the staff area, and headed toward a row of dogs that another volunteer informed her needed some TLC. Pat planned to work her way through every animal she could. She started off by approaching a male Labrador, named Dakota. Two years old, Dakota had a lovely chocolate coat and, like every dog there, had been altered.

"Hey, boy," Pat said, approaching his pen. Dakota's tail wagged. "Want to go for a walk?"

Pat halted outside of the dog's pen. She removed her glasses, rubbed her eyes, replaced the lenses, and re-examined the animal inside.

Dakota had two heads.

One of the heads was happy and grinning; the other snarled at her, showing teeth.

Pat put her hand against her lips, stifling a scream. She backed away from the kennel.

When she had first looked at the dog, he had appeared normal. Upon the next glance, he had two heads. Was she losing her mind?

Dakota continued to stare at her. His tail wagged. But that second head looked as if it wanted to rip out her throat. The eyes were ringed with crimson, and the teeth were disproportionately huge and sharp, as if they belonged in the jaws of a great white shark.

Clutching the leash in a tight grip, Pat retreated down the aisle and found another volunteer, a cheerful, fifty-something redhead named Susan.

"Are you familiar with Dakota?" Pat said. "The chocolate lab?"

"Yep, he's a sweetie. Is everything okay?"

"Is there anything . . . unusual about him?"

Susan frowned. "Umm, nope. He's a perfectly healthy, normal looking lab. Super playful, but most of them are at that age. Why?"

I've imagined the deformity that I saw, Pat thought. *If the dog really possessed two heads, Susan would have said so.*

"It's okay," Pat said, though she felt anything but okay. "I need to use the ladies room. I'll be back in a moment."

Pat turned away, and happened to glance at another kenneled dog. It was a black dachshund. But the length of its body was impossible to fathom. The canine was at least six feet long. It looked like an attraction in a carnival freak show.

The dachshund was glaring at her, too, dark eyes seething with menace.

Heart pounding, Pat hurried to the restroom. Along the way,

she saw a calico cat with eight legs. A German Shepard with three tails. A Yorkshire terrier with a pair of large, leathery wings protruding from its back.

By the time she reached the restroom, she was hyperventilating. She locked herself in a toilet stall, flipped down the lid on the commode, sat, and hugged herself.

What's the matter with me? I've never, ever been prone to anything like this--wild, vivid hallucinations.

They looked so real. It was impossible to simply tell herself that she was imagining things and prevent herself from reacting.

But she could not stay there at the shelter. She needed to get home, perhaps go to bed and let this spell pass.

Cold perspiration had beaded on her forehead. She tore a handful of toilet tissue from the nearby dispenser, used it to blot her skin.

The tissue came away soaked with bright red blood.

Pat stared at the blood-soaked paper, disbelieving. She shot to her feet, slammed out of the stall, rushed to the bank of mirrors above the sinks.

Her entire forehead oozed blood, as if the flesh had been ripped away. It streamed down her temples and leaked into her eyes.

This cannot be happening, it cannot be happening, it can't . . .

She twisted on the water. The mere effort caused her fingers to rupture and bleed, as if her skin were as thin and delicate as crepe paper. Blood poured into the sink, mingled with the water jetting from the faucet.

Weak-kneed, she backed out of the restroom. As she shuffled, blood dripped from her hands and face and spattered on the tile floor.

She didn't know whether the blood was genuine, or not. But she was feeling faint.

She nudged open the door with her shoulder, staggered out of the washroom. Blackness engulfed the entire facility, every light extinguished. Beyond the windows, darkness reigned, as if the entire city had plummeted into a blackout in the middle of the night.

It's only mid-morning, good Lord.

In spite of the darkness, she heard movement throughout the shelter, as though every caged animal had been freed. Barking, screeching, snarling, growling.

Something large and furry brushed against her. Pat flinched away. Cold, sharp teeth snapped onto her right hand.

Screaming, Pat ran. She fled the building and raced into the night.

And ran directly into the path of a roaring truck.

41

Monica spent the morning in her home office, performing research on the Internet. Discovering the basis of her escalating health issues had taken on a new level of urgency.

She felt as if she were, quite literally, falling apart.

Last night when she'd fallen at dinner, she had jarred loose a tooth: the mandibular second molar. She visited her dentist twice a year, and her last exam, two months ago, had shown her teeth to be in excellent condition, the bones strong and not bearing a single cavity.

The molar lay on her desk, beside her laptop, atop a patch of plastic wrap. The tooth didn't look healthy; it looked as if it had been extracted from an elderly individual suffering from poor dental health.

An examination of her remaining teeth revealed that many of them were decomposing, too. Her gums ached, and when she'd attempted to brush her teeth that morning, the pain and the quantity of blood leaking from her gums had forced her to put down the brush.

She'd also discovered more gray hair, but that wasn't the worst of it. She had fresh wrinkles on her face and throat, and other parts of her body, more than she'd ever seen.

It was no longer feasible to ascribe her symptoms to stress, grief, or any emotional state. Something else was going on with her, something far more insidious.

She was aging. Rapidly.

At the current accelerated rate, she was frightened to imagine what sort of condition she might be in by the end of the week.

Maybe in a coffin . . .

Although she had visited her primary care physician yesterday, she didn't have time to await blood work results. She needed answers immediately, or at least solid leads. The world of medicine often moved at a glacial pace, unless one was in an emergency room, and she didn't believe she had the luxury of waiting.

A pillow propped against her lumbar region, her fingers plodded across the laptop's keyboard. She wasn't able to type nearly as fast and accurately as she would have liked. Although she had taken Celebrex to combat the joint inflammation that had been plaguing her, she was as clumsy as if she'd been typing while wearing a pair of thick gloves.

It was maddening.

As a licensed pediatrician, she had access to a number of online medical journals and databases. Standard medical practice was to use the differential diagnosis process to rule out the existence of various causes. In theory, by narrowing down possible explanations, you ultimately hit upon the truth. Her PCP had kicked off that process by ordering blood work to check out her hormone levels, antioxidants status, and immune system function.

Instead of methodically weeding out all the possible factors, she was searching directly for a diagnosis that fit.

She found one relatively early in her searching, didn't want to believe it, looked in medical journals, found nothing satisfactory, and circled back to the original diagnosis.

Werner syndrome.

As stated on Wikipedia: *Werner syndrome (WS), also known as "adult progeria",is a rare, autosomal recessive progeroid syndrome (PS), which is characterized by the appearance of premature aging.*

Monica knew about progeria from her background in pediatrics, though she had never personally witnessed a case. Progeria was an extremely rare genetic disorder in which the symptoms of advanced aging manifested in children. Those afflicted lived only into their teens or early twenties.

Werner syndrome, the adult equivalent, was more common, yet still relatively rare, affecting less than one in one hundred thousand.

She read on:

Patients with Werner syndrome will display rapid premature aging beginning in young adulthood, usually in their early twenties. Diagnosis is based on six cardinal symptoms: premature graying of the hair or hair loss, presence of bilateral cataracts, atrophied or tight skin, soft tissue calcification, sharp facial features, and an abnormal, high-pitched voice. Werner syndrome patients are also generally short-statured due to absence of the adolescent growth spurt that usually occurs during puberty. Patients with Werner syndrome also display decreased fertility. The most common symptom of the six is premature graying and loss of hair.

She had to admit that the diagnosis didn't entirely fit. She was thirty-nine and just now experiencing symptoms. She didn't have any fertility issues. But she had many of the cardinal symptoms.

Even if she did have Werner syndrome, the prognosis wasn't encouraging. There was no cure. Most of those afflicted died of an associated disease such as cancer or arteriosclerosis, and treatment focused on managing the impact of those diseases.

She ran her fingers through her hair. It was a reflex action, something she had done unconsciously for years, but that time, several brittle strands of gray hair fell away from her scalp and landed like dead leaves on the desk.

Tears brimmed in her eyes. She put her fist to her mouth and squeezed her eyes shut, willing herself not to cry, but tears streamed down her cheeks.

God, please, what is happening to me?

There was a knock at the office door.

"My dear? May I come in?" It was Grace.

"Give me a minute." Sniffling, Monica snatched a tissue from the box of Kleenex on the corner of her desk. She blotted her eyes. "Okay."

"I brought you tea." Grace entered holding a cup and saucer. She placed them on the desk. "Just what the doctor ordered, child."

"Is it age reversal tea? If not, it isn't going to help me."

Folding her arms across her bosom, Grace leaned against the desk. Her gaze was sharp.

"Your medical research hasn't brought you answers?" Grace asked.

Monica shook her head. "Nothing that will help. Nothing that will reverse the effects of what's happening to me."

"There must be an answer. Don't give up. When there's a will, there's a way."

Monica felt like screaming at her mother. Grace's empty platitudes about willpower weren't going to do a damned thing for her. Meanwhile, Grace looked unreasonably stunning: smooth skinned and vibrant, younger than ever. Monica didn't know how it was possible for a woman her age to look so amazing, but she envied her.

That morning, when Troy had left the house for work, Monica had seen him pass by Grace in the kitchen. His gaze had lingered on her mother, while her mother had smiled, as if she shared some sort of secret with Troy. That look that passed between them had made Monica deeply uncomfortable, and an unspeakable thought had surfaced in her mind.

Could the two of them have . . . no, absolutely not, never.

"This condition I may have," Monica said, indicating the laptop display. "I think it may be Werner syndrome. Do you know anything about this? Ever heard about anything similar in our family tree? Maybe one of my sisters, or their children?"

"I've never heard of such an affliction in our family," Grace said.

"Can we call my sisters?" Monica asked. "I'd been meaning to ask you about that but there's been so much going on. I'd love to talk to them, not only about this illness of mine, but about . . . well, everything. Do you have their phone numbers?"

"I'd have to find them in my phone book. Perhaps later, dear." Grace clucked her tongue. "I'm so concerned about you. I wish I could fix this for you, but I am utterly mystified by your unfortunate condition."

Monica's shoulders slumped. She shifted back to her computer.

"I've got to keep looking," she said.

"I admire your spirit," Grace said. "Have some tea, child. It will help ease your mind."

"If that's the tea you normally give me, I'll pass. It makes me feel fuzzy. I need to stay focused so I can research." Monica rested her fingers on the keyboard and concentrated on the display.

"Then you leave me no alternative but to do this," Grace said.

"Huh?" Puzzled, Monica glanced at her mother.

Grace's tongue shot out of her mouth and stung Monica's face.

42

Troy got the call while at work. Shock hammered him so hard that he registered only fragments of what his mother's colleague told him.

Dr. Stephens, your mother . . . hit by a truck . . . critical condition . . . please come.

With barely any awareness of what he was doing, he was running out of the hospital and scrambling into his car; he roared across the streets, recklessly breaking traffic laws. He tried calling Monica, at home and on her cell, but she didn't answer. He punched the steering wheel. What the hell was she doing?

Somehow, he arrived at Grady Memorial Hospital in downtown Atlanta without incident. He raced inside.

He found a knot of his mother's colleagues from the humane society clustered in the waiting area. He ignored them—he would loop back to them later—and located a physician, a Dr. Khan.

"Patricia Stephens is my mother," Troy said. "What's her condition? I'm an MD."

Dr. Khan nodded crisply. "Critical. She has numerous severe internal injuries. We've stopped the blood loss, but she is unconscious. We're monitoring her very closely."

"All right." Troy felt dizzy, and had to struggle to stay on his feet. "Prognosis?"

"Uncertain," Khan said. "We've given her three pints of blood. She appears to have a strong heart, which is good, it will aid her recovery. We're doing all we can, I promise you."

Troy fired more questions at the physician, but it was for naught. Until his mother's vital signs stabilized no one could predict what would happen, and as expected, he wasn't allowed to see her, eldest child or not, MD or not.

Feeling as if he were dreaming, he shuffled into the waiting area and dropped into a chair. The colleague of his mother who had called him came to him. Her name was Fran. She was a white-haired, bespectacled lady that Troy remembered meeting in the past, at one of the shelter's charity events.

Fran sat next to him. Her eyes were ringed with crimson. She gently patted his arm. "Any news?"

"Critical," he said. He pinched the bridge of his nose. "Listen, what happened?"

"That's what all of us are out here trying to piece together. Pat had literally just arrived at work. I asked her to go and walk some dogs, and next thing we know, she comes out of the ladies' room screaming."

Troy couldn't imagine his mother behaving like that unless something truly terrifying had happened to her.

"Screaming?" he asked. "Any idea why?"

"She seemed terrified," Fran said. "But none of us could see anything wrong. It's like she had seen a ghost, or something worse. She ran out of the building as if the hounds of hell were on her heels. I called out to her, went after her . . . but I was too late."

Troy tented his fingers, lowered his head. Blood pounded in his skull.

"God in heaven, I've never seen anything like that," Fran said. Tears shimmered in her eyes, and she pressed a handkerchief to them, sniffled. "She ran right in front of a truck as if she didn't see it. The sound it made when it struck her, that's going to keep me up nights for a long time."

"It doesn't make any goddamn sense," Troy said. "I'd talked to her last night, she sounded fine."

"I know for a fact that she wasn't in her right mind," Fran said. "She couldn't have been. Pat's always been a cool customer, as dependable as the sunrise. Has she been on anything that would explain this, some kind of treatment?"

Troy ignored the question; a sentence she had just spoken had caught like a burr in his thoughts. Besides, while Fran was a concerned friend and colleague, his mom's medical history was none of her business.

She wasn't in her right mind.

His mother's bizarre and disturbing behavior supported that statement. Screaming at an invisible threat? Running into the street, heedless of the danger?

No.

A sensation like ice-cold water poured along his spine came over him as a terrible realization took hold. He shot to his feet, walking away from the group of his mom's friends, and called his house again. The line rang three times, and was finally answered. By Grace.

At the sound of her voice, his stomach tightened into a knot.

"Ah, so nice to hear from you, doctor," she said. "My daughter is resting. May I take a message, my dear?"

"What did you do to my mother?" he asked in a whisper.

"Pardon?" she said. "Whatsoever are you talking about, darling? Is your mother unwell?"

He could hear the smirk in her tone. The gentle mocking. He ground his teeth.

"Did you drug her?" he asked.

"I have no idea why you are hurling these awful accusations at me, doctor," Grace said, and managed to sound genuinely hurt. "I've been here, all day, with my daughter. What has happened to your dear mother? I'm *deeply* concerned. Pat's such a lovely woman, a wonderful asset to your family. If any harm has come to her, why, I would be so upset."

Troy hung up. He couldn't tolerate her bullshit any longer. He didn't know how Grace had gotten to his mother, and exactly what she had done to her. He wouldn't get those answers until his mom's vital signs stabilized and she regained consciousness.

If she ever did.

43

Monica awoke that afternoon. Bleary-eyed, she read her bedside clock: 2:11. Shadows filled the bedroom, the shuttered windows keeping out the sunshine.

I can't believe I've been lying here, sleeping the day away . . .

Yawning, she sat up. Her shoes were off, but otherwise she was fully dressed. She had no recollection of climbing into bed. Her last waking memory: sitting at her desk in her home office talking to her mother, and then . . .

Something shot out of my mother's mouth and stung my face . . .

The idea chilled her. But it was obviously a recollection of a bad dream. A patch on her forehead was mildly sore, as if she'd been struck by something, or maybe bitten. She touched the affected area and felt a slight lump.

Either she had bumped her head against the bedpost or something had bitten her while she had slept; whatever it had been, her subconscious mind had folded it into the weird dream about Grace.

She noticed a note lying on the nightstand, beside the clock. It was written in her mother's elegant script. She had to switch on the bedside lamp to read it:

> *Running errand to supermarket to replenish provisions;*
> *will pick up children on my return.*
> *Left your lunch wrapped in refrigerator.*
> *Love, Mother*

Monica smiled to herself. Her mother was so thoughtful and kind. While Monica suffered from this debilitating mystery illness, Grace had stepped in, without being asked, and picked up the responsibilities of running the family.

Troy's dislike of her mother bewildered her. Why couldn't he see and accept the truth of the value she added to their lives?

Although she had napped, presumably for many hours, her mind still felt foggy. She attributed it to the steady stream of medications she had been ingesting for the past several days.

Monica slid on her house slippers and shuffled downstairs. She had to move slowly, carefully, lest she send nails of pain blasting through her joints. Every joint creaked and crackled with pain.

At the rate she was going, she would soon need a walking cane, or perhaps a wheelchair.

In the kitchen, she opened the refrigerator and located her lunch sitting on a plate, wrapped in plastic. It was a ham-and-cheddar sandwich on wheat, layered with lettuce and tomato and accompanied by a bunch of green grapes, and a bowl of homemade vegetable soup.

Pangs of hunger twisted her stomach. She hadn't eaten much of anything all day.

After warming the soup in the microwave, she sat on a bar stool at the counter and settled in to enjoy her meal. She felt as if she were a little girl, happily munching away on a delicious lunch that a loving parent had prepared just for her.

She had to exercise caution eating the solid foods, due to the worsening condition of her teeth, but aching gums or not, she luxuriated in the simple pleasure of eating a meal that her own mother had fixed.

Halfway through her lunch, Troy shuffled into the kitchen.

"There you are," he said. His voice was edged with irritation.

She dropped her spoon into the bowl and stared at him. His eyes were rimmed in red, as if he'd been crying. Her stomach clutched.

"Baby, what's wrong?" she asked.

"What's wrong? I've been trying to call you for hours, Monica. Why the hell haven't you answered your phone?"

Monica glanced around the kitchen. She didn't remember where she had left her cell, probably upstairs somewhere. God, she felt completely out of sorts.

"I . . . I was napping."

"All you do these days is nap. You look like shit."

Monica bristled. "Go to hell."

"Whatever." He tossed his keys onto the counter, raked his fingers across his scalp. "Mom's in the hospital. She's had an accident."

"What happened?"

In a clipped tone, Troy gave her the highlights. Pat running into the middle of the street and getting struck by a car. In critical condition. Unconscious, her prognosis uncertain.

Monica couldn't believe such a bizarre, terrible accident had occurred, and Troy had no answers, either.

"I'll come to the hospital with you," she said, "as soon as my mother gets back with the children. All of us will go."

"No." Troy's lips twisted into a snarl. "I don't want Grace anywhere near my mother. All of this is her fault."

Monica had been putting away her food. She stopped and looked at Troy, and could only shake her head.

"Seriously, Troy?" she asked. "Let's add one more accusation to the pile, huh? How exactly is my mother responsible for this? What proof do you have?"

"Look around you, Monica. Hell, look in the mirror." His eyes seethed like hot coals. "You're falling apart. You need to get your ass to the hospital."

"My mother's taking care of me," she said.

"Is she?" He laughed. "Look at how our lives have totally fallen apart in only the past few days, starting when Grace arrived. Everything is her fault. I know that for fact."

"It's a good thing you went into medicine instead of law. Using logic like that, you'd be a horrible attorney."

His gaze was intense. "I'm beginning to suspect that Grace is responsible for Lily's death, too."

Monica was shaking her head.

"Falling down the stairs in her house while she was supposedly alone?" Troy asked. "I don't believe that any more. Not one bit. I believe Grace was there. I believe she pushed Lily down the stairs."

"Stop it." Tears streamed down her cheeks.

"Grace conveniently shows up at Lily's funeral, ready and willing to be a part of your life." He grinned, but it was a savage expression, without joy. "Capturing you while you're at an emotional low. After almost forty years, Mommy has finally come home, and you welcome her with open arms. How utterly predictable, and *perfectly orchestrated.*"

"Shut up!" Monica shouted, and in her sudden anger, knocked a plate off the counter. It shattered against the tiles.

Chest heaving, she glared at Troy, but he ignored the broken dish, and didn't meet her eyes. He appeared to be immersed in thought.

"The question is, why?" he asked, so softly she barely heard him. He ground his teeth. "*Why*, dammit?"

She opened her mouth to yell at him to get out, but he was already turning and walking away, leaving her alone in the kitchen, his accusations echoing through her mind.

44

Troy drove back to the hospital that evening. His baby sister, Nicole, had arrived from New York to be with their mother. He hadn't seen Nicole since that past summer. She worked as a senior analyst at a large firm on Wall Street and toiled long hours, but she dropped everything and flew in that same day when he called her about Mom's accident.

As he was pulling into the hospital's parking garage, his side chick, Liz, called him on his backup cell phone.

"Have you thought about my offer, baby?" she asked, purring like a cat. "I haven't heard from you."

So much had happened lately that Troy could scarcely remember what he and Liz had talked about the last time he'd seen her. But he knew his answer to her question.

"Sorry, Liz, but the answer is, no can do." He expelled a tight breath. "I can't do any of this, not anymore. My family needs me."

"Hmph. Is that your final answer? Better think about it, 'cause I won't make this offer again."

"Good-bye, Liz. You deserve better than me."

He clicked off. On impulse, he flung the cell phone out of the window, heard it shatter somewhere on the concrete. He immediately felt better, as if an anchor had been lifted away from his soul.

He should have ditched the backup phones and his philandering ways a long time ago. Coming face to face with an ongoing nightmare that had flipped his life upside down had given him a new, wiser perspective.

He had to be a better man. For himself. For his family. Life demanded nothing less.

He didn't know whether he would confess his sins to Monica. Right then definitely wasn't the time, as they had bigger threats encroaching on their lives. But if their relationship were to be made whole, ultimately, some day, he would need to come clean.

Inside, Nicole met him in the ICU's waiting room. More than any of his siblings, she had taken after their mother. Looking at Nicole was like viewing a photo of his mom from thirty years ago, and only intensified his anxiety over possibly losing her.

They hugged. "Thanks for coming, sis."

"It's Mom, Troy. You say the word, you know I'm here." Her eyes were bloodshot. A piece of luggage stood next to the chair in which she'd been sitting, the airline tag bristling from the handle. He realized Nicole had come there directly from the airport.

"Have they let you go back to see her?" he asked.

"Only for a few minutes." Sniffling, she blotted her eyes. "She's still unconscious, Troy. It was tough to look at her, the condition she's in . . ." Her words trailed off, and she pulled in a jagged breath. "I'm trying to understand why this happened to Mom and I can't. Hit by a truck? It makes no sense."

"I can't understand it either, sis." *But I've got some ideas on who's responsible,* he thought.

"How're Monica and the kids?"

"They're at home. I decided I won't be bringing the kids here. They don't need to see their nana like this. As for Monica—she's sick."

"What?" Nicole's eyes widened. "Sick? What's wrong?"

"I don't want to get the details right now, but you'll need to stay in a hotel while you're in town." The last thing he needed was Grace interacting with another of his kin. Grace was the equivalent of flesh-eating bacteria in his household, and it would be nothing short of reckless for him to expose anyone else to her needlessly.

"All right," she said. "I'm sure I can find a hotel downtown near the hospital. I'm only here for Mom."

"That would be best." He glanced toward the doorway. "I'm going back there to see her."

"They told me only one visitor at a time. Go ahead, I'll wait here."

At the visitor's check-in desk, the receptionist on duty noted his name, and buzzed him through the ICU doors. Troy hurried along the wide hallway.

He had spent many years of his adult life in hospitals, knew that great, life-saving work was done in these places routinely, but when you were there to visit a loved one, all of those years of experience faded and you were as worried as anyone coming there for the very first time. He found himself assessing the cleanliness of the floors, questioning the condition of the equipment, gazing critically at the nurses' station as he passed by and wondering about the competence of the staff.

The walls of his mother's room were see-through glass to facilitate constant supervision. He looked inside—and had to double-check the room number before he went in.

Oh, God, he thought.

Emotion constricting his throat, he pushed open the door.

Due to the upper body injuries she'd suffered, Mom was in traction. She was swaddled in so many bandages that looked as if she'd been mummified. Various monitoring pieces of equipment had been attached to her, screen displaying numbers that pulsed rhythmically, and an IV drip fed her vital nutrients.

Troy should have known the details of all of the vital signs being tracked, should have recognized the purpose of every instrument in the room—but all his years of training had vacated his brain when he'd crossed the room's threshold. He was a little boy again, terrified of losing his mother, his whole world, forever.

He went to her bedside. Her eyes were shut, much of her face wrapped in gauze.

"I love you, Mama." Tears wove down his cheeks. He leaned over her and kissed her forehead.

When he straightened, he found that Mom's eyes had opened. She blinked slowly, gaze unfocused. She licked her dry lips.

His heart slammed. Quickly, he grabbed the cup of water on the stand—it hadn't been touched—dipped his finger in it, and used it to swab moisture across her cracked lips.

"I'm here for you," he said. "You're in the hospital. You had an accident, Mom. Everything's going to be fine."

Her fuzzy gaze sharpened. Her lips parted, and in a raspy whisper, she asked: "How?"

"A friend says that you ran out of the animal shelter and into the path of a speeding vehicle." His hands tightened into fists. "I don't know how that happened, but I'm convinced that Grace had something to do with it."

"Can't . . . remember . . . what I did . . ." Tears leaked from the corners of her eyes. Gently, he flicked them away with a tissue.

"Does anything at all come to mind about Grace?" He hated to be questioning her about the woman, so soon after she had regained consciousness, when he probably should have summoned the nurse, but his need to know was like an ache in his gut.

"Purse . . ." Mom said. She tried to lift her head off the pillow. "Where . . ."

Troy looked around the room, found his mother's belongings inside the small closet near the bathroom door: her athletic shoes, clothes, and her leather purse.

He brought the purse to the bed. Mom watched him as he came to her. She might have been immobile and weakened, but her eyes were focused, and that gave him hope.

Standing beside her, he unzipped her bag.

"Gave . . . me somethin' . . ." Mom whispered. "A . . . gift . . ."

He emptied the bag onto her bed. A pocketbook, makeup, keys, business cards, and random items all poured out onto the sheet.

"That . . ." Mom said. She tried to use her arm but it was suspended in traction. "Cream . . ."

He found it at the bottom of the pile: A small, black glass jar. On the lid, calligraphic text read: *Lovely Hands, by Grace.*

"Yes." Mom nodded, winced from the movement.

Hands shaking, Troy twisted off the cap. The jar contained a creamy substance that emitted a strong herbal fragrance.

"Peace . . . offering . . . she said," Mom said.

"Peace offering, my ass." Troy ground his teeth. "No, Mom. Jesus, she was trying to kill you. The woman's pure evil. I'll bet you a year's salary that if I submit sample of this shit to a lab, they'll find it's swimming with hallucinogenic compounds."

"What . . . going . . . to do?" Mom blinked, appeared to be drifting off.

"Let's focus on your recovery," he said. "Leave Grace to me. I'm onto her now. I'm figuring out how she works. And I'm going to stop her."

45

As had become the norm lately, Grace prepared dinner that evening. The announced menu: baked salmon with a creamy dill sauce, French-grated carrot salad, roasted asparagus, and for dessert, peach cobbler. Monica had offered to assist in preparations, but as usual, Grace demurred. Monica hung out in the family room with Lexi and Junior, occasionally casting glances at her mother laboring in the kitchen.

Troy's outrageous accusations continued to rebound through her mind, like a perpetually caroming set of pinballs.

Look at how our lives have totally fallen apart in only the past few days, starting when Grace arrived . . .

I'm beginning to suspect that Grace is responsible for Lily's death, too . . . pushed Lily down the stairs . . .

Grace conveniently shows up at Lily's funeral, ready and willing to be a part of your life.

Monica refused to believe any of it. It would have made her mother out to be a monster, when she was in fact the exact opposite: understanding, considerate, loving. A mother any child, adult or otherwise, would have been overjoyed to call her own.

But the charges were so egregious that she couldn't fathom how Troy could entertain such ideas.

It had to be because of what had happened to Pat. That horrible freak accident. He was being overly emotional, desperate for a reason that could explain why something so awful had happened to his mother. Grace was a convenient scapegoat. It was obvious that Troy despised her anyway.

"Dinner is ready." Grace came into the family room. Before beginning meal preparations, she had changed clothes, yet again. She wore a sky-blue, fitted blouse and matching skirt that ended above the knees, and her hair was pulled back into a long braid. She was the most glamorous-looking grandmother that Monica had ever seen, and looked nothing remotely close to her true age.

"Pat is awake." Monica lifted her iPhone. "Troy sent me a text a few minutes ago. She's awake and alert."

"Well, isn't God good?" Grace clasped her hands together. "I pray Pat makes a speedy, full recovery." She paused. "Perhaps this will have taught her a lesson about the dangers of prescription drug abuse."

"What?" Monica dropped her phone in her lap. "Come again?"

"I was reluctant to share this with you and especially Troy—it would have only upset him." Grace pursed her lips, seemed to carefully select her words. "But when Pat stayed over here the other night, she and I shared the guest bath. She happened to leave her purse on the vanity, and it was open. I couldn't help but notice half a dozen bottles of prescription drugs virtually spilling out of her bag."

"What kind of drugs?" Monica asked. "Did you notice the names of any of them?"

Grace waved her hand. "I shouldn't have mentioned this. I apologize. Why don't we go in the kitchen and eat?"

"Please," Monica said. "It could be really important."

"She had sleep aids and anti-depressants. Lunesta and Lexapro are the brand names. I recognized them only because in a family for which I used to work, the wife was abusing those medicines, too."

"Pat doesn't seem like the drug-abusing type," Monica said.

"They never do, my dear." Grace took Junior's hand and led him toward the kitchen. "I wouldn't share this information with your husband, if I were you. He's so enamored of his mother, as any son ought to be. This revelation would crush him."

"He needs to know," Monica said. "If it's true."

"Pardon me?" Grace spun around, eyebrows arched. "If it's true, you say?"

"If it's true that Pat is abusing prescription drugs, yes. She might have those medicines, but that doesn't mean she's abusing them."

"The poor old girl ran into the street directly in front of a moving vehicle, an utterly illogical thing to do. I shared with you that she is ingesting drugs known to cause hallucinatory side effects and erratic behavior."

"Yes, but—"

"Don't be a fool, dear. It doesn't suit you. Now come into the kitchen and eat before dinner gets cold."

Glaring at her, Grace whirled away. Lexi followed Grace and her brother.

Chastened, Monica lowered her head. She glanced at the phone in her lap.

If what her mother said about Pat's drug abuse was true, it was her responsibility to share that information with Troy. It could be critical in understanding what had happened, and preventing any future problems.

But Monica simply didn't believe it. Pat was too well-balanced. Certainly, there was the situation with her supposedly forgetting Duchess outdoors the other night--

(our lives have totally fallen apart in only the past few days, starting when Grace arrived)

--but that seemed like an unrelated incident. There was no correlation between a memory lapse and a complete lapse of sanity.

"My dear?" Grace called from the kitchen. "Do you require assistance standing?"

"I'm okay, coming now." Pulling in a deep breath, Monica rose from the sofa. Her achy knees almost buckled from the effort. Beads of perspiration broke out on her hairline.

Although Monica had professed to be fine, Grace came to assist her anyway. After taking Monica by the arm, she slapped her rump with a vigorous swat that would have knocked Monica over if Grace hadn't been holding her upright.

"Hey, that hurt!" Monica's buttocks stung.

"Did it? My apologies, sometimes I don't realize my own strength. I was only getting a feel for your figure—you're becoming a regular bag of bones, dear. Mama's got to fatten you up. Men prefer women with curves."

Grace smiled as if to soften the blow, but Monica didn't believe the painful slap on her ass was a mistake. It was a rebuke. Monica had dared to disagree with her on the topic of Pat's possible drug abuse of prescription medications, and Grace hadn't liked it.

I'm starting to think like Troy, Monica thought. Which was wrong. Troy was wrong. Grace was an angel, a blessing for all of them, and they should have been grateful to have her.

But why couldn't she stop thinking about what Troy had said?

Grace helped her sit at the table.

"Have some iced-tea," Grace said. She slid a tall glass of a greenish beverage toward Monica. "I brewed it especially for you, darling. It will ease your mind and soothe your spirits."

"Sounds like exactly what I need," Monica said.

46

That night, Troy was driving home from visiting his mother at the hospital when Sullivan called him with an update.

Troy was in better spirits than he'd been earlier. Things were looking up for his mom. She had regained a firm hold on consciousness, and despite her weakness, her mind was as keen as ever, a clear indication that she had avoided the ugly specter of brain damage. Although she had suffered other, extensive physical injuries, and it would take time to determine when—or if—she would ever walk again, he was grateful that she was alive, alert, and talking. That was a blessing, and he would take them wherever he could get them these days.

He'd also taken the jar of that mystery cream Grace had gifted his mother: *Lovely Hands*. He had a vague notion of finding a chemist to run an analysis on the substances therein, though it didn't much matter anymore. The damage to his mother, the target of Grace's widespread malice, had already been done.

His phone buzzed as he was pulling out of the hospital parking garage. He had his iPhone paired with the BMW's Bluetooth system; he pressed a button on the steering wheel to accept the call.

"Hey, Doc, it's Sullivan," the detective said, his voice broadcast over the car's internal speakers. "The DNA results came in. Expedited like you requested."

"Monica and Grace are mother and daughter, like I've been saying," Troy said.

"Well." Sullivan cleared his throat. "Not exactly. The results don't make much damned sense. I think your samples were mixed up, pal."

"If there was a mix-up, someone at the lab you used is responsible," Troy said. "I collected the samples properly. Anyway, what did the results say?"

"The DNA is almost a perfect match." Sullivan laughed uneasily.

"What do you mean, almost a perfect match?"

"Looks like both samples probably came from the same person," Sullivan said. "They're almost exactly the same. My DNA tech tells me there's a small variation, but it's a level of variation you'd see only with identical twins."

"Identical twins?" Troy said, the words feeling like stones in his mouth.

"Crazy, right? Not sure how much you work with genetics, Doc, but I do a little reading on this stuff 'cause of my job. Identical twins, adult twins, don't have the exact same DNA like we used to think they did. They mutate, you know? Diet, lifestyle, environment—those things can alter someone's genetic profile over time. They'd still be pretty damned close, obviously, but not a hundred percent match."

Troy pulled into the parking lot of a gas station and nosed his sedan into a parking space near the corner. He stared out the windshield, but he kept seeing Grace's face.

"Anyway, it's gotta be a mistake," Sullivan said.

Troy didn't respond. He knew there was no mistake.

But identical twins? No way. Grace was *old*.

How old did she look last night, when she was working me over like a high-priced hooker?

The memory made his arms break out in gooseflesh.

It also forced him to question, anew, his perceptions of the woman. Grace had certainly looked old when he'd first encountered her at Lily's funeral, like any reasonably attractive older woman trying to conceal her age with artfully applied makeup. But more recently, such as that morning, when he'd caught her nearly naked in her bedroom, she didn't look a day past thirty.

She looked, in fact, as if she *could* have been Monica's twin, didn't she?

"You there, Doc?" Sullivan asked.

Grace had obviously drugged him last night. She had apparently drugged his mother, too, and he was increasingly convinced that she was doping up Monica to gain her continued compliance. But he wondered if Grace's scheming ran to an even more insidious level.

What if Grace wasn't Monica's mother at all?

What if she was really her twin? What if she'd been deceiving them from the start with a combination of makeup and wigs?

It was a far-fetched possibility, but their lives had become so crazy that he was willing to entertain almost anything.

"Did I lose you, Doc?" Sullivan asked.

"I didn't screw up the samples," Troy finally said. "But this variation in the DNA—what else can you tell me about that?"

"Funny you ask," Sullivan said. "There was a weird thing with a small percentage of the mother's sample."

"What weird thing?"

"The lab couldn't determine what it was."

"It wasn't in their database?" Troy asked.

"Foreign material, they called it." Sullivan chuckled.

Troy didn't laugh. He felt cold, though heat blew from the air vents surrounding him. Foreign material? How could that be possible?

How was any of this possible?

Because of the absurdity of it all, he doubted Monica would believe him. She didn't trust his motives and would assume he was fabricating a story to turn her against Grace. He saw little point in telling her.

"Get me some new, cleaner samples and we'll give it another run," Sullivan said.

Troy actually laughed at the request. "Not happening. Grace is on to me, now. Things with her have gotten a lot more serious."

"What happened?"

"The other night, she slipped me something, in some food, I think," Troy said. His face burned with shame. "It knocked me out. When I woke up . . . let's just say she had her way with me and leave it at that."

"Had her way with you, like, sexually?" Sullivan asked.

"Is there any other way? Yeah, man. She tied me up to a bed. It was some freaky shit."

"That's rape, Doc," Sullivan said. "It's a felony."

"I'd never be able to prove it. Me, raped by an old woman? No one would ever believe that."

"Yeah, hate to admit it but you've got a point."

"She did something much worse, to my mom. I think she drugged her, too. My mom's in the hospital now."

"And after all of this, your wife is still Team Grace?"

"All day long. I think Grace is slipping her something, too, to influence her. She won't listen to a word I say."

"What about the spy cam I gave you? That turn up anything?"

Troy's lips puckered. "Had a little mishap there, but it's back in place. You were going to run down the names in those address book pics I sent over."

"You'll have my report first thing in the morning—I think you'll find it interesting. Are you heading home?"

"I don't have anywhere else to go," Troy said.

"Be careful, Doc. I've got a really bad feeling about where this is headed."

Part Three

47

Monica picked at her dinner. Due to her sore gums and corroding teeth, she had to slice each piece of food into small portions in order to eat, and then chewing it still hurt—and she eventually became too weary with the overall effort. Perhaps it wasn't the attempt at eating that wore her out, but her declining state in general. Regardless of the reason, as she sat at the table with her family, she became so tired that her eyelids felt as if they were weighted with lead coins.

It's the tea, she thought, looking at the iced beverage her mother had served to her. Although it was different than the herbal blend her mom had been serving her each morning—which she'd also become convinced tended to make her drowsy—it seemed that soon after she had taken a few sips, her need to sleep had become more acute, like a pressure weighing on her brain.

After dinner, she intended to help her mother clean the kitchen, but she couldn't summon the energy. She was struggling to keep her eyes open.

"You need your rest, child," Grace said. "Relax, I'll attend to the dishes."

"It's barely eight o'clock in the evening," Monica said. "I've slept all day. I'm *sick* of sleeping. All I do is eat, sleep, and feel miserable in general."

"That's a natural condition when grieving the loss of a loved one." Grace came behind her chair. She kneaded Monica's shoulders. "You loved Lily so much. You loved that little fur ball

Duchess, too, and now, sadly, they're both gone. It's going to take time to adjust, dear."

Her mother's hands seemed to have magical properties, as they eased the tension out of Monica's muscles. The unfortunate result was that Monica felt an even greater wave of drowsiness pull her down.

"I've got to get the children settled for bedtime," Monica said thickly.

"Nana will take care of the children. Let's get you to bed."

Monica didn't remember making her way upstairs. It seemed that she closed her eyes for only a minute. When she opened them, she was lying in her bed, alone, wearing her nightgown. The nightstand lamp glowed at the dimmest setting. The clock read 8:47.

I've got to tuck in my kids, she thought with a sense of painful urgency. *What kind of mother have I become, sleeping away the days and nights and barely attending to my own children?*

Rising out of bed was like climbing out of a pool of quicksand. Her heavy limbs didn't want to obey her brain's commands to move. She gritted her teeth and *forced* her body to cooperate.

Trembling, forehead pebbled with perspiration, she finally got off the mattress. She felt light-headed. She sucked in several deep breaths, centering herself.

Slowly, she made her way across the bedroom, and out into the hallway. Ahead, the door to Junior's bedroom was partly open, light streaming from within. Lexi's door was shut, the frame outlined with shadow.

Her mother must have been preparing Junior for bed. Monica shuffled to the doorway, pushed the door open.

Grace sat on the rocking chair in the center of the bedroom. Junior sat on her lap wearing his *Spiderman* pajamas. Grace's blouse was unbuttoned, her hand cupping the back of his head, pressing his face against her bosom.

It looked as if she was breastfeeding the boy. Soft sucking sounds filled the air. Grace's eyes were shut, her face upturned to the ceiling, as if she were overcome with rapture.

Monica blinked. She couldn't believe what she was seeing.

"What's going on?" she asked.

Grace lowered her head, eyes snapping open. "Go back to bed, my dear. I'll be there shortly."

"You're *breastfeeding* my son?" Monica stepped into the room.

"I offered the breast to Lexi as well, but she wasn't interested. Junior was most amenable—I assume you breastfed him as an infant and he must have fondly recalled the experience."

"Are you serious?"

"Of course—Nana's milk is sweet and nourishing." Grace patted Junior's head, and carefully pulled him away from her nipple. "I never had the opportunity to breastfeed you. It's something I deeply regret."

"I can't believe you're doing this. Junior is five years old! He's not a baby!"

"I'm not a baby," Junior said, but his brows were knitted in confusion. "I'm a big boy."

"Yes, you are, sweetheart." Grace kissed him on the forehead, lifted him off her lap, and set him on the floor. "But no one is ever too old for Nana's milk. There is plenty for you as well, my dear, if you'd like."

"I don't understand why you're doing this," Monica said, "and I really don't understand *how* you're doing this. How can you be lactating?" She stared at her mother's breasts. They were smooth, round, and firm, and belonged on a much younger woman. "I can't believe any of it. I feel as if I'm dreaming."

"Perhaps you are." Smiling, Grace buttoned her blouse shut. "You've been ingesting heavy doses of my special herbal concoctions. They tend to muddle the perceptions."

Monica tried to take a step forward and felt dizziness warp through her. She squeezed her eyes shut, struggling to regain her equilibrium.

When she opened her eyes, she was back in her bed. Grace sat beside her on the mattress. Her eyes gleamed.

"The children . . ." Monica started.

"Are both tucked in and sleeping," Grace said. "Nana took care of them, don't worry yourself, dear."

"I saw something . . . you were . . . breastfeeding . . ."

"You were obviously dreaming," Grace said. "You still might be."

"Oh." Monica released a deep breath. "I . . . I don't feel well."

"You aren't well, my child." Grace traced her index finger along Monica's jaw. "You're dying."

48

At home, Troy discovered that the master bedroom door was locked, again.

He smiled to himself. Fine, then. He had the spy cam running. It would record whatever the hell Grace and Monica were doing in there in the evenings, and perhaps he could use the evidence to persuade Monica to trust him—and distrust Grace.

In the meantime, he would do some digging.

Downstairs in the kitchen pantry, he found a large Mason jar full of the individually-wrapped candies that Grace had been feeding his children. *Nana's Giddy Gum Drops* stated the label on the side of the jar, in elegant calligraphic text. He extracted a reddish gum drop from a wrapper and held it up to the light.

The candy was coated in granulated sugar. Or what appeared to be sugar. He brought it to the tip of his tongue, licked.

Sweetness spread throughout his mouth; definitely sugar. He chewed the gum drop, and it tasted like the juiciest strawberry he'd ever savored. No wonder his kids were fiends for this crap.

He searched the pantry for more Grace-concocted items. On a top shelf, he found a decorative tin labeled, *Nana's Easy Time Tea*. A giggle escaped him. Did she intend to launch a product line or what? What was next, *Nana's Knockout German Chocolate Cake*?

Again, he laughed, though from a logical perspective he didn't understand what was so funny. But he felt happy. Buoyant.

It's the candy, he thought. It contained some sort of mood enhancer, triggered the release of brain chemicals that stimulated feelings of euphoria.

Standing in the pantry doorway, he twisted off the lid of the tin. It was full of the fragrant, loose-leaf herbal tea that Grace had been brewing for Monica over the past several days. He inhaled deeply of the aromas wafting from the can . . . and felt a strong current of relaxation wash over him.

If Monica were drinking this tea every day, it was no wonder that she spent so much time sleeping. A mere whiff of it made him want to lie down and take a nap.

He had to get this crap, all of it, out of his house. He might not have been able to get rid of Grace, but he could toss out the bizarre paraphernalia that she was using to drug his family.

As he was standing at the open pantry, emptying the items into a large plastic trash bag, he had the distinct sense that someone was watching him. He turned—and almost shouted in surprise.

Grace stood only a few feet away, at the threshold of the kitchen. She puffed on one of her weird herbal cigarettes, blew out a column of smoke.

He wondered how long she had been observing him. She wore a soft smile, as if she found his activity mildly amusing.

She also wore one of his Chicago Bears t-shirts: dark navy blue with a roaring orange bear on the chest. The bottom of the shirt barely reached her knees. Her legs were bare.

"You're wearing my shirt," he said.

"Want me to take it off?" She grasped the bottom edge, began to peel it upward.

"*No.* I don't need to see you naked. Ever. Again."

"Don't need to isn't the same as don't *want* to, doctor." She strolled into the kitchen, swinging her hips. She took a pull from her cigarette, expelled another cloud of fragrant smoke.

"You shouldn't be smoking in the house," he said. "We've got children here."

"Going to make me stop?" she asked. She opened an upper-level cabinet, reached, withdrew a brandy snifter. The movement lifted the edge of her shirt, giving him a glimpse of her glorious, bare ass.

Troy swallowed. She was playing with him. All of this was only a shameless tease, a tactic to blur his thoughts, and it was working. Raw, naked lust clawed at him, and he had a sudden vision of bending her over right there at the kitchen counter and plunging into her from behind . . .

He squeezed his hands into fists, his fingernails digging into his palms, and the sharp pain brought his thoughts back into focus.

"I know what you did to my mother," he said. "She told me about your gift, those homemade creams you gave her. I know they were full of hallucinogenic substances."

"Is that so?" Grace crossed the kitchen. From another cabinet, she removed a bottle of brandy.

"I know about the candy you've been giving my kids, too, the happy candy. I know also about the tea you give my wife that makes her sleepy, compliant."

Grace poured a couple of ounces of brandy into the snifter. She swirled it around in the glass, inhaled deeply.

"Nightcap?" she asked, lifting the snifter.

"You aren't my wife's mother," he said. "I had a DNA test run on both of you. You and my wife have almost the same damned DNA, like identical twins."

Grace took a small sip of the liquor. She appeared thoroughly unconcerned by everything he had said.

"Who are you—really?" he asked. "My wife's twin sister? Separated at birth?"

She dipped her tongue into the glass. Except it was not a normal tongue—it was at least twice as long, like an obscene pink tentacle. It flicked the base of the glass.

Troy had taken a step back. *Did I really just see that?*

Grace had pulled the appendage back into her mouth, took a short sip of brandy. He was left worrying that his eyes had deceived him.

Foreign material, the lab had said about Grace's sample.

Something they hadn't charted in DNA before. Something unknown.

"Fascinating ideas, doctor." She swirled the liquor in the glass. "But I'm in a naughty mood and wouldn't mind another erotic episode with you, this time purely for pleasure. Are you game? You know I'll make it worth your while."

He knew she spoke the truth; the sex would have been spectacular. He had long considered himself a man of few foibles, but he had his limits: knowingly screwing his wife's mother—or twin sister, whatever she was—was out of bounds for him, no matter how appealing the prospect of another roll in the sack.

"I want you out of my house," he said.

"Do you?" She clucked her tongue. "Poor little Troy. Everyone wants Nana to stay except for him."

"I'll call the police," he said.

"Oh?" Grace grinned. "What would Monica think of that, eh? Calling the authorities to eject her long-lost mother from her home?"

His shoulders sagged. She had him beat, and both of them knew it. Without Monica's support, anything he did to get his woman out of their lives would probably destroy his marriage. Monica wasn't hearing a word he said, wouldn't tolerate any criticism of Grace. He'd need something damning to bring her on his side, something believable that even she couldn't deny.

The telephone rang: the landline. Troy checked Caller ID, and it was a number that he recognized. It was the old guy, the pastor they had met at Lily's funeral. He'd called at least once before to ostensibly check on Monica, but hadn't he alluded to something that he'd refused to confide to Troy? Troy vaguely recalled taking a message to pass along to Monica. So much had happened recently that he'd forgotten all about it.

Why did the pastor keep calling?

"Are you going to answer the phone?" Grace asked.

"I'm not in the mood to talk to anyone," he lied.

Grace's eyes narrowed, gaze traveling between him, and the ringing telephone. She stepped to answer it.

"Stephens residence," she said.

The reverend must have immediately hung up at the sound of her voice, because Grace returned the handset to the cradle. She stared at Troy, gaze edged with suspicion.

"What is it?" he asked.

"Tread lightly, doctor," she said. "I'm wise to your ways."

She picked up her snifter, flicked her tongue in it again—leaving no doubt about its inhuman length—and strolled out of the room.

49

Monica barely recognized herself.

Still wearing her nightgown, trembling hands braced against the vanity, she stared at her reflection in the bathroom mirror. It was like gazing into an enchanted looking glass that provided a glimpse of her in the far off future—thirty, forty years away.

"This isn't me," she whispered, her voice cracking on the words.

A web of fine lines and wrinkles had spread across her face. Much of her hair had turned gray by then, as if she were the victim of a bad dye job, and a good amount of it had thinned, too, exposing the shadow of her scalp.

She traced her quivering fingers along her face, down her chin and throat. She had developed the infamous old woman's turkey neck.

"It's not me," she said again. Tears spilled out of the corners of her eyes.

She cupped her breasts through the thin fabric of the nightgown. Both of the girls, as she used to proudly call them, sagged like deflated balloons.

Hot tears ran down her face and plopped onto the sink.

She was seriously ill and needed medical attention. She needed to be admitted to a hospital. Her mother's home remedies were failing her. Why hadn't she been able to see that? Why was she allowing herself to waste away?

She sniffled, wiped her eyes with the back of her hand.

She also needed to shower, but she feared she couldn't

manage the task without some assistance. Her mother would have to help her.

Afterward, she would put on a good wig, and lots of make-up. Then get out of the house and take in some fresh air, try to feel somewhat human again for a little while, and get to a hospital.

She was sick of being stuck inside, like a prisoner in her own home.

She ingested her daily dose of anti-inflammatory medicine, and shuffled out of the bathroom on achy knees and swollen feet.

Troy had already left. She didn't remember seeing him go; she must have been asleep. The clock read half-past nine in the morning. How long had she slept? Thirteen hours or so?

She couldn't remember any more. When she tried to focus intently on any one thing, her thoughts got fuzzy, as if her brain lacked the power to concentrate.

The bedroom door swung open. Her mother entered, pushing a cart laden with covered dishes.

"Good morning!" Grace said. "It's time for breakfast in bed for my sweet, lovely daughter."

Monica's stomach churned with hunger, but she was distracted by how fabulous Grace looked. She wore a tight yellow kimono-style outfit with green highlights, and matching heels. Her thick, jet-black hair cascaded to her shoulders in luxurious waves. Her complexion was radiant; save for her ruby-red lipstick, she wasn't wearing any makeup.

I don't understand how she does it, Monica thought. *It makes no sense.*

Slivers of memory surfaced in her thoughts. Something from last night, involving Grace and one of her children. Something Grace had said to her. She couldn't recollect any of the details, but the fragmented memories gave her a vague sense of discomfort.

"Last night," Monica said, her voice cracking on the words. "You said something to me . . . can't remember . . ."

Grace clucked her tongue. "Bad dreams, my dear, only bad dreams."

She wheeled the cart alongside the bed. She began lifting lids off plates. The delicious aromas of eggs, bacon, biscuits, and hash browns filled the air.

"I want to go to the hospital," Monica said.

"Hospital?" Grace paused in the midst of buttering a biscuit. "Why would you want to go to a hospital, dear?"

"I'm sick. Good Lord, isn't that obvious? Look at me."

"Watch your tone, child." Grace shot her a warning look. "I *am* your mother."

"Everything hurts, all I do is sleep, and I look old. I look older every day. I feel older every day."

"It's simply the change, dear." Grace poured hot water into a tea cup. "These are the things that happen to a woman as she ages. It's the burden we bear. Fortunately for you, I'm here to help you through it."

"I've picked up a disease, some sort of rare illness." Monica dragged her fingers through her hair. "I need to be in a hospital."

"Those dens of medical malpractice, those incubators of germs? Going to such a place is exactly what you do *not* need. You'll get back in bed and have some tea, and you'll eat this wonderful breakfast I've prepared for you."

She came to Monica and grasped her by the elbow. Monica tried to pull away her arm, but it was like trying to escape a robotic claw.

Grace's eyes simmered like smoking embers. "Behave, child. Don't test me."

"I want to go to the hospital!" Monica said.

The back-handed slap came so quickly Monica didn't see it coming. One moment, she was shouting at Grace. The next, she was on the floor, the right side of her face burning and the salty taste of blood filling her mouth.

She hit me? I can't believe this woman hit me. Lily never hit me like that when I was a kid.

Grace stood above her, bosom heaving, hands clenched into fists.

"You earned that, dear," she said. "I warned you to behave. I'd expect this sort of petulant behavior from a child like your daughter, not a grown woman."

A loose tooth rolled around like a pebble under Monica's tongue. Sitting up, her face throbbing, she spat the bloody tooth into her hand. It was another molar.

"I'll knock out every tooth in your mouth if you dare to defy me again," Grace said in a tone as cold as a January wind. "I've beaten grown men to a bloody pulp in my time. Now, get up."

Monica got up. It was a struggle, and Grace didn't come forward to assist her. She had to grab the nearest bed post for balance. Her stomach pitched, and she felt as if she might vomit, but she choked down the reflex, grimacing. She didn't want to give Grace the satisfaction of seeing her sick.

"That's my girl," Grace said with a hard smile. "You've got some spunk in you."

Monica glared at her. Grace matched her glower, hands still knotted in fists, as if to say, *try me, girl, and see what happens.*

Monica lowered her head. She was in no condition to tangle with Grace, and she remembered something Troy had told her earlier, about the woman possessing unusual strength. She had dismissed his comments then, as she had nearly everything else he had said about her mother. But what if everything he'd said was true?

"Get back in the bed," Grace said. "I won't ask again."

Obediently, Monica climbed onto the mattress. Grace adjusted the pillows behind Monica's back so she could comfortably sit upright. She placed the serving tray full of food and beverages on Monica's lap, and settled onto the bed next to her.

"Now, sip your tea," Grace said.

"The tea makes me sleepy," Monica said. "I don't want to sleep. Please."

"It will ease your mind. It's the cure for what ails you at the moment." Grace lifted the teacup and brought it to Monica's lips. "Drink it, dear."

Briefly, Monica thought about tossing the hot beverage into Grace's face. But what would she do after that, when Grace recovered?

It was too risky. There had to be another way.

Monica grasped the cup and took a small sip of the brew. Parting her lips hurt; her face was on fire.

"Better?" Grace asked. She smiled. "You put up such a fuss, child, but I think you enjoy my doting over you. You missed this, growing up, to my eternal shame."

"Where are the children?" Monica said, remembering the time.

"Your husband took them to school." Grace gave a wry smile, touched her stomach. "Men excel at certain duties, even the lesser members of their species."

Monica hadn't seen her own children since last night. She was sleeping their lives away. The thought made her want to cry, but instead, she yawned, wincing at the pain in her pulsing jaw. But the tea was having its usual tranquilizing effect on her. She put the cup on the tray.

I can't fall asleep, she thought. *I have to get out of here.*

"Biscuit?" Grace said. She brought one half of the buttered pastry to Monica's mouth. Her eyes twinkled. "Homemade, of course. My secret recipe."

Monica didn't want the tea, but she *was* hungry. She nibbled at the biscuit, chewing carefully, and of course, it was superb. She consumed the half that Grace had offered, picked up the other half off the plate and ate that one, too, leaving behind only a scatter of crumbs.

"That's my girl," Grace said.

"Can I have an ice pack?" Monica asked. "Please? My face is swelling."

"Indeed it is. It will leave an ugly bruise." Grace tenderly touched her inflamed jaw. "I'll fetch an ice pack in a moment."

"I'd like to go outside, too, please," Monica said. "I want to take in some fresh air."

And get the hell out of here, Monica thought. *Somehow.*

"Fresh air might do you some good." Her mother nodded her approval. "Fine. We'll do that upon my return."

"Where are you going?"

"I'm running an errand." Grace offered a mysterious smile. "I've got to pay a visit to an old friend."

50

Troy pulled into the parking lot of Roosevelt United Methodist Church, in East Point. It was a small, brown brick building set far back from the road. Although modest in scale, the building was fronted by white pillars, the roofline featuring a white stone tower that culminated in an ornate spire bearing a cross. Tightly spaced elm trees populated the property, their autumn-stripped branches trembling in the breeze.

It was ten o'clock in the morning. Only a few cars sat in the parking lot at that hour on a week day, but a black late-model Cadillac sedan was parked near the front door.

Pastor's ride for sure, Troy thought. McBride had kept their appointment.

Troy parked next to the Cadillac. Inside, the vestibule was dimly lit, but the doors to the sanctuary hung open.

A few lights glowed within, and they revealed a cavernous worship space. Looking at the building from the outside, he hadn't expected to find such a large area within. He walked along the carpeted main aisle, floorboards creaking under his footsteps. All of the oak pews were empty, except for one at the very front.

Reverend McBride sat alone, head bowed. He wore a dark suit as if he were prepared to deliver a Sunday sermon. A wooden walking cane lay beside him.

Troy cleared his throat. "Reverend McBride?"

McBride stirred, opened his eyes. He glanced at Troy, checked an antique gold timepiece.

"Right on time, son," he said in a gravelly voice. "Punctuality is the sign of the serious man."

"This is a serious issue, from what you've hinted at." Troy sat next to him in the pew. The pastor smelled of cologne and Bengay. "You wouldn't go into the details over the phone, but you kept calling."

"It's been heavy on my heart, young man. How is your wife, Monica?"

"She's sick. In more ways than one. Obviously she's dealing with losing Lily recently, but since then a lot has happened." Troy scrutinized the old pastor. "You know Grace."

Nodding, McBride wiped his eyes with a handkerchief, used it to mop perspiration from his face.

"I need answers, sir," Troy said. "What can you tell me?"

"All right." McBride tucked away his handkerchief. He gave Troy a clear-eyed gaze. "I'm Monica's father."

Well, I wasn't expecting to hear that, Troy thought. He could only stare at the older man, dumbstruck. McBride lifted his chin, as if owning up to the revelation.

"How is that possible?" Troy asked. "Grace told Monica she didn't know the identity of her father."

McBride barked a laugh. "That crafty jezebel? Oh, she knows plenty." He snapped out his handkerchief again, and spat into it. "We lost Lily over her. Lily used to be a highly esteemed member of this church, a veritable force of nature for the Lord."

"Lily had adopted Grace, from what I remember, correct? Grace was only a teenager, eighteen or so. Practically a kid."

"She wasn't no kid, son." McBride started to laugh, but it evolved into a spasm of phlegm-filled coughing. When he had composed himself, he went on. "Oh, she said she was eighteen or something. But she didn't act it, no sir. She was wise beyond her years."

"No disrespect, but it sounds like you took advantage of a very young woman, reverend," Troy said.

Crimson bloomed in McBride's cheeks. He adamantly shook his head.

Troy pressed on: "When you hear about grown men taking advantage of girls, one of their defenses is always, 'she acted wise beyond her years,' or some self-justifying crap like that. We're in your church, sir, before the altar. But you're going to sit here in the house of the Lord and lie to me?"

"Boy, how dare you speak to me like this, in my church!"

"Then tell me the truth, goddammit!" Troy shot to his feet.

McBride thumped Troy's thigh with his cane.

"Hey!" Troy's knee almost crumpled under him. "What the hell's the matter with you?"

"Not in this house, son." McBride pointed a long, gnarled index finger at Troy. "You will *not* use that foul language here. You will respect this house of God or you will leave."

Troy ground his teeth. He nearly charged out of there. Under any other circumstances, he would have given the pastor the finger and cut bait. He took pride in his reputation as a man who didn't tolerate foolishness, who didn't take any shit off anyone and did things his way, on his terms.

But he wasn't there for himself. He was there for Monica. He was there for his family.

He pulled in a deep breath.

All right, I can do this. For her.

He eased into the pew again.

"I'm sorry," Troy said. "But I need to understand what actually happened, reverend."

"You had this old man's heart jumping." McBride sighed, mopped a fresh layer of sweat off his face. "Thought I was gonna have to run this cane up your tail."

"We got off on the wrong foot," Troy said.

"Grace said she was a teenager, but she didn't behave or look like one, like I was saying." McBride shook his head. "She flirted with me, but I didn't encourage her, didn't take her devil's bait. To this day, I believe she sedated me."

"With food?"

"Yes." McBride's eyebrows arched. "A chocolate cake. She had brought it to the church. I ate some of it, and the next thing I knew . . ."

"She had tied you up," Troy said.

Quiet, McBride nodded. He hooked his thumb behind him. "Right back there in my office. Strung me up like a hog . . . got on top of me." His eyes got misty.

Troy wondered if the old man had enjoyed the kinky sex. He didn't dare to ask, lest the pastor thump him again with the cane.

McBride blinked. "I know what you're thinking, son. Did I enjoy that sinful experience? I may be a man after God's own heart, but I'm still a man, imperfect flesh, and that flesh is . . . weak."

"I wasn't going to ask," Troy said.

"Over the years, my memory has begun to fail me in many aspects, son. But for many reasons, that day is crystal clear in my mind. I saw things I can't explain with logic."

"Her tongue?"

"Is it some kind of deformity?" McBride asked with a quizzical frown. "I'm not a man of science. You're a physician."

"I haven't found any recorded cases that would explain it," Troy said, thinking again about Grace's DNA results: *foreign material*. "I checked."

McBride shuddered. But he continued to speak.

"When Grace turned up pregnant, she told Lily I was the father, merely to be spiteful, no other reason. Lily wouldn't believe my story." His lips quivered. "She quit this church, wouldn't speak to me again. She didn't want me involved with the baby. I'm sad she's gone now, that she died believing I purposefully did such a horrible thing."

The pastor lowered his head and sobbed quietly. Troy slid his arm around the man's frail shoulders, pulled him close.

He wasn't surprised that Lily had kept secret the truth of Monica's paternity. Lily had been of an older generation of ultraconservative, southern Black folk that didn't believe in sharing scandalous information, particularly when the church was involved. The woman had taken the secret to her grave, even when Monica had every right to know the truth. It was infuriating, but he understood.

"Lily is gone now," Troy said. "But you've got a grown daughter out there who needs to know who her daddy is. Now, more than ever, she needs you. Both of us do."

"I want to tell her." McBride sat up, blew his nose. "You think she'd be accepting of me?"

"First, we'll have to get around Grace. She's having a powerful influence on my wife. Monica's in a bad place right now."

"I can't be in that jezebel's proximity for one minute," McBride said with a firm shake of his head. "Heed my advice, son, and get that woman out of your family's home."

"I'm working on it, reverend. I'm working on it."

51

After his discussion with Dr. Stephens, Reverend McBride retired to his office. He had intended to write down some thoughts toward that upcoming Sunday's sermon, but the meeting with the doctor, rekindling those troubling old memories, had worn him out. He loosened his tie and lay across the plush leather sofa in the shadowed corner of the room, intending to enjoy a catnap, after which he would resume work on Sunday's message.

The moment he closed his eyes, he thought about *her*.

The passage of forty years had only intensified his recollection of the experience. He had been happily married for almost fifty years to a lovely woman, Claire—God had welcomed her to Heaven just last year—but sometimes, in his moments of weakness, his thoughts traveled back along that well-worn groove in his mind, like replaying an old song on a turntable.

Inevitably, shame followed immediately thereafter.

Take these thoughts from me, dear Lord, he prayed, as he drifted into slumber. *Cleanse my spirit to serve only you.*

He had been asleep for only a few minutes when a knock at his office door jarred him awake.

"What is it?" He sat up, reached for his glasses. Their office manager was on duty, but he'd told her he was going to be busy for a while and didn't want to be disturbed.

The door opened.

A young woman who looked exactly like his newly-claimed daughter, Monica, entered. She carried a white cardboard box.

241

Nana

The box was the perfect size to transport a cake.

A chill tapped McBride's spine. Hand trembling, he reached for his cane.

"Who are you?" he asked, though he was certain of the answer.

"It's been a long time, dear," Grace said. After locking the office door, she placed the box on the center of his desk. She lifted the lid. "I've brought you a chocolate cake. For old time's sake."

McBride barely noticed the gift. He couldn't stop staring at her. She wore a form-fitting yellow dress, and matching heels. The woman had to be at least sixty years old—or older—but she appeared to be only in her late twenties or early thirties. It was unbelievable.

An abomination, he thought. His hand closed around the handle of his cane. He rose to his feet, though his knees quaked.

"Get out." He pointed toward the door. "You are not welcome here."

Grace came around the edge of the broad desk. Her perfume reached his nostrils, a wave of warm rosemary, and the earthy scent made his mind whirl.

"Poor Reverend McBride." She clucked her tongue. "My, look at how you've aged. You used to be so tall and handsome. But you're an old man now, hunched over with a cane. How predictably pathetic."

Lips curling, McBride straightened as much as his deteriorated spinal column would allow. He shook his cane at her.

"Get from me, devil's harlot!" he said, and his voice was only an echo of the booming baritone he used to deliver the Word on Sunday mornings. Then he started coughing. He bent over, body wracked by spasms.

Grace came to his side. He should have pushed her away. But the fragrance of her, and the ripeness of her youthful figure, weakened his resolve.

Oh, the flesh is so weak, Lord.

Like a doting mother, she eased him back onto the couch. She brought him the highball glass of room-temperature water that had been standing on his desk, and helped him take measured sips. Drinking the water cured the dry, hacking cough.

She sat next to him, her leg pressing against his.

He should have thanked her, but he suspected her arrival had a malicious intent.

"What's your purpose here?" he asked.

She put her hand on his thigh. He stared at her hand as if it were an alien thing. She kneaded the soft, atrophied leg muscles. He made no attempt to push her away.

It had been many years since he'd experienced the sensual touch of a woman. He had forgotten how wonderful it felt to be the object of a woman's desire.

She doesn't desire you, you old fool. This is a devilish act of deceit.

But he didn't stop her. Encouraged, Grace rose, and straddled him right there on the couch.

The lenses of his glasses got foggy. Her cleavage was only inches away from his face.

Grace took off his glasses, leaned closer to him. Warmth radiated from her, her fragrance making him almost feverish with longing. Her bosom hovered close to his lips . . . so close that he could have tasted that sweet spot deep in the cleft of her breasts . . .

I'm failing my station, McBride thought, and it was the clearest thought he'd had since Grace had entered his sanctum. *I simply don't have the will to resist, I'm sorry, Lord.*

Grace took his hands and guided them to her hips. He didn't pull away. She put her hand on his hardening groin and squeezed.

"Old but not dead," she said. "Good for you."

McBride's throat was so tight it was difficult to breathe, impossible to speak.

In a fluid motion, she pulled her dress over her head, tossed it on the arm of the sofa. Her body was improbably nubile, skin glistening like a mahogany sculpture.

She wasn't wearing a bra. Her large breasts were engorged. She cupped them in her hands, played her fingers across the hard nipples, and watched for his reaction.

Involuntarily, he licked his dry lips.

Grace favored him with a knowing smile. She grasped the back of his head and pulled him toward one of her breasts.

His body would no longer obey his mind, was ignoring his conscience. He did the most instinctive thing in the world and took the offered nipple between his lips.

There was milk, plenty of it, and it was as warm and sweet as fresh cream.

He closed his eyes and drank deeply of her, hot tears of shame trickling down his cheeks, his arms encircling her narrow waist as if he were holding on for dear life. As he sucked, she clasped his head more tightly against her bosom and began to rock against his erection, creating a delicious friction.

In no time at all, an orgasm exploded through him, the most pleasurable sensations he'd felt in ages.

Sweet Jesus. He shuddered against her, his body quaking from the aftershocks of the climax.

"There, there now, reverend." She patted his head. "You needed this as much as I did, but that is good. A little pleasure before the end is always a blessing."

McBride pulled away, swallowed. He stuttered. "What . . . what . . ."

"You've been attempting to meddle in my affairs." Smiling, she traced a finger around his lips. "Disclosing old secrets, hmm? Stirring up the pot? I know you spoke to Dr. Stephens. You kept phoning their home and finally met with him this morning. I'm quite observant, you should recall."

He choked out the words: "I owe my daughter the truth."

"Oh, you dear old fool, the truth? None of you has ever known the truth."

She opened her mouth wide. He saw her tongue, that inhumanly long appendage, uncoiling from the depths of her throat like an awakening serpent, and it was more nightmarish than he remembered.

And he'd never known it could be a weapon, too.

52

Monica had dozed off. She snapped awake, blinking drowsily.

Although Grace had departed on her mysterious errand, before leaving she had forced Monica to consume the entire cup of herbal tea she had brought her. Monica worried the tea would have a sedating effect upon her, but she hadn't dared to resist. She fully believed her mother's threat to knock her around if she displayed any defiance.

The side of her face ached from where Grace had struck her. The ice pack Grace had given her had taken the edge off the swelling, but she was going to have a nasty bruise.

Sitting up, eyes still half-open, Monica felt something tighten around her neck. A coarse material. She touched it with her fingers, and her eyes went wide.

It was a rope.

She gasped. She pulled at it, to no avail. The rope was looped tightly around her neck, a perfect noose.

The length of rope traveled upward to the ceiling. It was tied around the base of the ornate wooden ceiling fan above the bed, in a complex-looking knot.

Panic swelled in her chest. Monica tried to draw up her legs, to stand on the mattress—and felt resistance around her ankles, too. She tore away the bed sheets.

Short lengths of rope had been knotted around both of her ankles. The ropes ran underneath the mattress, their ends tethered to the posts of the bed frame.

Before, she had complained of being a prisoner in her

bedroom. Now she had become a prisoner in her own bed.

"Help!" she shouted. Her voice broke on the word. Her throat was dry, her lips parched. "Somebody, help me!"

No one came to her aid.

A sheet of paper lay on the nightstand, next to the ice pack and a glass of water. She had to endure a painful, spine-burning stretch to reach the note.

She recognized Grace's handwriting.

This is for your own good, child. An ice pack, water, and bedpan are within reach if you require them.
I'll return soon and we'll conclude our time together.
Love,
Nana/Mother

Monica looked at the other nightstand, on Troy's side of the bed. A big yellow bedpan had been placed there.

No, no, no.

The handset for the telephone that should have been sitting on her side had been removed. She didn't see her cell phone, either.

Monica screamed.

As she screamed, she realized the futility of it. There was no one to hear and respond to her cries. Troy was gone. Her children were gone. She'd been isolated from her friends. She was all alone, forced to wait for her monstrous mother to return.

I'll return soon and we'll conclude our time together.

Monica had no illusions about the sinister connotations of that statement. Everything Troy had said about Grace, every outrageous accusation, was true.

Her mother had killed Lily. She had killed their dog. She had orchestrated the accident that had landed Pat in the hospital in critical condition.

And, Grace was the origin of the age-advancing illness that plagued Monica. Monica didn't know how Grace was doing it; she was a student of science and this defied all of her learning. But the how of it was irrelevant. It was sufficient to accept that her mother was the root of all the evil that had invaded their lives.

I have to get out of here.

Her clock read 11:23. She wasn't sure how long Grace had been gone, and didn't know the time of her return.

But she couldn't waste another second.

If she didn't escape before Grace returned, her mother was going to kill her.

53

Troy was driving when Sullivan called.

"You're in the car again?" Sullivan asked. "Are you a doctor or a Pizza Hut driver?"

"Comedy isn't your forte, man. You have that report ready for me or not?"

"Email is coming through now. I assume a hot shot MD like you has a mobile office set up in his Beemer?"

"You really ought to brush up on your client communication skills," Troy said. He drew to a stop at an intersection, flipped on his blinker to make a right into a Chick-Fil-A parking lot. "I'm pulling over now so I can review it."

"Before we get to that, my chef sister looked at some of those recipes you'd sent over," Sullivan said.

"The ones in Grace's old book," Troy said. "What'd she find?"

"Whatever cakes and other crap this woman is preparing, she's certainly not following any standard recipes, my sis said. Using a lot of unusual herbs. Some of them are even poisonous."

Troy thought about the chocolate cake that had rendered him unconscious, the creams that had fill his mother's head with lurid hallucinations.

"It's what she does," Troy said. "She seems to have a deep knowledge of that sort of thing, no idea where it comes from."

"I wouldn't recommend that you or your family eat anything else she prepares."

"No shit." Troy laughed. "Oh, and before I forget—the clock spycam you gave me? Ugly, and worthless."

"It didn't work?"

"I got hazy footage of Grace climbing into the bed with my wife and burrowing under the sheets next to her. I didn't see anything else. I need to know what she's doing under those covers. Something tells me she's not snuggling."

"Doc, it's a camera, not an X-ray," Sullivan said. He paused. "You get my report?"

"Just came in. Let me take a look."

The LCD display on the dashboard provided a view of the home page of Troy's Gmail account. The email from On the Move Investigative Services, with an attachment, sat in the inbox. Troy opened the attached PDF.

He had initially sent Sullivan photographs he had taken of Grace's journal: names of women, addresses, and dates spanning a wide range. Sullivan had researched each entry Troy had provided and given notes on each.

Viola Easley – June 14, 1947
1752 Arthur Lane
Los Angeles, CA 90287
September 5, 1987 – September 16, 1987

Viola Easley died on September 17th. She was born on June 14th—at the time of her death she had recently turned forty. She was adopted. Cause of death unknown.

A fuzzy color picture of Viola Easley was included.

Troy was stunned. The woman looked remarkably similar to Monica. She had a Jheri curl, but the two women looked enough alike to pass for sisters.

"This is incredible," Troy said.

"Keep looking," Sullivan said.

Mary Jackson (Williams) – December 5, 1924
22543 Cumberland Avenue
Boston, MA 54319
April 20, 1963 – May 1, 1963

Mary Jackson died on May 3rd. She was born on December 5th—at the time of her death she was approaching forty. Adoption status uncertain. Cause of death unknown.

There was a black-and-white photo of Mary Jackson, too. Different hairstyle, again, but she bore an uncanny resemblance to Monica.

Charlene Johnson (Trice) – August 27, 1968
909 Williams St, Apt 3
Milwaukee, WI 45102
October 5, 2007 – October 18, 2007

Charlene Johnson died on October 19th. She was born on August 27th—at the time of her death she was approaching forty. She was adopted. Cause of death: undisclosed illness.

The included photograph of Charlene might as well have been a picture of Monica.

Christina Devereaux – March 17, 1980
8879 Rice Ferry Road
New Orleans, LA 24501

Christina Devereaux is still alive. She is a high school administrator in New Orleans. She was adopted.

The picture revealed the woman to be another Monica lookalike.

Troy leaned back in his seat and ground his teeth.

"I don't understand it," he said. "They look so much alike, it's as though all of them were cloned."

"My thoughts exactly, Doc," Sullivan said.

"Cloned, or something like it, and Grace is the blueprint," he said. "She's the mother. She's having these children, these girls, and at birth, she puts the babies up for adoption."

"Meanwhile, she goes off and works various jobs," Sullivan said. "Seems that she typically works as a live-in nanny, based on her employment history."

"She has a talent for running a household," Troy said. "My guess is she's also using her herbal formulations on the families that employ her, testing and refining her recipes. If we could find out exactly whom she's worked for over the years, I've no doubt we would find a history of deaths and accidents."

"Right," Sullivan said. "As for her daughters, she comes back to them when they're around forty years old. Pays the lucky ladies a visit, and they die soon thereafter."

"Why is forty the magic number?" Troy asked. "Because some folks think that's over the hill?"

"There's a lot of pressure on women as they get older, I guess," Sullivan said. "Hell, my wife, when she turned forty a few years back, didn't even want me to celebrate her birthday. She tells me, 'Nicky, I'm officially an old lady now. Why would I want a party?'"

"Grace is draining these women, her daughters, of life, of their youth." Troy thought about how Monica's physical condition had deteriorated in the past several days: the graying hair, the wrinkles, the arthritis. "Meanwhile, she somehow reverses her own aging process, and starts looking younger and younger."

"Okay," Sullivan said cautiously. He cleared his throat. "That isn't ah, quite scientific, Dr. Stephens."

Troy went on: "Some of the entries in her journal go back to the eighteen hundreds. Eighteen eighty-three, from what I remember. I hadn't sent them to you because they seemed unrelated."

"If this woman was around giving birth in eighteen eighty-three, she would be well past a hundred and forty-some years old," Sullivan said. "Even some of the cases I checked into, where these women were dying back in the nineteen sixties . . . how the hell could Grace be only fifty-nine?"

An image of Grace popped into Troy's mind: the amazingly youthful figure . . . the elongated tongue.

"I don't think she's completely human, Sullivan," Troy said softly.

The detective was quiet.

For a heartbeat, Troy worried that Sullivan was going to declare him insane and hang up on him. Then he realized he didn't care.

"I've been dancing around the acceptance of that fact," Troy said. "But I can't ignore it any longer. I don't know *what* she is. She's got human DNA mostly, but there's something else there, something uncharted. I don't know if we'll ever know because she doesn't seem inclined to tell anyone the truth."

Sullivan still hadn't responded, but Troy heard the guy breathing hard, perhaps struggling to comprehend their situation.

Troy went on: "I'm convinced she's assumed multiple identities over the years, too. This name, Grace Bolden, is only her current incarnation. If we researched further, dug deeper, I'm convinced we would find out more."

"Does it matter?" Sullivan asked. "All of this is damned strange, maybe unexplainable, but your wife's in danger. We can both agree on that, Doc."

"Damned straight." Troy sat up and punched a search into his phone. "I need to get my hands on a gun. Monica always argued against me keeping a firearm in the house but I can't think of a better time."

"Think you'll need backup?" Sullivan asked.

54

Monica grabbed the glass of water off the nightstand, liquid spilling over the rim as she strained against her bonds. She drank much of the water in three thick swallows.

With her thirst satiated, she assessed her predicament.

The ropes around her neck, and both ankles, severely restricted her range of motion. The noose about her neck prevented her from bending forward far enough to reach the ropes knotted around her ankles. The bonds on her ankles ruled out standing on the bed and getting ahold of the knot at the base of the ceiling fan.

But she still had the use of her hands.

She seized the rope tethering her to the fan. Clenched it in both hands and pulled, trying to use all of her weight. Her shoulders ached in protest, and her fingers throbbed.

Dust motes drifted from the fan blades, and the unit creaked softly, but it held firm.

This isn't going to work. Besides, do I want the ceiling fan to collapse on my head?

She wiped dust off her brow, drew a couple of deep breaths. She leaned forward as much as she could, the noose tight around her neck, and extended her left arm while bending her right leg, attempting to bring her ankle within reach of her hand.

Her limbs shook from the effort. But her reach was several inches too short.

She let her body relax. Perspiration seeped into her eyes, and she brushed it away with the corner of the bedsheet.

She needed a sharp object, such as a knife. Something that could slice away the rope.

She turned to the nightstand on her side of the bed. Stretching, she grasped the handle of the drawer, tugged it open.

She didn't have sufficient range of motion to peer inside of the drawer, but she could get her fingers in there. Her fingertips scrabbled through the contents. She felt loose coins, a small bottle of something, a pencil, random slips of paper. Nothing with a cutting edge.

Troy had a matching small table on his side of the bed. She got that drawer open and performed another blind search. Coins, foil-wrapped condoms, keys, a watch. Nothing useful to her present circumstances.

She dropped back onto the pillows, panting, sweat pouring into her eyes. She flicked away the moisture with the bedsheet.

Look around the room again.

The wheeled serving cart on which Grace had delivered her breakfast was still in the bedroom. It stood beside Troy's nightstand. Grace had been in such a hurry to leave for her mysterious appointment that she hadn't cleared the dishes, either.

Monica remembered a sharp knife among the flatware Grace had brought in. She had used it to halve the biscuit she had served Monica.

But the cart was out of reach. There was no way to pull it toward her with her hands alone.

She sat up in the bed, thoughts racing.

If her arm was too short to snag the cart handle, she needed to extend her reach.

The tangled bedsheet lay against her legs. She grasped one corner of it. The fabric was sodden with cold sweat.

She dug into her nightstand drawer again and extracted the pencil. It was new, with a length of about seven or so inches.

She glanced at the serving cart, assessed the dimensions of the narrow gap between the handle grip and the flat surface of the cart.

This can work.

The clock flashed 11:45. Time was galloping past.

She yanked the bedsheet from underneath her body, freeing it from the mattress. She knotted about six feet worth of the sheet, tailored it into a long braid.

Next, she tied the corner of the bedsheet around the center of the pencil. It required several attempts. Her fingers trembled and ached, and she lacked her usual hand-eye coordination. But she finally got it done.

Now, to hook it.

Carefully, she inched to the edge of the bed, as far as she could go without the noose choking her out. Holding the corner of the sheet in one hand, the pencil dangling from the knotted tip, she pitched it toward the serving cart.

The pencil clattered to the floor.

She almost laughed. She wasn't even close.

She reeled it in, and tried it again.

It bounced against the edge of the cart. Close, but no cigar.

She pulled in several deep breaths. She was drenched in sweat, her entire body throbbing in pain. But she hadn't felt so invigorated in days.

Desperation was the cure for fatigue.

Once more, she pitched the pencil toward the handle.

That time, it worked. It lodged in the gap between the handle and the flat edge of the serving area.

She gave it a gentle tug. The pencil held firm in the aperture. The cart budged toward her.

Like a fisherman reeling in a great fish, she slowly pulled the serving cart across the carpet, toward the bed. The cart was heavy. The pencil bent and swayed—and finally, snapped in half.

By then, she could reach forward and grab the handle without assistance. She pulled it toward her.

She flipped away the silver lid atop the plate, uncovering the remains of her meal.

The flatware was gone.

She nearly screamed with frustration. Was Grace always one step ahead of her?

There was a fistful of napkins beside the plate, silver winking at her from underneath. She tore away the napkins and found a fork, spoon, and the knife.

Thank you, God.

She levered the knife against her thumb, pressed carefully. She winced. The blade had a nice, sharp edge, and it should have; she couldn't remember ever using any of this flatware. It had sat in the dining room, unused, until Grace had begun preparing her elaborate dinners on their best china.

The clock read 12:01pm.

Gotta hurry now. Any minute she can return.

She positioned the knife's edge against the rope, focusing on the segment slightly above her head that trailed upward to the fan. It required her to raise her chin so she could see what she was doing, and to extend her arms a bit. She sliced at the rope, and promptly lost her grip on the blade. It slipped from her hands and dropped against her leg, stabbing her thigh.

"Shit," she said, pain fanning through her.

She had to slow down. If she tried to rush this she could inadvertently hurt herself.

Balancing the knife against the rope again, gripping a piece of it in her left hand to hold it steady, she began to saw with her right hand. She cut back and forth, with slow, firm strokes. She kept the blade in the same deepening groove in the threads.

The muscles in both of her raised arms quickly began burning as lactic acid built up. Her shoulders throbbed. Perspiration gathered on her brow, dripped down the bridge of her nose.

Monica kept going. The rope had started to loosen; she could see threads of it falling away.

The aching in her arms soon became too much to bear. She had to take a break. She let her arms drop.

The clock read 12:16. She couldn't believe time was passing by so rapidly.

She tugged at the rope. She had made good progress, but needed to cut deeper to free herself.

Gathering in a deep breath, she resumed working.

She had been at it for perhaps a couple of minutes when she heard an ordinary sound that was suddenly terrifying: the groan of the garage door opening.

Grace is back, no.

Trembling, she jerked at the rope. Still, it held. She positioned the blade in the deep groove she had created, pushed against it hard, and cut, cut, cut.

The garage door closed.

She tugged at her bond, and the damaged rope snapped free.

There was no time to celebrate her victory. She still had to free her ankles.

Noose dangling from her neck as if she were a convict who'd escaped a hanging, she bent forward.

Her legs were filmed with cold sweat. The perspiration acted as a lubricant. Using her hands, she was able to slip each knot off her ankles.

She didn't hear Grace, but her mother had to be downstairs. Perhaps on her way up.

Monica swung her legs to the side of the mattress. She clutched the knife.

What if it's Troy?

She didn't dare to call out. If it was her mother, and not her husband, the only advantage she enjoyed was that her mother still believed she was bound in place.

Rising off the bed, she winced. Her knees ached. Hell, *everything* hurt. She was in no condition to run.

She only had to get out of the house.

The far side of the bedroom had a set of doors that opened onto a balcony, but that was not an option for her. The balcony was at least twelve feet above the ground. She'd have to jump off the railing, and in her current fragile state, that would be the equivalent of leaping off a ten-story building. The only way out was through the doorway, and to risk Grace seeing her.

She tipped across the room, knife held in front of her. Her nightgown hung limply on her slender frame, drenched in sweat. She slipped on a pair of house shoes lying near the bathroom door.

Faint noises downstairs. It sounded as if someone were in the kitchen.

Monica reached the door. Twisted the knob.

It opened soundlessly.

The hallway beyond the threshold was quiet, steeped in shadows.

She heard heels clicking on tile, downstairs. There was no doubt that it was her mother.

She tightened her grip on the knife handle.

She didn't want to engage in a physical confrontation with Grace. She suspected she would lose that battle, armed with a knife or not. She wanted only to get out of the house without alerting her mother.

But if it came down to a fight, she wasn't going to back down.

She crept along the long corridor. The hardwood floor masked the sound of her soft-soled shoes.

She paused at the closed door to her office, lips pressed together, thinking.

She had a landline in her office. She could get to the phone and call 911, tell them there was an intruder in her home, and that she feared for her life.

She liked that idea more so than attempting to escape her house undetected.

The door opened with a creak.

Shit, Grace is going to hear that, she thought, cringing. But she moved forward across the threshold. The room was dense with shadow, but she had spent so much time in there that she could have navigated the space in full dark.

The wireless handset stood in its cradle on the edge of her desk. The red battery light blinked.

With a sinking feeling, Monica plucked the handset out of the cradle anyway.

No dial tone. She examined the telephone base. The power cord had been snipped in half.

The bitch has been planning this.

"My child?" Grace said. From the nearness of her voice, it sounded as if she were ascending the stairs. "Your mother has returned. Did you slip your bonds? Hmm?"

Monica crept to the office door. She heard Grace's footsteps on the staircase.

She hid behind the door.

"I brought someone home with me." Grace chuckled. "It's an old friend I think you'd love to meet."

Monica was so focused on the nearness of Grace that couldn't think about what her mother was saying. Her mother's heels clicked along the second-floor corridor.

Grace passed by the office doorway, leaving a scent-trail of her beloved rosemary fragrance. She headed toward the bedroom, where Monica had left the door ajar.

Monica edged from behind the door and crossed into the hallway.

"Aren't you a plucky girl?" Grace said, out of sight in the master bedroom. "I'm quite impressed. But you are *my* child, so perhaps I shouldn't be so surprised by your resourcefulness."

Monica reached the staircase. Gazing down the twenty or so steps almost made her dizzy. She clutched the railing, and started going down, each step driving stakes of pain into her weakened legs.

"You and your many, many sisters have so much in common," Grace said, from somewhere above and behind her. "All of you tend to fight so valiantly once you realize the end is nigh. But ultimately, your mother always wins."

Monica kept going down the stairs, sweat trickling into her eyes.

"To be forever young is my destiny," Grace said. "To think I once believed it was a curse. I was such a fool in my youth, so many, many years ago."

When Monica made it to the bottom of the steps, she heard Grace's footsteps closing in. She risked a look over her shoulder.

Grace stood at the top of the staircase. She appeared amused by Monica's escape attempt, lips turned in a gentle smile.

"You can't leave, child," Grace said. "We have a guest waiting for you in the living room. Don't be rude, go say hello."

"Stay away from me," Monica said.

Nothing mattered more to her than getting the hell out of there, but she would have to pass by the living room to get to the front door. She hobbled as fast she could along the entry hallway. One of her house slippers had fallen off. The knife swung loosely in her clammy hand.

Someone sat in a wing back chair in the living room.

Monica had to look, had to shout at this person that Grace was crazy and dangerous and they had to get out while they could, that no matter how beautiful and charming Grace seemed it was all a trick. She staggered toward the visitor. It was a man, and he looked familiar.

"Reverend McBride?" Monica said.

McBride sat in the chair, head sagging against his chest. He looked as if he had dozed off, but he wasn't moving, wasn't breathing.

The doctor in her compelled her to touch his hand, to check his pulse.

His skin was cool. She didn't need to feel for a pulse to know he was dead.

"Say hello to your father, child," Grace said, sweeping past Monica to stand beside the chair. She seized a wisp of McBride's hair and jerked his head upright. The reverend's lifeless eyes regarded her. "He wanted you to know the truth of your parentage and I thought it would be kind to fulfill a dead man's final wish."

Monica screamed.

55

At Dunwoody Guns & Ammo, Troy purchased a firearm. It was a surreal experience, as he was no one's soldier of fortune. He'd never bought a gun and had fired one only once in his entire life, while hanging out with some buddies from med school. He was amazed at the fluid ease of the purchase process: after a quick criminal background check run through the computer, he was allowed to acquire his weapon of choice that very day.

He bought a Sig Sauer P226, a nine millimeter semi-automatic pistol with a fifteen-round magazine capacity. The sales guy, an older tanned gentleman with white eyebrows and a mane of thick black hair so out of place it had to be a toupee, boasted that it had long been the preferred weapon for Navy Seals.

If it was good enough for special ops, it was more than adequate for his purposes.

He bought five magazine clips of ammo. A consultant at the store led him to their on-site firing range. He demonstrated to Troy how to load and unload the pistol, and Troy practiced the process. He fired several practice shots at a cardboard target, missing badly with most of them.

"Aim for center mass, and you'll be fine," the consultant said. "Perfect head shots between the eyes happen only in the movies."

"I'll keep that in mind."

Troy drove back to his neighborhood in Dunwoody. He made

a quick circuit past his house, saw nothing concerning—not from the exterior anyway—and circled around to the community clubhouse.

The clubhouse and surrounding grounds had been decorated for the holiday season. Every year, their HOA hosted a sumptuous Christmas party that Troy usually looked forward to, but in his present state of mind, he was so far removed from such things that he could summon no interest whatsoever in celebrations of any kind.

He checked his watch. It was one o'clock in the afternoon.

Right on time, Sullivan pulled into the parking lot. He swung his black Ford F-150 into the spot next to Troy's sedan and hopped out.

"Armed and ready, Doc?" Sullivan asked.

Troy had hired Sullivan for yet another task: back-up. The detective wore a holstered handgun on his hip. On the surface, it seemed excessive, two grown, armed men teaming up to kick a woman out of a house, but Troy couldn't ignore the butterflies of anxiety fluttering in his gut.

Neither of them had any clue how Grace would fight back. They didn't even understand *what* she was, the extent of her capabilities. She was strong, perhaps inhumanly so, but there might be more she could do to defend herself, and that possibility frightened him.

"I'm ready," he said. "I have to do what's best for Monica, for all of us."

"You show her the evidence about her mother, I'm sure she'll come around."

"And her father, too," Troy said.

Sullivan nodded. Troy had shared with him the revelation about McBride's paternity. He was eager to disclose the news to Monica, but he was looking for McBride to fulfill that task, as it was his right and responsibility as a father. Once he got Grace out of their lives and Monica learned the truth, he prayed she would be willing to see things his way.

But first, they had to deal with Grace.

263

Troy got back in his car. Sullivan followed him in his vehicle. Troy parked in front of the house instead of pulling into the driveway next to Grace's rented Chevy, and Sullivan nosed his truck right behind him along the street.

Troy used his remote control to open the garage door. Monica's X5 was parked in its usual spot.

Together, he and Sullivan stood at the mouth of the driveway.

"Well, she's still here." Sullivan nodded toward Grace's sedan.

"Yeah, she's been driving my wife's car," Troy said. "She's taken over everything, like I said."

"How do you want to play this?" Sullivan hitched up his belt, fingers twitching.

"Go in there and tell her that her stay in this house is over. She can pack her shit and get out."

"Think it'll work out like that, nice and easy?"

"Not at all."

They advanced along the driveway, into the garage. Light streaming from the garage door opener alleviated the shadows. He noticed, on the floor, droplets of a dark, glistening fluid that he initially assumed had come from one of their vehicles, but the spatter trail led directly to the interior door.

He bent, touched a droplet. His fingers came away red, and smelled of metal.

"Holy shit, is that blood?" Sullivan asked.

"We've gotta hurry." Troy rushed to the door, shouldered it open. Sullivan followed close behind.

The blood trail continued across the hardwood floor of the main hallway, and led around the corner, out of sight. Troy looked along the hallway and didn't see Grace or Monica.

He followed the droplets toward the living room . . . and to where they ended at a familiar figure sitting in a chair.

"Oh, shit," Troy said. It felt as if the bottom had fallen out of his stomach.

"Who is that?" Sullivan asked.

"Reverend McBride—Monica's father." Troy had seen his share of recently deceased human cadavers, but he couldn't bear to look at the man. "Grace must've gotten to him after I saw him this morning."

Sullivan drew his pistol.

"She figured out what you two were doing," Sullivan said. "She's raised the stakes, doc. We've gotta find your wife, now."

Troy hurried away. The kitchen, family room, and other rooms were empty. There was only one place Grace in the house that could be with his wife.

"Let's go upstairs." Troy drew his gun, too. "To the bedroom."

56

The door to the master bedroom was locked, of course. Troy had anticipated nothing less.

"Gonna kick it in?" Sullivan asked.

"I have a key, but what the hell." Troy grunted, took a couple of steps backward.

"I kicked down my share of doors, back when I was a cop," Sullivan said. He examined the hinges. "This one opens inward so you can do it. Use your heel. Aim for the spot near the keyhole where the lock is mounted."

Drawing a breath, Troy rushed forward, lifted his leg into a front kick, and slammed his heel against the door. The wood rattled and buckled in the frame, his thigh muscles twanging like a tuning fork. He kicked the door again, and heard something snap.

One more kick sent the door flying open.

Raising the gun, Troy charged inside. The blinds were shut and the lights were off, drenching the room in shadows. He flipped the light switch.

The ceiling lights blinked on. A ragged length of rope dangled from the overhead fan, but Troy focused his attention on the bed beneath. Concealed underneath blankets, shapes shifted and thrashed. He heard the soft sucking sounds of someone feeding.

Feeling weak in the knees, he moved forward. He grasped the bottom of the blanket and snatched it away.

Behind him, Sullivan said, "Dear God in heaven . . ."

Grace and Monica lay on the bed together, face to face. Both of them were clothed, Grace in a yellow dress, Monica in a nightgown. Monica's eyes were wide open with terror and her mouth hung open wide, too. A long, pinkish appendage, that ghastly tongue, extended from Grace's mouth and snaked deep into Monica's throat. The tongue throbbed in a sinuous, slow rhythm, tiny beads of a glowing crimson substance traveling along that alien feeding tube, out of Monica and into her mother.

She's feeding on her, sucking the life out of her, Troy thought.

As he watched, his hand limp on the gun, Grace drew that monstrous tongue out of her child with a wet, slurping sound. Monica started gagging.

Sitting up in the bed, Grace smiled at them.

"Welcome, boys," she said in a low purr. "Here for a ménage a trois? You'll have to wait until I'm done eating."

Sullivan had a Glock. He aimed the pistol at Grace with the practiced ease of an ex-cop. Troy raised his gun again, too, though his arms shook.

"Step away from the bed, ma'am," Sullivan said. "Hands in the air."

"Or you'll do what?" she asked.

Immediately after she spoke the last word, her tongue darted from her mouth like a striking cobra. The tip of it lashed against Sullivan's left hand. He screamed and dropped to his knees, clamping his good hand over his injured one, freshets of blood leaking between his fingers.

Troy fired the gun. He was less than ten feet away from Grace, and he aimed for center mass as he'd been taught.

But he missed. Grace quick-crawled like a spider away from the bed, and she moved faster than he'd ever seen anyone move. The round hammered into the drywall behind the bed, chips spraying. Grace scrambled to the balcony doors. Troy fired at her again, and again. The glass door shattered. Grace shrieked as one of his rounds hit her. He shot at her again, but she lunged through the broken doors and onto the balcony. He ran after her, stumbling over furniture.

She was gone by the time he got outside. Bright red drops of blood stained the wrought iron balcony railing.

He slammed his fist against the railing, went back inside.

"Got a first aid kit, Doc?" Sullivan had gotten up, both of his hands drenched in blood. He grimaced.

"Look in the bathroom," Troy said.

On the bed, Monica was trying to get up. It seemed unbelievable, but she actually looked older than she had when he'd left that morning, and he wondered that if he and Sullivan hadn't arrived when they did, if it would have been the end for her.

The thought chilled him.

He braced his arm behind her back and helped her sit up. Her nightgown was cold with sweat, and her body trembled against his.

"I'm here with you now, baby," he said. "It's over."

"Water . . ." she said in a raspy voice.

He picked up the glass of water from the nightstand, helped let her sip.

"Your mother is gone," he said. "I know you may not agree with what I did, but you've gotta hear me out, okay?"

"She's gone?" The stress lines bracketing her eyes seemed to disappear. "Are you sure?"

He'd expected an angry reply from her and was thrown off balance by her apparent relief. But the sound of a roaring engine cut off his response.

He leaped off the bed, ran to the front-facing window.

Monica's SUV ripped out of the long driveway with a squeal of tires, nearly clipping the bumper of Troy's car parked at the curb.

"Shit!" Troy said. "Grace is taking your car!"

Monica put her hand to her forehead as if afflicted by a sudden migraine.

"The children," she said.

57

Wanda Washington had been working at the front desk of North Springs Elementary for seventeen years. She had seen a lot of things over the course of her career at that wide L-shaped desk: teachers and students carted out on stretchers due to some health issue or another; affairs between faculty members that they failed to keep hidden; a bareknuckle brawl between the P.E. teacher and a parent; teachers stalked by former lovers who tried to get into the school to see them; and one of the most common, domestic squabbles between parents, always over the issue of who controlled the children.

So when Dr. Troy Stephens called her and said, due to a family emergency, don't allow *anyone* except for him to remove his two children from school that day, Wanda didn't miss a beat.

Domestic squabble, she scribbled on her notepad. She added the names of the Stephens children.

One of the aspects of working at a public school that had changed during her tenure was that an armed police officer remained on the school campus throughout the day. Sadly, these days, such precautions were necessary. They kept all doors locked between classes, too, including doors that controlled access to various areas of the school.

It had become a bit like a prison, Wanda thought, and it was only an elementary school.

The cop on duty that day was Officer Leon Tyson—or, as she called him, "Officer Chocolate," because he was the sexiest man she'd ever seen in a uniform. She picked up her two-way radio off her desk and summoned him.

Officer Chocolate sauntered up to her desk a couple of minutes later.

"Domestic situation, huh?" he said. "I need to be concerned with these people?"

"Both of the parents are doctors," she said. "The mother, Dr. Monica, is a sweetheart."

"The father ain't?"

Wanda didn't reply, just offered a sour expression. Her mother had taught her that if you can't say anything nice, don't say anything at all. The truth was, the dad, Dr. Troy, was one of those *I'm-an-MD-and-I'm-better-than you* types that Wanda had always despised. He might have been a fine man, but his demeanor rubbed her the wrong way.

"I get you," Officer Chocolate said with a curt nod. He nodded toward the school entrance. "Looks like we got a visitor."

Wanda checked the surveillance display, which gave live color footage of various parts of the campus, including the front door. A woman that Wanda immediately recognized as Dr. Monica approached the locked front entrance.

"That's the mother," Wanda said to Officer Chocolate.

"Didn't waste any time, did she?" he said.

Dr. Monica rang the buzzer at the door. The bell on Wanda's desk chimed.

Don't allow anyone except me to take my children out of school, Dr. Troy had said.

With only the slightest hesitation, Wanda hit the button to unlock the doors.

Dr. Monica swept inside. Her hair was tousled, and she wore a winter overcoat and heels. She was unexpectedly glamorous. Usually when Wanda had seen the pediatrician she was wearing scrubs.

Officer Chocolate gave her a once-over and appeared to like what he saw, too. Jealously nibbled at Wanda's heart, but what did you expect from a man?

Dr. Monica approached the desk. "Good afternoon. I'm here to pick up my children, Troy and Lexi Stephens. There's been a family emergency, I'm afraid."

There's something different about her, Wanda thought. Something about her tone. It was oddly formal.

"Your husband called, a few minutes ago," Wanda said, just to gauge the woman's reaction.

"Of course, he would have," Dr. Monica said, and her eyes narrowed. "He's trying to use our children as pawns in a selfish little game of his."

Whoa, I wouldn't want to be on her bad side, Wanda thought.

"Anything you want to discuss, ma'am?" Officer Chocolate asked, thumbs hooked on his belt.

"It's important for the children to be with their mother during this family crisis," Dr. Monica said, and her gaze shifted to Wanda. Her eyes had softened. "Woman to woman, I think you understand."

"Of course I do." Wanda offered what she hoped was a sympathetic smile.

She picked up her two-way radio to notify the teachers to bring the Stephens children to their front desk so their mother could take them.

58

Driving to the school, Troy broke almost every traffic law to get his kids before Grace could grab them. Although he'd told the woman at the front desk to release the children only to him, no one else, he wouldn't relax until Junior and Lexi were safe with him and Monica.

Monica had demanded to come with him. She was in poor condition, had been literally drained of energy by Grace as one sucks water through a straw, but the flash of resolve in her eyes made it clear to Troy that she was not staying behind at home.

"This is my fault," Monica had said. "I ignored your warnings about Grace, put all of us in jeopardy. I'll be damned if I don't do my part to make it right."

Sullivan was coming, too. He'd wrapped a bandage around his wounded hand and hopped in his pickup truck to follow them.

As Troy sped down the roads, he gave Monica the highlights of what he'd learned.

"She's done this before," he said. "Many times, over the years, with families just like ours, with children of hers, *daughters*, who look exactly like you."

Monica blinked in surprise, but didn't disagree. He wondered what had happened between her and Grace that finally opened her eyes. Among other things, perhaps McBride's dead body sitting like a wax figure in their living room had something to do with her newfound acceptance.

"We had a fight." Monica sucked in her bottom lip. She was bundled in a white puffer coat, and she had lost so much weight recently that the coat looked much too big on her. She touched the purplish bruise on the side of her face. "Hit me when I asked to go to the hospital, tied me up. She was . . . she was *sucking* stuff out of me when you got back, I was powerless to fight back, paralyzed."

"Hang on." Troy swung the car through a sharp turn.

"She killed my father, Reverend McBride." Monica's lips trembled. "I didn't even . . . I didn't even get a chance to know him, Troy, and he was trying to reach out to me. I believed her lies about him."

"So did Lily," Troy said. "But Grace is the root of everything. She brought about this mystery illness of yours, the rapidly advanced aging. She was feeding on you every night."

"I don't remember any of that happening," Monica said. "But she was sedating me with her damned herbal teas. I've been so sleepy, so agreeable to everything she says . . ."

"It's how she works. She did the same thing to your sisters, over the years."

"My sisters," Monica said in a flat voice.

"Look at the pictures in the report." Troy pointed at the display embedded in the console. "I had a DNA test run on both of you."

"You did? When?"

"Couple days ago. Didn't ask your permission, sorry, but I had to know. Your DNA is almost identical, but a small portion of hers is unknown."

"Unknown. Jesus."

"There are other things I need to come clean about, too," Troy said. "I've done some things I'm not proud of, baby. You need to know the truth about what I've done."

Monica shuddered, glanced away from the screen and met his eyes. Her gaze was so clear, so incisive, that he realized she knew everything about his affairs, that perhaps she'd known all along and had never wanted to acknowledge it.

"You're here now," she said. "We're in this together. We've got to get our children, Troy. That's all that matters to me in the world right now."

Troy veered into the campus parking lot. Grace had perhaps a ten-minute lead on them, but he prayed that his advance call to the school had derailed her plan, that the front desk receptionist had listened to him. Grace looked so much like Monica, could pass any visual test as Monica that he worried about how the school faculty would respond.

"Not seeing your car in visitor parking," he said. "Maybe she didn't come here."

"Or maybe she's left already." She was shuddering.

Troy didn't bother to find a parking spot. He slammed to a stop outside the front entrance and hustled out of the car. In his peripheral vision, he saw Sullivan turn into the lot, too.

Troy tugged at the front door, found it locked. He mashed the buzzer and shouted into the intercom.

"It's me, Troy Stephens! I called about my kids!"

He expected the receptionist to immediately disengage the locks, to let him in to collect Lexi and Junior, but almost a full minute passed before someone came to the door and pushed it open, and it wasn't someone he expected.

It was a cop. The officer scowled at him.

"I need to get my kids, man!" Troy said.

He tried to go past the cop, but the guy stuck out his long arm, blocking the entrance.

"Brother, your wife already left with the children." The cop put his fists on his waist. "Is there a problem here that we need to discuss?"

Troy felt as if the ground had opened up beneath him. He took a step back, his knees wobbly.

Monica had gotten out of the car, too. She hobbled toward him, shaking her head in a stout refusal to accept what she knew had happened.

As if from across a great void, Troy heard his cell phone ringing. It was the ring tone he had assigned to Monica's mobile number, in a fit of mean humor: the mad cackle of a witch. Dazed, Troy accepted the call.

"I'd like to propose a trade," Grace said.

59

At Stone Mountain Park, Christmas was in full effect. Troy had been to the theme park and historical site before, but had never brought his family there during the holiday season, and he was floored by the extent of the decorations on display and the attractions available for children and adults alike.

Snow Mountain, a vast area full of cold, man-generated snow, offered tubing, a zone with activities such as a snowball shooting gallery and snowmen building, and slides. A market offered seasonal food from various vendors and holiday shopping. The Wonderland Walkway, a tunnel of thousands of lights, led to a snow palace and a show that took place during regular intervals. And there was the requisite visit and photo op with Santa Claus...

At four o'clock that afternoon, the overcast day had brought about a premature twilight. Troy advanced through the park, hand-in-hand with Monica. Picking her way forward carefully, wincing from time to time, she clasped his hand so tightly that his muscles tingled, but he needed the close contact as much as she did.

Troy gripped his iPhone in his other hand. He checked it continuously for text messages.

They got in line for perhaps the theme park's most famous attraction, the Summit Skyride. At that afternoon hour on a weekday, there wasn't much of a wait at all. After a delay of only a couple of minutes, they boarded the Swiss cable car.

Grace had told them to meet her at the top of Stone Mountain.

There, they would execute her proposed trade: Troy would get back their two children; Grace would get Monica.

It was a deal with the devil, and he prayed that everything worked out in their favor.

Monica eased onto one of the benches bolted against the wall, while Troy stood, clutching a nearby hanging strap for balance. Rocking gently, the passenger cabin slowly ascended via the cables.

"Of all the places she could have picked," Monica said under her breath.

"I know," Troy thought.

Stone Mountain not only provided a stunning view of the Atlanta skyline, the north face of the rock also featured the largest bas-relief in the world, a depiction of three personalities from the Confederate Army. In the last century, the Ku Klux Klan had met there to revive their hate group, and the site had been home to various race-based controversies over the ensuing years.

In Troy's mind, not even a billion sparkling Christmas lights could have erased the troubling history of that place.

Troy glanced out the window, and felt a brief spell of vertigo. The aerial tram took them more than eight hundred feet above ground. He'd never been comfortable at great heights. Swallowing, he looked away from the glass.

A text message came through on his phone. He showed it to Monica, and she smiled for the first time in hours.

The cabin slid into the end of the tramway.

They disembarked, into the glass-paneled visitor's center. Outside the boarding area, a big sign overhead declared: "Welcome to the Top of Stone Mountain – elevation 1683 feet above sea level."

Troy and Monica headed to the exits, emerged in the cold, crisp air at the summit. A long paved walkway led to a covered area with seating; beyond that, a path led to the uneven stone surface of the mountain summit.

They went to the sitting area, and waited, per Grace's instructions. It was twenty after four.

Ten minutes later, Grace emerged from the main building of the visitor's center. She wore a long faux fur coat and heels. She strolled along the walkway like a model, and Troy realized that though he had shot her earlier, the injury had been far from fatal.

Grace didn't have the children with her, as she had promised she would. Monica gave Troy a knowing look. Troy took her hand in his, squeezed it.

"Let's do this," he whispered.

60

"Here we are, family." Strutting toward them, Grace took a final draw from her cigarette, flicked it to the ground. "Yes, I realize you were expecting to receive the children. They were having such a fine time in another area of the park that I left them to their own devices." She winked at Troy. "Play by my rules and I'll tell you where they are, doctor."

Troy said nothing. He glanced at Monica, but she was already stepping forward, trembling with emotion.

"We know what you did," Monica said. "What kind of grandmother, or nana as you like to call yourself, would abandon her grandchildren in a theme park?"

Grace blinked. For the very first time since this monster had invaded their lives, she looked flummoxed.

"What in the hell *are* you anyway?" Monica asked. "What am I, to have come from you?"

"You're mine, that's what you are, child," Grace said, teeth flashing.

"We're two steps ahead of you," Troy said. "If I've learned nothing else about you, it's that you can't be trusted. We invited you into our home and you took advantage of us. You drugged my wife, my mother, my kids, *me*."

At that, Grace grinned, and caressed her stomach. "I can feel your seed inside me, doctor, growing. Our memorable night together will pay rich dividends for me in the future, another child for me to harvest once she ripens."

Troy was disgusted by the revelation that he had impregnated

Grace, that he'd provided what she needed for her to continue her cycle. Although she looked exactly like Monica, she was a thoroughly alien thing, and he wanted nothing more than to be done with her for good.

He pressed on: "You would have loved nothing more than to slip away with Monica while I run around the park like a chicken with its head cut off, trying to find my children." It was his turn to smile. "It was a devious plan, I'll give you that. But my man, Sullivan, he got here over an hour ago, he was watching you from the moment you came in with Lexi and Junior. You left the kids in the food court. My sister, their aunt—who happens to be in town because of what you did to my mom—is with them now. This madness is over. There's no damned trade."

"No." Grace shook her head.

"Why kill Lily?" Monica said. Tears tracked down her cheeks, and she wiped them away. "She was more of a mother to me than you could ever be. You're nothing to me."

Grace clenched her hands into fists, and she looked ready to charge them. Troy pulled back his jacket and showed her the pistol holstered on his hip.

"I shot you earlier and you recovered, but whatever you are, you can bleed, you can be hurt," he said. "You stay away from my family, understand?"

"Stay away," Monica said.

Grace glowered at them as they backed away. They hurried toward the visitor's center. She didn't follow, but they continued to watch her from afar as they entered the building.

They were the only passengers to enter the cable car returning to the ground. Troy was grateful for the privacy. Monica came into his arms, and he folded her into a tight embrace.

"It's over." He kissed Monica's forehead.

"Do you really believe she'll leave us alone?" she asked.

"We've got a unified front now. She knows we'll both fight back. If she dares to mess with us, it will be a battle, and I don't think she's used to that. I think she'll move on."

"There are so many things I don't know." Monica tilted her

face up at him, her eyes glassy with tears. "Like I said to her: if she's a monster, what does that make me?"

"It makes you the bravest woman I've ever met—the woman I love more than anything," he said.

"But I still don't know what I am, Troy. Even my father, a man I had met only once, is dead now." She blinked back tears, looked away from him. "I've never felt so . . . so empty."

"Well, you know what? You've got two young children down below who love you and can't wait to see you. I think that's a fair trade off."

"Right," she said, but she still looked troubled.

He didn't know what else to tell her that would ease her worries. Before any of this insanity had entered their lives, he had considered himself Mr. Fix-It, always ready to dispense sage wisdom to solve everyone's problems.

He realized he had been an arrogant fool. Sometimes, there simply were no answers, and you learned to live one day at a time in spite of life's uncertainties.

The passenger cabin descended along the cables at a painfully slow pace. He heard a thumping sound above them, and felt the car rock.

"What is that?" Monica asked, gaze traveling to the ceiling.

He heard another thump on the roof. It came from the area behind Monica. Troy tensed. He put his hand on his gun.

Another knocking sound, near the edge of the cabin.

Heart hammering, Troy stepped forward, putting himself in front of Monica.

"It's her, isn't it?" Monica said. "God, I knew she wouldn't quit."

Grace's face slid into view. Upside down as she hung from the roof, she stared at them through the glass, teeth bared in fury.

"Give me my child!" she shrieked.

Monica screamed. Troy raised the gun.

Grace's face vanished as she ducked back onto the roof. Troy heard her scrambling about above them. He looked to the set of doors on his left, and realized what Grace had in mind.

"Give me something," Monica said, sounding short of breath. "A gun, a knife, something to defend myself."

Troy dug into his pocket and drew out his Swiss army knife. He handed it over to Monica, his hand shaking so badly he almost dropped it. Trembling as badly as he was, Monica accepted it and unfolded one of the longest blades, a cutting edge less than two inches long.

With the sinuous grace of a serpent, Grace slid down from the roof, positioning herself directly in front of the closed double doors. Her hair blew in the wind, the ends of her coat rippling like wings.

She began to pry the doors apart. Troy looked for a way to bar the entrance, but there was nothing; they were secured from the outside with some sort of locking mechanism. Grace was strong enough to force them open with her bare hands.

"Stay behind me," Troy said.

He and Monica backed up, putting as much distance as possible between themselves and the doorway. He aimed the pistol.

Cold air gusted into the cabin as Grace slammed the doors open. Scraps of paper, stirred by the wind, whirled around them.

Remembering to aim for center mass, Troy lined her up in his sights and squeezed the trigger.

But Grace's tongue was lightning-quick. It darted forward and popped against the gun's barrel, throwing off his aim and knocking the pistol out of his hands. The fired round blew a hole into a pane of glass, and the gun's report in the small, enclosed space made his ears hurt.

The pistol had landed on the cabin floor, out of reach. Troy lunged toward it. Grace lashed at him with her tongue, the appendage striking his arm.

Troy cried out. It was like being hit with a bullwhip. He staggered, lost his balance.

On hands and knees, he searched the floor for the weapon. Tears of pain obscured his vision, but he could see the black shape of the gun. It had clattered underneath a row of seats. He crawled after it.

By then, Grace had entered the cabin. As he reached for the pistol, she stepped on his hand, grinding her heel on his fingers. He howled.

She picked him up by the scruff of his neck as if she were a lioness plucking up a misbehaving cub.

And flung him toward the cabin's open doors.

61

Screaming, Monica watched her mother toss Troy into the gray maw of the cable car's yawning exit. Troy hurtled into the chasm, and Monica was overcome with such horror that she forced herself to look away.

"Look at me, child! I am your mother and you are mine."

Grace loomed in front of her, hair blowing around her head in a dark nimbus. Her tongue slithered from between her lips.

As if waking from a dream, Monica remembered the small knife in her hand.

The tip of the appendage flicked toward Monica in a pinkish blur and snapped against Monica's lips, and the sharp pain snatched a scream out of her. The instant her mouth went open, her mother's feeding tube plunged inside. Monica felt the alien thing fill her mouth and quest down her esophagus, while her mother's eyes shone with savage pleasure.

Monica sank to her knees.

As her mother's tube filled her, it felt as if she were choking, unable to breathe. Darkness clawed at the edges of her vision.

Intuitively, she realized that once the sea of darkness overtook her she would never surface again. This was her mother's final feeding, her last opportunity to siphon the remaining life out of Monica.

Monica clutched the knife.

Above her, Grace's eyes shone with triumph.

Using what little strength she had left, Monica swiped at the appendage with the blade. The knife ripped a deep gash in the strange flesh. Blood spurted. Reflexively, Grace reeled the tentacle out of Monica's mouth with such speed that it left Monica's throat bleeding and raw.

Grace gagged. Hanging out of her mouth, the tongue flopped like a fish in a boat, leaking great gouts of blood.

Shrieking, Monica surged upward and shoved Grace toward the yawning doorway as hard as she could.

Grace tumbled backward, off balance. Her eyes flew wide with shock, and she pin-wheeled her arms to try to brace herself in the doorframe.

A hand came over the lip of the doorframe and seized Grace's ankle. It snatched her leg from underneath her, breaking her balance and pulling her through the doorway.

Screaming, Grace dropped away from the cable car and plummeted into the twilight.

Troy flung his leg inside, crawled into the cabin.

Monica pulled him into her arms.

Quiet, they held each other close as the cable car glided back to earth.

62

Nine months later

"Are you ready for this, babe?" Troy asked.

Late on a Saturday afternoon in August, they stood in the lobby of the Holiday Inn in College Park, Georgia. Lexi and Junior twittered around them, restless with anticipation.

Monica clasped Troy's hand. Holding his hand didn't hurt anymore. After several grueling months of physical therapy, cosmetic surgery, medication, and extensive nutritional support, she had regained nearly all of her former strength and pushed back the symptoms of premature aging. While she had needed orthodontic surgery to repair her teeth, her hair had grown back, thick and dark. Her skin reacquired its elasticity. Her joints were flexible, her bones strong.

Troy's mother, Pat, had recovered as well, though she would walk with a cane for the rest of her life.

Psychologically, Monica had mostly found her way back to a good place, too. Sometimes, though not as often as before, she still had nightmares about her mother, heard her voice echoing in her dreams: *You belong to me, child.*

But the thing that had once been known as Grace Bolden was gone forever. Upon falling hundreds of feet through the air and striking the ground, its body had erupted into flames, an incinerating fire that had left behind only a mound of harmless ashes that soon fluttered away in the wind.

They were safe from Grace. But going inside that hotel

banquet room was going to be a major step into a new chapter.

With her blessing, using Grace's journal, Troy had undertaken the task of organizing a family reunion of sorts. Of her sisters, and their families. There were seven of them, including her, between the ages of forty and seventeen.

Seven of them with identical DNA. Seven of them with a story to tell of how their lives had unfolded.

But only one sister had encountered their mysterious common mother and lived to tell the tale.

"Seven Sisters Reunion," read the printed sign standing on the small table outside the closed banquet hall doors.

"I'm ready," Monica said. "It's time I finally meet the rest of my family."

Gathering her husband and children around her, she went inside.

Get on the Mailing List!

Enjoy this story? Visit www.brandonmassey.com now to sign up for Brandon Massey's free mailing list. Mailing list members get advance news on books, the chance to win autographed copies, and much more. Sign up now!

Also by Brandon Massey

Novels

Thunderland
Dark Corner
Within the Shadows
The Other Brother
Vicious
The Last Affair
Don't Ever Tell
Cornered
Covenant
In the Dark
Frenzied

Collections

Twisted Tales
The Ancestors
Dark Dreams I – III

About Brandon Massey

Brandon Massey was born June 9, 1973 and grew up in Zion, Illinois. He lives with his family near Atlanta, Georgia, where he is at work on his next thriller. Visit his web site at www.brandonmassey.com for the latest news on his upcoming books.